For my big sister, Charlie, who led the way.

THE CHERRY HARVEST

If you imagine that your right palm is the state of Wisconsin, your thumb will be Door County, jutting into the depths of Lake Michigan. This far north, it's a short season of blossoms and fruit, so you have to catch it just right. Come late May, take a low-flying plane from Cherryland Airport clear up to Rock Island, and you'll glide over three thousand acres of pink and white fluttering blossoms. In the best of years, these trees supplied the entire nation with cherries.

But that was before the war.

CHAPTER ONE

THE RAIN CAME AGAIN, harder this time. Charlotte pulled her knit hat tight, pushed up the collar of her gray wool coat, and stared through the chicken wire at the rabbits. Kate's prize rabbits.

She entered the pen and chose a plump one, furry and warm in her cold hands. Its heart thumped like a tiny sewing machine. Charlotte brought it into the dim barn and stroked its fur until it calmed, trusting. She hesitated a moment—*stealing from my own daughter*—then picked up the butcher knife.

When she cut the jugular, the sewing machine stopped. The muscles loosened and the body flopped open. Blood spattered and dripped from strands of Charlotte's white-blond hair. After stringing up the animal by its heels, she clipped the skin at the hind legs and pulled it down over the thighs and fat belly, turning it inside out like a glove.

A ribbon of dusty light slanting through the window illuminated the slick white body, front paws hanging together as if in prayer.

Charlotte lopped off the head. She'd chop it up later for chicken feed. The hide would serve as lining for a hat or mittens.

Two of the mousers darted from the shadows and rubbed against Charlotte's legs, mewing. Lulu and Ginger Cat. She ignored their pathetic cries. It was their job to keep rodents from the granary and compost heap. Best if they were hungry.

When she slit the carcass down the front—"oh!"—six tiny bodies slid into her hand, wriggling with life. Trembling, she closed the sink drain and pumped in water. She knew better. She should have palpated the rabbit's underside before cutting her open. She stared at the floating dead things. Not just one of Kate's rabbits, but seven.

Shaking off the guilt, Charlotte placed the butchered animal on the cutting board and sliced it into quarters. She scooped the babies from the sink and chopped them into unidentifiable pieces.

THE RAIN HAD SUBSIDED and the sun was low in the sky when Charlotte saw Kate pedaling down Orchard Lane toward the barn. Watching through the kitchen window, she marveled at how her daughter had grown from an awkward skinny girl into a lovely young woman, a slim figure in her knit sweater and wool skirt, pinky-white skin, long wispy blond hair.

"Saw your Kate in town yesterday," Ellie Jensen had said at the dry goods store that very morning. "All grown up now, so pretty. Reminds me of that Swedish actress, Ingrid Bergman. Same as you."

Charlotte smiled at the thought. What was that motion picture she and Thomas had last seen? *Intermezzo.* Back when they were carefree enough to afford a few hours at the picture show. She remembered that evening, that night. It had been so long now since desire stirred her. Damn war changed everything.

When Kate came in, Charlotte braced for an encounter.

Kate set her schoolbooks on the hall bench. "Mmm. Something smells good." She grabbed the vegetable basket. "Be right back."

Charlotte's mind raced with possible explanations. She had to speak with Thomas first. She needed him on her side.

Kate returned too soon with a basket of morels and spring greens. "I spied them in the woods on my way home." She took her bounty to the deep porcelain sink and dumped it into the colander.

"Beautiful!" Charlotte reached for the basket. "I'll take care of it. Why don't you go on upstairs and get a start on your schoolwork. I'll call you when supper's ready."

Kate happily picked up her books and hurried upstairs to her room.

Charlotte was setting the table when Thomas came through the back door. He flipped his straw hat up onto the hall shelf, took out his red handkerchief, and wiped his forehead, then breathed in deeply. "Ah, the aroma of Char's kitchen."

Thomas Christiansen was a lanky six-foot-three. In his early forties now, his sandy-colored hair was going a bit gray at the temples and crow's feet crinkled the corners of his blue eyes. He put his face near Charlotte's neck and sniffed playfully at her skin. "What you got cooking?"

She pulled away. "I have something to tell you." Because he'd know as soon as she took it out of the pot. She could lie, say she trapped it or shot it. He'd believe her. Thomas believed anything she told him. But not Kate. Kate kept track of her rabbits. She knew exactly how many she had on a day-to-day basis, how many more she needed to pay for tuition at the university. Her piggy bank. Like stealing from her piggy bank.

Thomas turned to the sink to wash up under the pump.

Charlotte stirred the mushrooms into the stew, then put the cover back on the pot. "Olga cut off my credit at the butcher shop."

He picked up the towel. "Why do you need credit? You have ration stamps."

"I swapped them for kerosene and soap and toilet paper and so many other things. Oh, Thomas . . ." *Say it, just say it.* "I had to butcher one of Kate's rabbits. She doesn't know—"

"One of her rabbits? What about your chickens?"

"If we ate my chickens today, we wouldn't have eggs tomorrow or the next day or the next. I need to put food on the table every single day, Thomas."

"The eggs then. Why didn't you trade the eggs for supper? Or cook them? We could be eating eggs tonight instead of—"

"They go just so far . . ." She couldn't bring herself to tell him about the yarn.

"You could have made a vegetable soup—"

"Enough!" She whirled toward him.

He looked stricken. Oh, Thomas. He had no idea how difficult it was. It wasn't her place to complain, it was her duty to keep the household going. The mama duck floating serenely on the surface, paddling like mad below. "Thomas, it's what I had to do."

He threw down the towel and left for the parlor, escaping into one of his books, no doubt. Charlotte lifted the stew pot from the cast-iron stove and set it on the wooden countertop. She stirred the juices with a bit of goat's milk. One day this will be over. But until then, we do what we must.

When the rabbit was cooked through, Charlotte put a piece of meat on each plate, covered it with mushroom sauce, and added the wild greens. She called Kate and Thomas into the kitchen.

Kate was about to sit when she looked at her plate. "That's a . . . is that one of my rabbits?" She stared at Charlotte.

"I'm sorry, Kate, but—"

"You killed one of my rabbits?" Her blue eyes blinked fast, but not fast enough to keep a few tears from falling.

When Thomas reached for her hand, Kate pulled away and rushed out the door. With an irritated glance toward Charlotte, Thomas stood and left.

Charlotte watched through the window, Thomas following Kate to the barn, the two of them off in their imaginary world.

Waiting for their return, Charlotte fussed about the kitchen, wiping counters, rearranging things, glancing every few moments through the window. After half an hour, she scraped the plates of food back into the stew pot. All that trouble for nothing.

Finally, there they were, walking to the front of the house, Thomas's arm around Kate's shoulders. Charlotte heard the front door open and close, Kate's footsteps on the stairs.

Thomas came into the kitchen and stood over Charlotte, arms crossed. "It's not just the rabbit, it's the principle, that you didn't ask—"

"She wasn't here—"

"Selling rabbits, that's her savings. You know the university means the world to her."

Charlotte nodded as if she agreed, but she didn't. What was book learning in the face of putting food on the table? Kate would never make a good homemaker, and Thomas wasn't helping.

He reached for his chair as if to sit down.

"You need to get to that county meeting."

Eyeing the clock, his shoulders dropped. He went to the back hall and picked up his hat.

"I've got Dorothy's letter for you." She pulled it from the pocket of her housedress.

He raised a hand, dismissing her. "The growers must have something better to offer, else why would they have asked for the meeting?"

"And what if they don't?" Charlotte untied her apron. "I'm going with you."

"What?" He swung around. "Women don't go to these meetings."

"Then I'll be the first." She grabbed her hat and gloves, opened the back door, and led the way along the flagstone path to the garage.

Thomas liked to please, that was the problem. He wasn't one to stir up trouble even if it was for his own good. He didn't care much for business either. He was happiest with his books, reading made-up stories and poetry.

He ground the Chevy pickup into gear, and they lurched word-lessly down the bumpy gravel lane. The sun had set and bits of purple lingered on the horizon. Sitting on the other end of the cracked leather seat, Charlotte held her gloved hands quiet in her lap.

"What's the point of you coming?" He glanced her way.

"Watch the road."

"Damn it, woman." He stared straight ahead. "This risky plan of yours . . ." He gripped the steering wheel so tightly the horn blared.

Charlotte flinched but didn't contradict him.

At the end of Orchard Lane, Thomas turned south onto County Trunk Q. They were quiet now, skirting the bay where a pale moon climbed through clouds. Fishing boats creaked gently against their moorings. A single gull swept over the water, piercing the evening with a shrill call. Frogs, crickets, they all had their say. These creatures didn't care about boys dying, ships lurking. If we disappeared, they wouldn't even notice Charlotte thought, staring out the window. This cold beautiful world didn't give a damn.

When they reached Highway 57, Thomas shifted into high gear and continued south toward the county seat.

Approaching Sturgeon Bay was like entering a new world. With the need for more and more warships, the shipyard had attracted thousands of workers, and the close-knit harbor community had been overtaken with acres of prefabricated houses and men from all parts.

Thomas pulled into the gravel lot of the Door County Courthouse. He wasn't smiling. Charlotte didn't wait for him to help her down from the truck, but she did wait for him to lead the way. The men would respect him more for it.

As soon as Thomas opened the door to the meeting room, Charlotte felt eyes on her. Indeed, she was the only woman. Though board members nodded toward her, she noted the looks they exchanged with each other.

Mike Peterson had an oversized presence that reminded everyone he owned Big Mike's Lumber & Building Supply. With all the new construction, he must be rolling in money.

Ole Weborg, who ran the bait and tackle shop, was a short, stocky fellow, red in the face with sunburn or windburn, depending on the season. Friendly to everyone, he knew the run of the fish, the time to go out and the time to be patient. Likable guy, but more cautious than wise, Charlotte thought.

Bo Jenson, county administrator, the only man in a suit, was friendly in a political way, pumping hands, asking to hear about business and family, smiling, winking.

The door opened and Sheriff Bauer, big thick-chested German, came in uniform, gun in his holster. And right behind him, Pastor Duncan, tall, calm. There were other members Charlotte didn't know, nine in all.

Charlotte followed Thomas to the audience section, where growers sat in metal folding chairs, not members of the board but here because the topic was the harvest. Most were in bib overalls stained with whatever kind of produce they grew. Thomas's stains were pink from years of cherries. At Charlotte's approach, the growers stood respectfully. Thomas took off his hat and shook hands with the men and held out a chair for Charlotte. After they were seated, Thomas pulled his empty pipe from a pocket and sucked on it as if it held tobacco.

Once the board members had taken their places at the front table, voices quieted. Someone coughed. Cigarette smoke curled up through the dusty light, giving the room a sickly pallor.

Bo banged his gavel. "We've called this meeting at the request of the growers." He scanned the audience, about twenty men. "So what do you have to say?"

Ralph Sundgren stood and cleared his throat. He had cherries in southern Door. "I'm not ashamed to say we need help." He regarded the board. "Our best men and boys are off to war. The rest, taking jobs right here at the shipyard. Migrant workers too, Mexicans and Indians. And why shouldn't they? Steady work, good pay."

"Even the girls will be down here once school's out," said Gus, who owned an apple orchard. "And who's left to pick the fruit?"

"I barely made it through '43," shouted Artie, a major grower up near Sister Bay. "Another year like that'll drive me out of business."

"It's not just the harvest," Ralph said. "We need men *now*, to prune and spray. The county's gotta subsidize workers so they'll come back to the farms."

Other growers called out, echoing Ralph's words.

Bo banged the gavel. "The county can't afford to match the wages at the shipyard."

"Then tax 'em!" Artie pumped a fist. "All those laborers coming in, getting wealthy right under our noses. Tax 'em to pay the pickers. Hell, they make so much they won't even notice."

Mike put out his hands. "We can't institute a tax without a public vote. Next election isn't until September."

"Then what are you gonna do?" Ralph challenged.

Charlotte touched Thomas's hand. He tucked his pipe into his pocket and slowly stood. The room quieted. He glanced about, taking his time, then cleared his throat and spoke. "The Army's going to be bringing in German prisoners, setting up camps."

A murmur surged through the crowd. "What'd you say?" Faces stared up at his tall frame.

"Prisoner-of-war camps, here in Wisconsin," he said a bit louder. "The prisoners can do the work."

Charlotte breathed in deeply and sat up straight.

"Are you saying we get Nazis to work the farms?" Big Mike crushed his cigarette into a stone ashtray.

"It's what they're planning down in Beaver Dam." Thomas motioned toward Charlotte. "My wife's cousin wrote they'll be working the canneries, living in tents at the fairgrounds—"

"Those are killers you're talking about," Mike cut in. "We can't just let 'em loose!"

The sheriff cleared his throat. "They're boys, like our boys. Just on the wrong side."

"Boys?" Mike turned on the sheriff. "They killed my son!"

The room went quiet until Ole broke the silence. "I hear it on the QT, Canadians captured a German submarine in the Saint Lawrence Seaway."

Men gasped.

Ole held up a hand. "It's not in the news 'cause of the media blackout, but just think about it." He scanned the shocked faces. "The Saint Lawrence leads into Lake Ontario, Erie, Huron—and right to us, right to Lake Michigan. And you can bet they'd love to come on in and stop the shipbuilding here in Sturgeon Bay and down in Milwaukee and Chicago. Why, they might be mining the lakes right now."

Big Mike pounded his fist on the table. "All we need are some Nazi spies on our shores signaling to them German subs, telling 'em how it is."

Ole appeared frightened. "Nazis are trained solders, and we're the enemy. They'll escape—"

"Where they gonna escape to? They don't even speak English, for God's sake," Ralph said.

Bo looked to the growers. "What else you got?"

"We got nothin' else." Artie nodded toward Thomas. "I like what he says."

"Yeah. I say put 'em to work." Ralph stood, hands clasping the straps of his overalls. "They owe us."

Growers' voices rose in agreement until Bo banged his gavel. "Quiet. One at a time."

Thomas spoke up. "Our son, Benjamin, is serving with Clark's Fifth Army in Italy now. As you can imagine, we hate those Nazis as much as any of you."

Charlotte rose beside him. At five-foot-ten, her height was an advantage when dealing with men. "We worry about our boys over-seas, but we have nothing to feed our families here at home." She herself wondered over the consequences of the plan, but she wasn't going to let her doubts show, not with the family farm at stake.

"Time, that's our worst enemy. And these prisoners, they're the only way we can get our crops in before we lose another year."

"Where're they gonna stay?" Ole demanded.

"We have a migrant worker camp," Charlotte said. "Enough for fifteen, maybe twenty men on our property."

Thomas nodded.

"I have a camp too," Ralph shouted.

"Put the sonsabitches to work," one of the growers called out. "Labor's labor."

The sheriff cleared his throat before speaking. "What do we do to get these PWs here?"

"It's all in the letter," Thomas said. "We petition the Army for however many men we need. They bring guards in with the workers. We give the Army the workers' pay. But we can delay payment until after the harvest."

"You saying the Army's going to pay the damn Nazis?" Mike said.

"They'll be sitting in the back of the movie house," Ole said. "With our girls."

Thomas shook his head. "The Army'll pay them in scrip, only good in the commissary. They won't be buying any movie tickets."

Pastor Duncan cleared his throat and after a few moments of silence began. "I know the pain this community is suffering. I sit with families who've lost their men and boys. I see farms and businesses going under. Forgive your enemies, Christ teaches. These prisoners, we must forgive them."

"You gotta be kidding!" Mike shouted.

The sheriff started to stand, but when Mike scowled he resumed his seat. "I move we vote," Mike said.

The growers rose, cheering.

"I second the motion," Bo said. "But only board members."

Amid the grumbling that followed, Bo brought down the gavel. "All in favor of petitioning the Army for prisoners of war to work the farms, raise a hand."

Charlotte watched as Pastor Duncan's hand went up, then the sheriff's. A few men who hadn't spoken raised tentative hands. Mike sat rigid, his face smug.

The room grew quiet until Bo shouted out the verdict: "Four in favor, five against."

"Then what are you going to do for us?" Artie jumped up.

"Cherries is what makes this county," Ralph yelled.

Charlotte stood again and faced the board. "If we don't have a harvest, we won't be buying at your stores." As the growers mumbled their assent, she realized that her voice was the strongest in the room. The men at the table had nothing to offer but fear. "You businessmen are wealthy now because of the shipyard. But once this war's over, if the orchards are gone, the tourists won't be back. And there won't be any growers either. What are you going to do then?" The room went quiet. "It's not about politics, it's about survival."

"Here, here!" Artie led the growers to their feet.

Thomas gave Charlotte's hand a squeeze.

Bo wasn't smiling now. He nodded down the table toward Ole and Mike.

"Fine, then. Do it." Mike's voice boomed. "But let the record show . . ." He pointed to the growers, his eyes focused on Charlotte. "Let the record show that you—*you*—are making a bargain with the devil."

CHAPTER TWO

A SHAFT OF LIGHT swung across the ceiling and disappeared. Kate could count the minutes before it came again, pulsing through the night from the lighthouse half a mile up the coast.

A cool evening breeze flowed in through her open window along with the gentle lapping at the shore below. She was over the rabbit now, but even more determined to leave this place in the fall. Snuggling under her quilt, Kate chose a novel from the stack on her nightstand and opened to the first page: "Last night I dreamt I went to Manderley again . . ." Oh, this was going to be good.

Bingo jumped onto the bed and purred for attention. Kate plumped her pillows behind her, nestled the cat in her lap, and fell readily into the story.

The rumble of Father's truck broke the spell. Kate continued reading, but when she heard Mother and Father coming up the stairs—were they arguing?—she could no longer focus. Family conversations were generally respectful, though lately Kate sensed tension beneath the polite words. It was Father's voice now. "If even one of those PWs sneaks off . . . I'll be out in the orchard . . . who will protect you and Kate?"

Kate slipped out of bed and stood near her door, listening. *German war prisoners in the orchard?*

A gust off the lake brought gooseflesh to her skin. She hugged her flannel nightgown tight around her. If only Ben were here. Since he'd left, nothing was right. She had to talk to Josie.

After closing her door, she pulled on overalls and a thick wool sweater. She switched off her reading lamp, reached out her window, and grabbed hold of a thick oak branch.

Her Schwinn bicycle was her way out. It didn't take her far, not nearly far enough, but it took her to Josie's. Before gas rationing, she could have taken the motorboat, but now she wasn't allowed to use it. Besides, it would make too much noise in the quiet night.

The path followed the scoop of bay, edging between the beach on her right and the front yard on her left. Approaching the woods, Kate rode through the cedar trees and passed by the caretaker's cottage. Designed as a smaller version of the house, the cottage had been abandoned for years. This was where Josie wanted to live after she and Ben were married, and she had been bringing things to it, little by little—a framed mirror for the bedroom, a watercolor of a house with a white picket fence for the living room, sheets and pillows and a quilt for the double bed. Kate had promised to make lacy curtains.

Just beyond the cottage, a crackle in the cedar branches startled her—a white-tailed doe and two speckled fawns. She rode quickly past, not worried about the deer but about the coyotes that would be attracted to the little ones. She didn't want to be in their path if they came yelping.

When she reached Island Road, Kate leaned her bicycle against a birch tree, kicked off her canvas loafers, and rolled up the legs of her overalls. The channel was about twenty yards across. Until a few months ago, a footbridge had connected the island to the mainland, but a winter storm brought it down. The lighthouse keeper ferried to the mainland by boat, and for anyone who might venture by foot, he had fastened a rope alongside the fallen bridge. Today, because of the storm surge, the water was high. Kate grabbed the rope and stepped barefoot into the cold water, which reached nearly to her knees.

She was about halfway across when a splash on the surface stopped her. A dark creature dove under. She froze, anxious for what might attack her from below. But when a beaver surfaced, heading toward an inlet stream, she laughed at her silliness.

Once she reached Loon Island, Kate ran through the woods, well-worn piney needles soft under her bare feet. When she came to the yard, she hurried past the outbuildings—oil house, icehouse, smokehouse, woodshed, barn, privy, summer kitchen—and finally stopped below Josie's second-story window. She threw a small stone, their signal. Josie's face peered out, then disappeared.

Soon Josie opened the door to the dark hallway between the keeper's residence and the tower. "C'mon," she whispered. Her parents would be asleep, but on a night like this, their windows would be open. Holding an oil lamp before her, Josie led the way to the circular brick lighthouse and up cold cast-iron steps—118 of them—spiraling up and up and up.

At the top, while Josie held up the lamp, Kate pushed open the hatch. They climbed through to the watch room, which was surrounded by thick glass. Josie opened the door to the outside gallery, a gray cast-iron balcony encircling the tower.

A short wall-mounted ladder led to the lantern room above, where the huge lens turned. Only Josie's father was allowed up there. The lens illuminated the world around, scene by scene—the watery horizon to the east, the gravelly shore to the south, the woods on the mainland, and the rocky shore leading to the Potawatomi Islands far to the north.

Sitting next to Josie on the metal lattice floor, Kate pulled her sweater close against the chill night air. Josie offered her a Chesterfield, and Kate leaned in for the light.

Josie had large features, full lips, dark eyes, and next to Kate's slim figure, she was all curves. Though Josie was a year older, Kate had skipped a grade, so the friends were both high school seniors. Josephine, the teachers called her. The boys called her sexy.

"Look what I found," Josie whispered, pulling a magazine from inside her jacket. Kate had encouraged her to read poetry and fiction, but Josie was more interested in magazines, *Good Housekeeping, Ladies' Home Journal.* She even kept a scrapbook of favorite articles—"The Good Wife's Guide," "How to Keep Your Man Happy," and other sappy advice.

At least this magazine looked more interesting than the others. *Esquire.* Josie opened it to a pen-and-ink drawing of a redheaded woman lying back provocatively, wearing black lingerie that hid nothing, her long legs angled up as if she were lying on an invisible couch, feet pointed in black high-heeled slippers. "One of the Vargas Girls." Josie said it as if the girl in the illustration was a personal friend. She flipped the page and started reading aloud from an interview with Hugh Hefner.

"Hugh who?"

"I don't know who he is either, but you can learn a lot about what a boy wants by reading these things."

"Oh, Josie. Why do you waste your time on this?"

"Hah! You're the one wasting your time on made-up stories. Where's that going to get you? I'm more interested in real life."

"Real life isn't nearly as interesting."

"That's because you're not in love." Josie's face beamed for a moment in the revolving light, smiling as if she knew more than she would tell. "You just need to meet the right boy."

Kate took a long drag on her cigarette.

Josie nudged her. "My mother got me a subscription to *The Bride's Magazine.* I want you to help me pick out a wedding dress that Benny would like."

Kate had to control herself to keep from laughing. Ben couldn't care less about wedding dresses.

"Say, I saw Timothy Peterson watching you in English class." Josie paused for attention. Timothy was seventeen, not yet old enough to enlist. "He's smart and handsome, and his father owns that lumber and building supply place. Big Mike's." Josie paused to take a puff. "His big brother was killed, you know. He needs someone to talk to. You could have a good life with him."

"I don't want a good life with him or anyone else. I want my *own* life."

"Oh, Kate. You've never even kissed a boy, let alone . . ." Josie entwined an arm in Kate's. "When you're in love, it makes all the difference."

The two friends were quiet for a bit, gazing out across the dark lake. Josie broke the silence. "I'd like to make something special for Benny. What do you think?"

"Chocolate. He likes chocolate. Cookies, brownies." That's what Kate would do if it weren't for the rationing. Here at the lighthouse Josie had access to so much Kate didn't have—sugar, butter, and any book she wanted—all brought in by the Coast Guard.

"I'm thinking of something he could wear." Josie gave a sly smile. "You could help. You like to sew—"

"I'm sure the Army gives Ben all the clothes he needs."

"Something intimate." She faced Kate in the dark and whispered, "We could make him underpants."

"What?"

"Shh . . ." Josie admonished, then continued in a low voice. "A soft fabric . . . I'd embroider a little heart with my name—"

"Really! How could you think such a thing! Anyway, you don't know his size."

Josie blew smoke out the side of her mouth. "I bet he left a pair in his room. You could—"

"I will not!" Kate took an angry puff on her cigarette and flicked the butt through the gallery railing.

"Or I could ask your mother . . ."

"And that would be the end of that." Mother did not like Josie one bit.

Thoughts of Mother brought back the image of the quartered rabbit, punishment, no doubt, for spending time at school, studying, instead of coming straight home to help with chores. "Mother wants me home all the time now. It's gotten worse since Ben left."

Josie lit another cigarette and gave it to Kate.

"I'm not good at the things he does." Kate sucked in the smoke.

Josie peered off into the darkness. "Nobody can compare with Benny."

Kate pulled her legs up under her.

"He's so popular. And the best dancer in the world." Josie stood and spun small circles, disappearing off around the gallery.

It was true. Everyone loved Ben. He couldn't play on the football team because of his chores, but before every home game the players would rub his blond hair for luck. During the games he ran up and down the field, cheering the plays, getting the crowd cheering as well. He was strong and handy and helped neighbors fix fences and raise barns. Friends would show up in the orchard or the barn and talk with him while he worked; he'd give them things to do. Groups of boys would drop by after supper. In the summer they'd swim in the lake and sit on the dock; in the winter they'd go down to the cottage to talk their "man talk," Ben called it, shooing Kate away when she tried to join them.

Josie came dancing back around the gallery and tried pulling Kate up with her. "All the girls want to be with Benny, but he chose me! I just want to dance with him. Dance and dance and dance! C'mon."

Kate shook her head. "I have something to tell you."

"A secret?" Josie sat down and leaned in close. She loved secrets.

Kate put a finger to her lips. "German war prisoners are going to work in our orchard."

"Nazis in your yard?" Josie cried. "Benny's fighting them and your family is going to—?"

"Shh!"

"I can't believe it! Does Benny know?" She grabbed Kate's arm. "I have to write to him about this."

"No!" Oh, she shouldn't have told.

Ben's letters to Josie were different from those he wrote to the family. Letters to Josie were often stained with muddy fingerprints, written from cold foxholes, he told her. They had passages blacked out by Army censors, and Josie figured he was talking about his buddies dying beside him, gunned down by the Nazis. In the parts that weren't blacked out, he said that only two things kept him going: his hatred for the enemy, and his anticipation of holding Josie once again in his arms.

Josie's face hardened. "When those Nazis are in your orchard, I might just come by with Papa's rifle and shoot them out of the trees." The light swung around and her eyes glowed. "Benny would like that."

IT WAS WELL BEYOND MIDNIGHT when Kate climbed back up the oak tree in the light of a million stars. Inside, she undressed before the open window, then lay naked on her sheets. After the heated bicycle ride home, she welcomed the chilly night air on her skin.

Sometime later she startled awake. Eyes staring in at her. It wasn't a new dream—it came with the rustling of branches, raccoons in the tree or deer in the brush below—but this time the eyes belonged to Nazi prisoners. Leering, laughing.

A shaft of light drifted across the ceiling and disappeared. She shivered and pulled up her covers.

CHAPTER THREE

CHARLOTTE WOKE TO THE SOFT COOING of mourning doves and slipped quietly from under the warmth of her covers, careful not to wake Thomas. She pushed aside the curtain and peered out across the wide lake. Many a morning Charlotte had looked through this window to see Ben on the dock or out in the blue wooden motor-boat with Scout, his black retriever. He'd fish until he had enough for the family's supper, then he'd clean his catch and bring Charlotte beautiful fillets. All before he left for school.

Thinking of the vest she'd finished knitting yesterday, she smiled. She had stayed up well beyond bedtime perfecting the cabling that ran down the front. Now it sat next to her bed in the canvas satchel, ready for mailing. She imagined Ben fingering the precious stitches, thinking of his mother keeping him warm in the icy Alps.

The last time she saw Ben was at the train station, tall and solemn in his Army uniform. If he was frightened, he didn't show it. She certainly was—frightened that the war would change him, frightened that she'd never see him again. She studied his face, full rosy cheeks, big blue eyes. She hugged him tight to her breast until the whistle of the steam engine blew them apart.

Off near Loon Island, a man in a motorboat stood casting a line. He reeled something in and caught it in a net, too far away to see what it was, but it had to be a fish. Food, that's all she seemed to think about these days. She had stretched the rabbit stew to three suppers; the next two nights they'd had a watery soup she'd made from wild greens and mushrooms and a few of her last pathetic vegetables from the root cellar—a flabby carrot and a potato full of eyes. She would have eggs and goat's milk for breakfast and lunch today, but what about supper? A pheasant would be nice, or a grouse. Ben used to come home from school, pick up his gun and go into the woods with his dog, and bring home splendid dinners. Charlotte hadn't written him that Scout had died.

Thomas fished and hunted through the winter, but in the spring he had the pruning and spraying to do, and in the summer he managed the harvest. Charlotte herself was a good shot, but she wasn't patient enough to sit still and be quiet. So much to do. Until a week ago, she had counted on Olga's credit. What would she put on the table tonight? And tomorrow? And the next day? Just thinking of it made her hungry. Only thin soup last night! Thomas and Kate must be hungry too.

She pulled on her wool flannel robe.

Could that be the lighthouse keeper in the boat? She had never seen him in anything but his dark-blue uniform and cap, neat and well groomed, proud like a military officer. The man out on the water wore a casual jacket and flat cap.

Remy Lapointe wasn't a military man but a civilian, an engineer of some sort, employed by the Coast Guard with privileges Charlotte could only imagine. The Coast Guard supply boat routinely stopped at the island, bringing anything the lightkeeper and his family wanted. He certainly didn't need to fish for supper.

Charlotte watched as he reeled in another and captured it in his net. Fish weren't among the rationed items up this way, but those who caught fish these days kept them. What a waste for the lightkeeper's family to have the fish! Charlotte turned from the window. *What can I trade?* Glancing about, her eyes landed on the canvas bag. *That's it! If Marta provides the yarn, I can knit her something, something special she can't buy.* She slipped into a freshly washed housedress and grabbed the canvas satchel to show Marta the quality of her work.

Downstairs in the chilly kitchen, Charlotte opened the cast-iron stove, added a log from the wood box, and lit the kindling. Kate and Thomas would appreciate a hot stove when they came down for morning tea. Soon the scent of cherry wood filled the room.

Charlotte opened the back door, picked up the *Door County Advocate,* and scanned the headlines. No new war news today. She put the paper on the kitchen table for Thomas, donned her coat, hat, and gloves, and went out the door.

Down in the boathouse, Charlotte turned the winch and the blue wooden motorboat rolled down the track alongside the dock. A silvery fish flashed briefly near the surface. She stepped into the boat, pushed off, and lowered the propeller into the water. Floating beyond the dock, she pulled hard on the starter rope, then again, until the motor finally caught and growled into motion. Oily fumes permeated the air. Charlotte shifted the throttle, and the bow lifted and bounced on the waves as she guided the boat across the bay to the island.

Through a rising mist, the eastern horizon shifted from purple to orange, and by the time Charlotte reached the lighthouse the round fiery sunball was dancing on the lake's surface. *When was the last time I danced?* She had taught Ben and Kate how to dance in the living room—the waltz, the foxtrot, the Lindy Hop. Ben was so light on his feet, laughing and singing along with the music. All the girls wanted to be his partner.

She tied the boat at the dock below the lighthouse and headed up the walk. Charlotte didn't know these people well, Remy and Marta Lapointe. They had arrived in 1939 when the former keeper received a new assignment. Charlotte and Thomas had gone to the welcoming party—a square dance at the armory. She recalled Remy, dignified in his uniform; Marta, his plump wife reaching out to greet everyone; and their four children—two boys, two girls, Josie the oldest. Was that where it started, Ben and Josie dancing together?

Charlotte stepped along the stone walkway near the massive brick tower and rounded the corner to the front of the residence. When the door opened, Marta looked startled, wide dark eyes, brows lifted. "What is it? Did something happen?" Her French Canadian accent so foreign to Charlotte's ears, the nasal *o*, the missing *h*.

"I didn't mean to startle you, Marta. I've only come for a visit." Charlotte wasn't one to make neighborly calls—for one thing, she didn't want neighbors knocking at her own kitchen door—but for the sake of business, she was prepared to do so now. "If this isn't a good time . . ."

Marta opened the door further. "Please come in, if you don't mind speaking softly lest we wake the brood." She paused. "I do love my mornings before the children are up and about, eh?"

"I'm disturbing you."

Five years earlier, shortly after the couple arrived in Door County, Charlotte had called on Marta, bringing a cherry pie. Marta was friendly then, but now she wasn't smiling.

Handing Marta her coat, Charlotte noted the woman's resemblance to Josie—the high cheekbones, large features, thick dark hair and eyelashes.

"I was about to make coffee."

Charlotte took it as an invitation. "How delightful." She hadn't had coffee for ages, just chicory once in a while. She drank mostly mint tea from her window garden.

A good seven inches shorter than Charlotte, Marta led the way to the kitchen. She wore the latest military-cut slacks and matching cardigan sweater—a style Charlotte had seen on the covers of magazines at Schwarz's Drug Store. And shiny new leather loafers! The only shoes available in Turtle Bay were canvas.

In the kitchen, Marta nodded toward a chair at the round fruit-wood table. The previous lightkeepers had kept the place in the original brown and gray, but now it was painted bright blue and yellow, a cheerful look. A large bowl of fresh fruit sat on the wooden counter—grapefruit, oranges, lemons, bananas—and baskets of vegetables hung on a rack, not just root vegetables but fresh garden greens—lettuce and cucumber and ripe tomatoes. How did she get them so early in the season? So as not to appear wanting, Charlotte swallowed her question and said, "Such a cozy kitchen."

Just then, Marta opened the coffee tin and oh, that rich dark aroma! She poured beans into the grinder and turned the handle. "It's not like Boston . . . but for now . . ." Marta said, as if this were quite a comedown from her husband's former assignment. Remy and Marta didn't have an easy life here on the island—no electricity, not even a pump at the sink because the well water was bad. Goods had to be shipped in. Still, Charlotte envied their easy access to things because Remy worked for the government. Charlotte's son worked for the government too, but his family was suffering while this family remained above it all.

Marta lifted the cover to the bread box and pulled out a tray of pastries. Charlotte couldn't help but stare. No one had sugar or flour for such treats these days.

"Apple or apricot?"

"Apricot," Charlotte said too quickly.

Marta put two pastries into the bun warmer on the stove. "Have you heard from Benny? Such a handsome, capable boy. You must be proud, eh?"

Charlotte cringed at Marta's use of the nickname Josie had given him. "Thank you, yes, we hear from *Benjamin* often."

Marta's eyes remained on Charlotte, expecting more, but Ben's letters were none of her business.

Marta poured steaming water over the crushed coffee beans. "Josie gets letters . . ."

"Letters?" Charlotte felt the sting. "From Benjamin?" *What does he say to* her?

Marta laughed. "Lovers . . . who knows!"

Charlotte didn't laugh. Josie was one of those clever girls who would do whatever she needed to get what she wanted. And what Josie wanted was Ben. Some might call the girl attractive, but she was far too free with her body to suit Charlotte, walking with a deliberate swing of her hips, standing too close, breasts pushed forward. Charlotte wished Ben had chosen one of his own kind—a farm girl, a Norwegian, at least a Protestant. That was the worst of it: these people were Catholic. Charlotte wasn't fond of any church, but it was the Catholic allegiance to the pope that galled her. A Catholic marriage would mean Ben would have to be baptized and, worse yet, swear to raise his children—her own grandchildren—Catholic.

Josie had even drawn Kate into her little web, luring her with books—to get information about Ben no doubt. The Coast Guard brought a roving library to the island regularly, and Josie ordered whatever books Kate asked for. Impressionable as she was, Kate spent far too much time with the older girl.

When Marta brought the coffeepot to the table and poured steaming dark liquid into the cups, Charlotte nearly swooned with the seductive scent.

"Sugar and cream?" Marta asked.

Sugar and cream! Charlotte hadn't seen such a casual display of luxuries since before the war. She tried to act nonchalant as she reached forward. "Was that your husband I saw out on the lake fishing?"

"Remy? Yes, it's his way of relaxing."

Charlotte laughed. "I tried fishing a few times, but all I could think about was everything else I should be doing. The fish bite early morning and evening, just when I need to be preparing breakfast or dinner. Benjamin was the one . . ."

Marta set the pastries on the table and sat across from Charlotte. She wasn't smiling. She wasn't friendly, as she had been in the past. *What's this about?*

Charlotte chose the fat one dripping with apricot jelly. "Thank you." If only she could take this home to share with Kate and Thomas. She was about to bite into the sweet when Marta cleared her throat for attention.

"Let us say grace." Marta lowered her head.

Charlotte dropped the pastry to the plate and, out of respect, followed Marta in the sign of the cross, but inside, her blood bubbled with resentment. She didn't want Ben to feel the shame if he might pick up his fork too soon.

Just as the prayer ended, the door opened and Marta looked up. "Ah, here's Remy."

The lighthouse keeper came into the kitchen.

He tipped his hat—"Mrs. Christiansen"—but he didn't smile. He carried a mesh basket of perch, tails flicking, iridescent scales catching the morning light, and put it into the sink. "I do hope nothing's amiss."

"Charlotte's just come for a visit." Marta's voice had an edge. Husband and wife exchanged looks, frowning.

What's going on?

Remy gave a slight bow. "Please excuse me. I must dress for work."

Footsteps pattered upstairs. Charlotte had to finish her business while she still had a chance. She smiled across the table at Marta. "You're lucky to have a husband who brings your family supper."

"The children turn up their noses at fish, except Josie." Marta sighed. "Remy does it for sport."

Sport? So they didn't even want them! Charlotte could get by with trading something small, a hat or mittens perhaps. She took a sip of the rich coffee. "The last time I enjoyed my fill of fish was when Big Mike's eldest son was married."

"The boy who was killed in the Kasserine Pass, killed by that

Nazi Rommel!" Marta stared into Charlotte's eyes, pursed her lips. "We heard what you did at that county meeting."

Charlotte's cup rattled on the saucer.

"How could you, with your own boy over there? My future son-in-law!"

Not if I can help it! Charlotte sat up straight, much taller than the other woman. "We don't have a boat bringing us food and supplies. We need men to pick the fruit. Surely you understand."

"What *you* don't understand, Charlotte"—Marta splayed her hands flat on the table—"is that you are putting my husband and all the others who watch out for your safety at risk. With Nazis loose right here on the shore—"

Charlotte shook her head. "The prisoners will have Army guards. You don't need to worry—"

"Worry? In addition to all they had to do before, lighthouse keepers are now charged with protecting our shores from the enemy. The shores of the Saint Lawrence Seaway and the Great Lakes." She leaned in. "And you think a few prison guards can protect us from that madman Hitler, who's bent on controlling the world?"

Charlotte shivered. What if a prisoner did escape? If there were submarines in Lake Michigan . . . no, no, she wouldn't let herself be drawn in by the fear.

"This is war, Charlotte." Marta stood, hands on hips. "What do you want? What did you come for?"

Charlotte was stunned by Marta's hostility. She wanted to leave. Walk out. But what she wanted more were those fish. She took a deep breath and bent down and opened her canvas satchel. "I came to show you something I made." She pulled out the blue vest.

Marta's eyes brightened. She sat back down and took the vest. "You can't buy anything like this." She held it up. "It's just about right for Remy. Yes, just his size."

"I could knit something for you, Marta."

Marta's mouth opened, her eyebrows rose in a question.

"I'm willing to trade," Charlotte said. "I have nothing for supper."

Marta smiled. "The fish, eh?"

Charlotte nodded.

"You'd trade this beautiful vest for a basket of fish?"

"No, not this vest. But I'll make something special if you provide the yarn. Mittens, a hat, a scarf." She paused, waiting. "Even a vest. I would do that for you."

Marta touched the cable stitching. "I like this one."

"I'll need eight skeins. Ellie's Dry Goods—"

"No, *this* one."

Charlotte shook her head. "I made this for Ben."

Marta looked at the vest, then at Charlotte, her mouth twisted into a self-righteous smirk. Charlotte felt tears welling. *I need those fish!*

Marta's head cocked toward the ceiling, children prancing above, coming down the stairs. Charlotte stood and walked to the window. Three gulls cut through the sky, a freighter slid northward on the horizon. *What's the vest worth to this woman?*

"Well?" Marta demanded.

Charlotte turned to face her. "I'll trade the vest for the fish." She scanned the room. "And those grapefruit and oranges and lemons. That basket of green vegetables. A tin of coffee."

Marta opened a cupboard and pulled out a burlap sack and began filling it, then another. "The Coast Guard boat comes tomorrow." She said it as if she had won.

Charlotte looked at the table. "Cream and sugar." *What else?* "And three of your pastries . . ."

"Three pastries?" Marta hesitated. "I promised the children."

"One then, for Kate. Apricot."

Marta wrapped an apricot pastry in butcher paper and added it to the sack.

Charlotte picked up the vest and fingered the blue cable stitching one more time before letting it go.

CHAPTER FOUR

AFTER MOTORING BACK ACROSS THE BAY, Charlotte tied the boat to the dock and stopped for a moment to gaze up at the house. To others it might look like any old farmhouse—traditional two-story, white clapboard—but to Charlotte it was beautiful. It was home.

Built in the 1860s, the Christiansen homestead sat on a knoll that rose up from the shore, and now the early sun shone golden on the wide front porch where honeysuckle vines blossomed. A bench swing hung from the rafters, and next to it was the wooden rocking chair Ben had made for her.

Charlotte hefted Marta's burlap sacks from the boat and carried them up the stone walk. On the porch she gave the rocker a little push to set it going.

Inside, the front rooms—living room on the right, dining room on the left—were bright with morning sun. All was in order.

Charlotte carried the sacks down the hall, set them on the kitchen table, and peered out the back door to the orchard. That was what drew her, Thomas's cherry orchard. It extended across sixty acres of flat, fertile soil, ninety trees to the acre, 5,400 trees in all.

Thomas had grown up here, and his father before him. Now Charlotte had lived here longer than she'd lived on the dairy farm down near Kewaunee. There she had learned about animals from her father and housekeeping from her mother. But what she enjoyed most was the vegetable garden—the dark rich scent of the earth, the miracle of seeds, and the feel of the cool soil on her bare feet when she ran between the rows, her cotton pinafore kicking up in the breeze.

Mama had served as cook and housemaid for the Romanos, the family that owned the dairy where Pa was foreman. Every evening, after an early supper, Charlotte helped her mother serve the Romanos and their dinner guests. Charlotte liked to peek in on them eating the vegetables she had nurtured—salad greens, tomatoes, cucumbers, carrots, beets, squash. They all cooed over young Charlotte—"Did you really grow these beans yourself? Oh, such a pretty child!" Then they'd turn away and go on discussing their grown-up things.

That is, until Mama served them pie. That was what everyone liked best, Mama's pies—strawberry, blueberry, and rhubarb in the summer; apple and pumpkin in the fall; and finally, minced meat at Christmas. The secret's in the dough, Mama told her. So Charlotte watched and listened and learned until Mama let her make the pies herself.

Charlotte was fifteen when the Romano boys took a calf to the state fair and invited Charlotte to ride along with her pies. She didn't win a prize that time, but people who tasted the pies wanted more.

The blue ribbon came later, the year she met Thomas. She was seventeen; he was twenty. "Your apple pie tastes like coming home," he said. He was tall and lean with a pleasant face, and his eyes crinkled at the edges when he smiled. She was glad she had worn her baby-blue sundress.

After another taste, he said, "How many pies do you have left?" He spoke in a quiet, thoughtful way.

"Only three." She smiled from under her lashes and pushed a strand of white-blond hair behind an ear.

He pulled a leather wallet from his pocket. "I'll buy them all."
He paused. "If you'll tell me your name."

Heat spread to her cheeks. He winked and said,

> *There is a garden in her face,*
> *Where roses and white lilies show;*
> *A heavenly paradise is that place,*
> *Wherein all pleasant fruits do grow.*

"Charlotte," she finally whispered.

"Charlotte." He closed his eyes as if savoring a favorite dish, and said,

> *Werther had a love for Charlotte*
> *Such as words could never utter;*
> *Would you know how first he met her?*
> *She was cutting bread and butter.*

What's he talking about? "Who's Werther?"

He chuckled. "Just a fictional fellow in a poem by Thackeray."

Thackeray? How was she to respond to that?

"Pleased to meet you, Charlotte." He held out his hand, long
fingers like a piano player, light touch. A mellow fragrance of cherry
tobacco. "My name's Thomas. Thomas Christiansen."

He wore a freshly pressed linen shirt, beige linen trousers, and
fine leather shoes. He looked a bit askew—his jacket slung over a
shoulder, his shoes dusty—but given the quality of his clothes and
his educated manner, she judged him prosperous.

"I don't know many poems," she said. She didn't want to tell
him she thought poems silly, all those nursery rhymes about someone named Jack—Jack Be Nimble, Jack and Jill, Jack Sprat, Little
Jack Horner. Her mind raced forward until she recalled one about
Tommy and the words flew from her lips:

Little Tommy Tucker
Sings for his supper.
What shall we give him?
White bread and butter.
How shall he cut it
Without a knife . . .

She stopped. She hadn't thought it through.

"How will he marry / Without a wife?" Thomas concluded with a grin. "And now that you have no more pies to sell, Charlotte, would you go walking with me?"

When she blushed, he leaned in and said, "Your cheeks are like cherries. I'll just bet you make the best cherry pie." He held out an arm for her and sang,

She can make a cherry pie
Quick as cat can wink its eye—

"I've never made a cherry pie."

"Never? Well, whaddya know. I have an orchard filled with cherries, and no one to make me a pie."

She took his arm. "You have an orchard?"

They strolled through the fairgrounds noisy with carnival rides and pitchmen hawking tickets to sideshows. Calliope music piped all about. She sat on a painted horse circling round the carousel. He stood beside her, his hand on her horse's mane, and told her he had intended to pursue a literary career, but when his father and brother died in a fire, he gave up his university studies and returned home to take care of his distraught mother and run the family orchard.

Over the years Charlotte would sense that Thomas had left behind more than just his studies, but she never asked because she was afraid he'd say yes. And even if he'd said no, she wouldn't have believed him.

Charlotte was a good wife. She took care of Thomas's mother

until the sickly woman died. She ran an efficient home, managed a bountiful garden, cooked and sewed, did the bookkeeping, and taught Ben and Kate the responsibilities of farm life. Thomas loved her, she knew. But he loved other things too. He loved his books, and whatever he had wanted before, whatever he had left at the university, Charlotte couldn't give him that.

She turned from the orchard and walked down to the dock to reel in the boat. Out in the yard, Mia, the nanny goat, gazed up from where she was munching newly sprouted grass. That first year without a harvest Charlotte had butchered the other two goats and kept this last one for milk. Who knew the war would last this long. Only families with small children got ration stamps for store-bought milk, so even goat's milk was in demand.

Chickens pecked about, ignoring her. Just five hens left. One night some weeks ago the rooster didn't return to the coop. With all his strutting and cock-a-doodling out there in the dark, he must have been easy prey for a fox or coyote. Until Charlotte had another rooster to fertilize the eggs, she couldn't afford to serve her family chicken.

She thought of the eggs she had traded for the yarn, deep blue like Ben's eyes. She had seen it in the window of Ellie's Dry Goods. How could she resist, even if it left her nothing to trade for stew meat? She had counted on Olga's credit. But now she had fish for two or three dinners and a bounty of fruits and vegetables, so the trades had worked well. A half-dozen eggs for all this.

No. She glanced toward the rabbit pen. Not when she factored in all the hurt and anger and mistrust. And the beautiful vest Ben would never wear.

After reeling in the boat, Charlotte returned to the kitchen and picked up yesterday's *Door County Advocate*. She spread open the pages to the local ads and brought the bucket of fish to the table. One by one, she scaled and gutted them, then put the pinky-white fillets into the icebox.

Charlotte typically saved knitting and mending for evenings, sitting in the parlor with Thomas while he read his books. She had her daily chores—today was washday—but right now she wanted to make something for Ben. She carried her canvas satchel to the parlor and switched on the Philco—Glenn Miller's band playing "I Dream of You." From the couch she could see the grove of budding birch and maple and the orchard beyond. Off in the distance Thomas was pruning. He couldn't possibly prune all the trees before the blossoms came. *When will those PWs arrive?*

She opened her satchel—not much yarn left. What could she make with so little? Bingo jumped onto Charlotte's lap, startling her. Charlotte petted the cat in long strokes until he purred and settled.

When she looked up again, her eyes focused on the War Mother's Flag hanging in the window. Its big blue star told the world her boy served in the armed forces. According to the news, General Clark's army was positioned in the icy mountains of Monte Cassino. Charlotte didn't know much about the geography of Italy, but she knew the pattern for socks: knit one, purl two. Picking up her knitting needles, she cast on forty-two stitches.

Marta's children didn't like fish. Charlotte shook her head. She might have gotten the lot of them with a simple scarf. If only she hadn't taken the vest.

The music ended, and the local newsman announced a clearance sale at the dress shop, a woman injured in an accident down at the shipyard, a boy from Egg Harbor killed in the Battle of Saipan. *Killed!* Johnny Malone . . . in Ben's class!

The cat jumped away.

Charlotte's hands clenched the couch cushion, eyes focused on the War Mother's Flag, heart racing. She gulped for air. Gulped again and took a ragged breath. Then another.

The newsman was talking about the weather—mostly sunny— then Bing Crosby's voice was crooning "I'll Be Seeing You." Charlotte tipped back her head to keep the tears from falling. Her shaking hands took up the needles. Keep going. Knit one, purl two.

CHAPTER FIVE

KATE READ EAGERLY TO THE END. "And the ashes blew towards us with the salt wind from the sea." Ashes of Manderley.

After reading those last lines, she reluctantly closed the book and stared at the yellow book jacket—*Rebecca*, Daphne du Maurier. Kate wanted to meet this author, learn the impetus for the story. The biographical note on the inside flap said that du Maurier lived in Cornwall, England. Worlds away.

Kate put down the book, switched off her nightstand lamp, and lay back on her pillow. She decided she liked sad endings best. Why was that? She was eager to discuss it with Professor Fleming.

An owl hooted from the woods: *hoo h'hoo hoooo.* Another echoed in the distance. The beam from the lighthouse swept across the ceiling.

Professor Fleming. Kate closed her eyes and brought it all back—four years ago, when she was thirteen.

From the time Kate was a little girl, Father had taken her to every theater production in the county—community plays, school performances, even puppet shows. Mother and Ben weren't interested, but

Kate loved escaping into the stories. When Father proposed to take Kate to a play at the university in Madison, Mother wasn't pleased. But it was November, the orchard was dormant for the winter, the root cellar was full, and Ben volunteered to do Kate's chores while she was away.

"It'll be just one night," Father had said.

With overnight bags in hand, Kate and Father boarded the train in a flurry of feathery snow and traveled south through small towns and open countryside, passing snow-covered red barns and carrot-nosed snowmen and children skating on backyard ponds.

Once on their way, Father opened his valise and pulled out a book. *Show Boat.* "The play's based on this novel." He handed it to Kate. "Written by a Wisconsin girl, Edna Ferber. Grew up in Appleton. We'll be going right through there on the way."

Greedy for a new story, Kate pushed off her shoes, pulled her legs up under her wool plaid skirt, and opened the book.

The train stopped now and then. Passengers pulled parcels down from overhead racks and hurried off. Others entered with a cold draft, shook snow from their coats and hats, found spaces for their things. Kate barely registered these changes, so engaged was she in the story.

She was about halfway through the novel when Father touched her arm. "I'll be right back." After the whistle blew a second time, he returned with a bouquet of flowers. He seemed eager, excited. "We're nearly there."

"Who are those for?"

"Someone I'd like you to meet."

When they disembarked in Madison, a woman waved from the platform. She had dark hair and big brown eyes and wore a belted raccoon coat and matching hat and very high heels.

Father gave her the flowers and introduced her as Miss Fleming— "Professor Fleming," he quickly corrected himself. "She wasn't a professor when we met, how many years ago?" He didn't wait for her response. "And now her stories are published in *Atlantic Monthly, Harper's* . . ."

"Oh, Thomas." She hugged his arm. "That's enough."

Miss Fleming—Father was soon calling her Deenie—drove them to the university. Bundled in winter coats and hats and gloves, they walked along shoveled sidewalks to a grand stone building. "The Memorial Union," Miss Fleming told them.

"It's like a palace," Kate said.

The union stood on the shore of the frozen lake. A single skater twirled and danced on the ice, casting a long shadow in the low orange sun. Two boys on the beach pushed off in an iceboat, and once the sail was up, the little skiff tacked back and forth, then raced out across the lake faster than any boat Kate had ever seen.

Inside, Miss Fleming led them to a noisy dining hall, Der Rathskeller, permeated with the scent of wet wool and beer. When Father helped Miss Fleming out of her coat, she looked stunning in a slim green wool flannel skirt and jacket. The three of them sat in front of a fireplace painted with German murals and ordered bratwurst and beer, a cherry soda for Kate.

Students came and went—some lingered in serious conversation, others laughed in groups or flirted in corners. The girls looked sharp in neat wool skirts, knit sweaters, and leather saddle shoes. Boys wore V-neck sweaters over shirts and ties. Kate took note of the clothes, the way the coeds wore their hair, the flirting, the jostling.

Kate was wearing her best cardigan sweater and white cotton blouse. "The fire feels good," she said, rubbing her arms.

Father smiled and launched into his poet voice: " 'Some say the world will end in fire, / Some say in ice.' "

"I'll take fire," Miss Fleming said, glancing toward Father with a grin.

"My favorite Frost poem is 'The Road Not Taken,' " Kate said. " 'Two roads diverged in a yellow wood, / And sorry I could not travel both . . .' "

Once she'd finished, Father said. "If only we could travel both." He looked at Miss Fleming.

She cleared her throat, and then, after a pause, turned to Kate. "Your father tells me you like to write stories."

When did he tell her that?

"Speaking of favorites," Father said, "my favorite Kate story is 'The Deer and the Wolf.'" Then to Kate, he said, "May I tell it?"

Kate blushed. But when Miss Fleming looked her way, expectant, she nodded.

Father put down his beer and began. "A female deer finds a wolf cub abandoned in the woods and takes it in to replace her fawn, which had been shot by a careless boy." He paused to sip his beer. "Once the wolf is weaned, he goes off on his own. Then, one day the wolf is running with a pack, running down the very deer that raised him. Kate has a way of showing how conflicted the wolf is as he bites into his mother doe."

Miss Fleming touched a paper napkin to her lips. "That's quite a story, Kate. Do you recall where the idea came from?"

Yes, she recalled it clearly. "I was walking through the woods and saw a doe and her fawn and wondered what might happen if the fawn were to die and the doe had milk coming for her baby. And the story came all at once."

"Would you be willing to share some of your writing with me?"

Kate thought of the notebooks filled with poems and stories and random thoughts, simple reflections on everyday things. "Not much happens in my stories."

"It's not what happens but how your characters react," Miss Fleming said. "Want to give me an example where not much happens?"

Kate put down her bratwurst and wiped her hands on her napkin. "I was milking one of the goats, and she nearly kicked over the pail of milk. I started a story about what would happen if she did. But it's silly—"

"Tell me."

"Well, I'd need to make the milk really important, right? Maybe they need it to survive." She paused. "Oh, this sounds childish!"

"Not at all." Miss Fleming patted her hand. "Go on."

Kate took a big breath. "The protagonist doesn't want to disappoint her mother, so instead of telling the truth, she sneaks into a neighbor's barn and milks their goat. I don't know what happens next. I haven't figured that out."

"It could go in so many directions," Miss Fleming said. "That's the best kind of story. Once you decide how to end it, I'd love to read it."

"When I finish it, I'll send it to you." Kate paused. "But I'd never show it to Mother."

Father coughed as if choking, then sipped his beer.

"Writers don't have parents," Miss Fleming said, giving Kate a wink.

Kate blushed with Father right there.

"Your dad's on your side. He would have made a fine English professor."

Father smiled. "Well, I don't know about that—"

"Your father and I once talked about opening a bookstore together."

"What about the orchard?" Kate blurted.

Father frowned and looked away.

THE THEATER LOBBY WAS ABUZZ with students calling to each other, talking, laughing. A group of boys and girls came up to Miss Fleming, and when the professor introduced Kate as a friend, the students seemed eager to know her. "When will you be coming here?" "What do you want to major in?"

Before Kate could answer, a bell sounded and everyone headed toward the auditorium.

They had front-row seats, and as the curtain rose and the orchestra swelled with "Ol' Man River," Kate felt herself right up there on the levee in Natchez, Mississippi, boarding the riverboat.

When the curtain fell for intermission, Kate followed Father and Miss Fleming to the lobby café, where they ordered drinks.

Kate took a sip of hot chocolate and asked them how they met.

"It was freshman year," Miss Fleming said. "Homecoming dance." She picked up her beer mug.

Father laughed and clinked his mug against hers. "So long ago."

Kate tried to imagine Father at a student dance.

"I was studying agronomy, but Deenie persuaded me to take a literature class."

"And do you regret it?" Miss Fleming challenged in a teasing voice.

"I wouldn't have signed up for more if I did." He touched her hand. "You know how I enjoy reading. Tell her, Kate."

"Father loves his books. But Mother thinks it's a silly waste of time."

Father frowned at that last part. "Well, things change."

"Indeed," said Miss Fleming, a pensive look.

After a pause, Father took a sip of beer and grinned. "Remember the time the sailboat dumped us into the middle of Lake Mendota?"

"The picnic!" She turned to Kate. "I made your father a batch of brownies with a bit of brandy, my own special touch. The fish who found my sweet treats must have had a fine afternoon."

"Your sweet treats." Father winked her way.

"But hey, TomTom." She gave a light punch to his shoulder. "You were strong enough to right that big boat."

TomTom? Kate's eyes widened.

"It was a small boat, Deenie. Your memories are larger than my capabilities."

Kate put down her chocolate. "I had no idea how fun college could be."

"Tell me, Kate," Miss Fleming said. "Are you interested in coming here to the U?"

"Oh yes! But . . ." She looked at Father. *Was it possible?*

He nodded. And with that nod, the window to Kate's little world blew wide open.

After the play, they walked to the freshman girls' dormitory where Miss Fleming had arranged for Kate to stay the night. Kate introduced herself with her full proper name, Katrina Linn Christiansen, because if she was to be an author, that was how she wanted to be known.

The girls stayed up well past midnight, discussing the play and answering Kate's questions about college life.

That was where she wanted to be right now. She wanted to live in that dormitory with those girls forever.

CHAPTER SIX

CHARLOTTE LOOKED UP at the sound of an approaching vehicle and peered out the back door. Finally! An Army truck, green with a big white star on the door and a canvas-covered bed, rumbled down Orchard Lane. She wiped her hands on her apron and went out to the porch.

Thomas was directing the truck off to the far side of the property, toward the migrant workers' camp, a collection of whitewashed wooden buildings that included a bunkhouse, cookhouse, outhouse, and dining hall. The prisoners would stay through the fall, working first here in the cherry orchard, then in Gus's apple orchard over on Plum Bottom Road. That was the agreement. The Army had erected a snow fence around the camp, a meager defense, but they also sent guards who spoke German. They had culled the dangerous ones—the SS were identified by tattoos of their blood type etched on the underside of their left arms, Charlotte was told. The men sent here had been approved and were glad to have the work.

The migrant camp was not visible from the house, but Charlotte was curious to see the prisoners. She waited on the porch until Thomas, flanked by two Army guards with holstered pistols, led about a dozen men into the orchard. Thomas was speaking to one of the guards. Charlotte couldn't hear their conversation, but intermittently the guard would shout out orders in what must have been German. The prisoners stood at attention in brown and tan outfits, a large "PW" imprinted on the backs of their shirts. Even from this distance, Charlotte could see that most were mere boys, like Ben.

When Thomas turned to take the PWs to the barn, Charlotte ducked inside. Peeking through the kitchen window, she watched as one of the prisoners caught up to Thomas and walked alongside him. The two appeared to be in conversation. Thomas didn't speak German, so this man must know English. She watched until the group emerged from the barn, carrying pole pruners and loppers, saws, hatchets, rakes, and ladders.

Finally, we will have our harvest.

CHARLOTTE FINGERED THE SOIL in her garden. The rain had let up for nearly a week, and the beds were dry enough for planting. It was a sweet little quarter-acre of rich loamy earth surrounded by chicken wire to keep out deer and rabbits. She noticed a few places where the fence needed mending. She had always counted on Ben to help her. She glanced toward the barn as if expecting to see her handsome son heading her way with his toolbox, whistling, happy to fix whatever wanted fixing.

There'd be time for fence mending later. She had to get the seeds into the ground while the weather held. She went to the barn to fetch the tools.

Back in the garden, Charlotte picked up the heavy cultivating fork, put a foot on the crossbar, and pushed the chisel-like steel tines into the ground. She worked up one row and down another, preparing the earth for planting. It was hard, physical labor, turning the soil, but she loved the smell of earth, the scent of abundance.

It was late in the day when a bicycle bell jangled Charlotte's attention away from her work. Kate was riding down Orchard Lane on her way home from school, long blond hair blowing in the breeze, white cotton blouse pressed against her young breasts, skirt flapping up, revealing shapely legs.

Just then, one of the prisoners dropped his rake and charged toward Kate. Charlotte threw down the pitchfork and ran, shouting, but the others were too far away to hear. From this distance, she couldn't make out the prisoner's face, but he was squat and solid, barrel-chested, with a short blond crew cut.

Thomas was running as well. He rushed the man, tripped him, and the prisoner hit the ground face-first. Kate's bicycle wobbled and toppled, spilling Kate with her books and papers onto the gravel. One of the guards stood over the prisoner, pistol pointed at the cowering man. When the PW scrambled to his feet, the guard pushed him off in the direction of the migrant camp.

This was what the county board had feared, what Charlotte herself had feared. And the season was only beginning.

Thomas helped Kate to her feet and picked up her things. He put an arm around her shoulders and walked her down the lane to the yard. Kate was not one to cry, but her face was puffed with tears, her blouse was ripped, and she had bloody bruises on her bare knees.

Thomas nodded to Charlotte, then returned to the orchard.

"Oh, Kate!" Charlotte wanted to hug her close, but that wasn't her way.

"I can't believe you let those killers into our yard!" Kate choked out the words. "That Nazi wanted to kill me! Don't you care? Aren't you afraid?"

"Yes, I am afraid. But we're not going to let them know that." They walked to the barn with Kate's bicycle. "They'll be gone in a few months." Charlotte tried to sound cheerful. "Just steer clear of them."

"And they better steer clear of me." Kate's voice trembled.

THE ONLY ACCESS TO THE ROOT CELLAR was from the back of the house, through double wooden doors that angled up against the foundation. When Charlotte went out, a breeze lifted the hem of her housedress. It was dusk now, and the setting sun had pulled the warmth down with it. She rubbed her arms briskly to warm herself.

As she bent over to grab the metal ring on one of the cellar doors, she sensed eyes upon her. She looked up to see the German prisoner, the one who had spoken with Thomas, loitering at the edge of the orchard. Was he watching her? He turned away and rolled a wheelbarrow of pruned branches to the woodshed.

Charlotte shivered as she stepped down into the cool stone cavern beneath the kitchen. She struck a match and lit the kerosene lantern she kept on the shelf. Opening the grain bin, she silently celebrated her find—a handful of wild rice had fallen into a corner. She brushed it into her palm and went back up. The prisoner was gone.

AT THE SUPPER TABLE, Thomas was filled with enthusiasm about the progress in the orchard. "These fellows are good workers. We should be done with the pruning in a week." He paused. "But there might be some bad ones out there," he said to Kate, "so you keep clear of them, all right? Especially that one who knocked you down . . . Fritz Vehlmer's his name."

"He has crazy eyes," Kate said. "And that scar on his cheek. I don't want to see any of them ever again. And I don't want them looking at me either."

"Glad to hear it," Thomas said.

"You need to send that one away," Charlotte said.

"I told the Army guards to send him back to the prison and bring me a new man, but they said the Army wouldn't replace him. They assured me that Vehlmer was only interested in Kate's bicycle. He's a mechanic, and he heard a rattle as she rode by." Thomas paused. "They say this fellow's good at fixing things. I'm going to have him take a look at the tractor. And your bicycle, Kate."

"I don't want anyone touching my bicycle!"

"Fine. Fine." Thomas patted Kate's hand.

Kate took a drink of water.

When Thomas put a forkful of fish into his mouth, he said, "This is heaven, Char. Lord knows how you do it. Lemon for the fish. Green vegetables." He stabbed at his salad.

Charlotte had put most of the food into the icebox. Orange slices would be a surprise after dinner. Grapefruit for breakfast. And coffee with cream and sugar.

"Kate, your mother's a culinary magician."

Kate nodded. "It's really good."

After a pause, Thomas said to Charlotte. "You were up late last night."

"I was knitting . . . something for Ben." Her eyes clouded with the thought of the vest she had traded this morning. No, she wouldn't think of that now. "Would you like more spinach?"

"Ah." Thomas accepted the bowl from her.

"I was surprised to see you talking to one of the prisoners," she said. "Do they speak English?"

"Just the one, Karl Becker."

Charlotte debated about telling Thomas that Becker had watched her going into the root cellar, but Thomas continued. "He's a math teacher. Smart, well read it appears. Went to Oxford." He paused, then quoted:

Ye sacred nurseries of blooming youth!
In whose collegiate shelter England's flowers
Expand, enjoying through their vernal hours
The air of liberty, the light of truth—

Kate waved a hand, stopping him. "I don't know that one."

"Wordsworth. A bit obscure, I'll admit. He wrote it while at Oxford," Thomas said with a wink. "Say, how's Hawthorne coming?"

"*The Scarlet Letter?* I've just about finished it."

Thomas smiled. "Original sin exposed." He took a sip of water and picked up his empty pipe. "So what do you think of Hester Prynne's decision?"

"It's not fair that Hester's the one who's condemned, but it's her own fault for not telling the truth about her baby's father."

"She's filled with guilt." Thomas sucked on his pipe. "She tempted the minister. As Eve tempted Adam in the garden."

"Kate?" Charlotte stood to clear the table.

The girl continued the conversation with her father as she rinsed the dishes. "Hester takes all the blame while the minister says nothing. He's the one who should feel guilty. He should wear a scarlet letter too."

"But she's the stronger character, don't you think? She makes the choice, she's the one who lives, while he disintegrates—"

"That was Chillingworth's doing, that's what I think."

Enough of this silly talk. Charlotte put her hands on her hips. "Let that be a lesson."

Kate looked up from the sink. "About what?"

"Keep your legs together."

"Mother!" Kate's cheeks went red.

Thomas coughed and looked away.

Charlotte smiled to herself. If they had to talk about made-up stories, they could at least find a practical message in there. She opened the icebox and chose one of the oranges to slice.

AFTER SUPPER, CHARLOTTE WENT to the parlor and switched on the Philco. She sat on the couch, opened her sewing basket, and pulled out a sock that needed darning. Thomas sat in the green brocade wingback chair, sucking on his empty pipe, a book open in front of him. Frank Sinatra was singing, "All or nothin' at all," when the music abruptly stopped: "We interrupt this broadcast for a special bulletin. Allies have taken Monte Cassino. Repeat. Allied troops have driven the Germans from Monte Cassino."

Charlotte dropped the sock and stared at the radio. Thomas put down his book.

The announcer went on: "In the early morning hours today, May 18, 1944, a patrol of the Polish 12th Regiment serving in the US Fifth Army under the command of Major General Mark W. Clark raised a flag over the ruins of Monte Cassino Abbey. The only remnants of the defenders were a group of thirty Germans, all wounded. The road to Rome is open. And now we return to the previous broadcast."

Sinatra's voice came back.

"Oh, Thomas! They've done it. Ben's finally out of those terrible mountains."

Thomas smiled. "I'm sure we'll read all about it in the paper tomorrow."

Bingo mewed and jumped on the couch. Charlotte scooped him into her lap and pushed her fingers through his soft gray fur. "Thomas, what is the first thing you want when we have money again?"

"The tractor needs new tires."

"Damn tractor. Horses are more reliable."

"You want to manage the orchard?"

"What else?"

Thomas studied his pipe. "I'll get myself a good stash of tobacco." He paused. "What about you, Char?"

The cat was asleep now, but Charlotte's fingers didn't stop massaging his neck. "I need a rooster. And enough layer hens to replenish the flock. And two more goats. And cows. Dairy cows. I'll start with two." Charlotte's mind wandered to her past. Fresh sweet milk, as much as she wanted. Yes, after the war, when Ben came home, Charlotte would go to the county fair and choose two prize calves.

"Cows, they take a lot of work, Char."

"You forget I grew up on a dairy farm."

"I haven't forgotten." He gave her a wink. "My sweet rosy milkmaid."

Charlotte cozied into the couch. "Just think, if we had had a cow these past few years we'd be doing so well, selling milk and butter and cream and cheese. And buttermilk. I don't recall when I last had buttermilk. If we had a cow, we could feed the whey to the goats and chickens. Hire a bull every spring to get a calf to slaughter at a year. Self-sufficient."

"You got it all worked out, my pretty cowgirl. A rooster. A stud bull. I see where that mind of yours is going."

She laughed. "You're always searching for hidden meanings."

"Isn't that what women are about? Hidden meanings?"

"I'll make vanilla bean ice cream. Oh, I can almost taste it! With cherry sauce."

"Cherry sauce. Hmm." Thomas stood and held out his hand for her to follow.

CHARLOTTE SAT BEFORE HER DRESSING TABLE and reached for her hairbrush. When Thomas touched her shoulders, she let him take the brush, pulling it gently through her long blond hair. Charlotte closed her eyes, savoring the sensual delight of the simple act.

It had been so long since she had taken pleasure in his touch. Thomas had always been a lusty man, and they had enjoyed their time together in bed. But since Ben left, Charlotte merely went through the motions. As his wife, it was her duty. But she hadn't wanted it, not as she used to.

"*You* didn't keep your legs together, my sweet," he whispered in her ear.

Charlotte opened her eyes to meet his in the mirror. "I couldn't resist you, Thomas."

When they married, Charlotte was already pregnant. It happened in the hayloft at the dairy, rain pouring down beyond the barn window, cows stomping and bellowing below, the fertile pungent earth, and a future with a man who had inherited his family orchard. Yes, for Thomas, Charlotte opened her legs.

And now, as she lay next to him on their bed, she opened again, and Thomas moved toward her, his lanky body coming warm against her own, his hands on her breasts, on her buttocks, knowing them, coming into her, full and familiar.

"You are my downfall," he whispered. "My original sin."

She smiled at his wordplay.

"You will wear my scarlet letter." He thrust forward.

She slid her hands up his back, recalling that first time. Grasping him close, the physical presence of Thomas, the man she had wanted so many years ago, now touching her face, breathing into her hair. Whispering her name.

And now, right now, her body wanted him, needed him. Whispering back.

CHAPTER SEVEN

KATE WOKE TO THE SHARP ODOR OF SKUNK. Rising on an elbow, she peered out to the lake where the morning mist floated over still water in that gray-white light that comes just before dawn.

She listened as if she might hear him—Ben—whistling in the room next to hers. He had always risen early to do his chores. He'd often do hers as well, then pop his head into her room, singing "Lazy Katie, will you get up, will you get up, will you get up . . ."

She raked her fingers through her tangled hair. She didn't mind the skunk so much. No, it reminded her of a spicy pine forest, tramping through the woods with Ben. She slipped out of her flannel nightgown and pulled on a cotton shirt, wool sweater, and overalls.

Downstairs, the warm scent of burning cherry wood emanated from the stove where Mother was sterilizing milk pails, humming the way she used to back when everything was normal. Must be because of the war news, Ben on his way to Rome.

"Morning, Kate."

"Morning."

Kate put on her wool jacket and cap and picked up the covered pails. Outside, the cold climbed in and she pulled her jacket close. She had always felt safe in the yard any time of day or night, but now she imagined prisoners lurking in the shadows. The snow fence encircling the camp served more as a perimeter than a barricade, light enough to be knocked down by anyone determined to escape. She pictured the wild eyes of that Nazi who had rushed her, and she shivered.

Sliding aside the heavy wooden barn door, Kate inhaled the calming warmth of animal sweat and dung and headed toward the goat pen.

What's that? A rustle and thump in the hayloft. Kate froze.

Ginger Cat jumped to the floor and dashed off toward the empty stalls after something too quick for Kate to spot. Kate let out a heavy breath.

The stalls once held two draft horses, Getup and Sunrise. Father sold the horses a few years back to buy the tractor. Mornings were easier for Kate now that she didn't have to care for the horses, but she missed them. The barn seemed bigger, empty. Almost scary.

Stepping into the goat pen, Kate petted Mia in long strokes and murmured softly to her. Mother had taught her how to relax animals before milking. Mia shook her stubby tail. Kate put a bit of hay in the feed tray, helped the goat onto the milking stanchion, tethered her to the post, and cleaned her udder. Sitting on the milking stool, Kate took one of the nanny's warm, fuzzy teats into each hand, gently working the milk down the soft tubular appendages, squirting it into the pail. She wondered what it was like for Mia, this touching and squeezing. The first time she had milked a goat she was embarrassed with the intimacy of the act. Mia bleated as if she enjoyed it.

While she worked, Kate's mind wandered to the university, the girls in the dormitory. She had read the acceptance packet numerous times, memorized the schedules and campus map. Her roommate would be Libby Huntington from Shorewood Hills. Libby.

She had never met anyone named Libby. She hoped this Libby Huntington from Shorewood Hills liked to go to plays and discuss literature.

After Kate let Mia into the yard, she tossed out feed for the hens and gathered eggs from their nests. She swept out the stalls with the big push broom, then climbed the ladder to the dusty hayloft and pitched a forkful of hay down to the floor below. All the while, Kate longed for the day she would be away from here, reading and writing and conversing with interesting people like Miss Fleming and the girls in the dormitory. But behind it all was the guilt, guilt about leaving her mother. *What will she do when I'm gone?* Everything would be better when Ben came home. But when would that be?

Kate wandered over to Ben's workbench. He would sit on his stool for hours, whittling fallen limbs and burls into furniture and figurines, listening to the hit parade on that old radio he'd fixed up. She blew dust from the radio and switched it on. Bill Austin with his "Is You or Is You Ain't My Baby." Louis Jordan on the trumpet. She knew the singer because Ben always guessed the songs and the singers as soon as the music started, and he'd challenge Kate to do the same. Ben would whistle along. He tried to teach her to whistle, but her mouth wouldn't make the shape right.

Ben's wood-carving kit sat neatly on his workbench alongside hunks of wood, just as he had left it all. A log lay near the lathe, ready to make into some piece of furniture, no doubt. He had made the kitchen table and chairs, as well as Mother's rocking chair on the front porch.

Kate picked up one of his carvings—a rearing horse with well-defined muscles and mane. The eyes were wild with fear. Ben must have been working on this before he left. "He'll be home soon now," Mother had said a few days ago. "I can just feel it."

Nat King Cole was signing "Straighten Up and Fly Right." Kate put down the figurine and turned off the radio.

On the other side of the barn, Kate opened the rabbit hutch. She gently drew Mama Bunny from the hutch, stroked her soft gray fur, and put her into a holding pen. She changed the fat rabbit's straw bedding and added fresh water and spring greens.

Out in the rabbit pen, Kate cuddled a few of the little ones, then scattered feed pellets. "Spring's here and soon you'll be dining on new clover and dandelion leaves."

Kate returned to the barn to clean up, and when she finally emerged back out into the morning, songbirds greeted her—melodious finches, cheery robins, squeaky little chickadees. Sparrows hopped among the chickens, pecking the ground. Near the edge of the woods, a doe with two speckled fawns fed on green sprouts.

The sun was just peeking up from across the lake, the rim of a ball, huge and red. Kate stood transfixed as the gray-blue mist turned shades of pink and rose from the glassy surface. Reflections of trees rippled along the shore. A family of ducks floated by like paper boats. She thought of Thoreau—"drifting meadow of the air." The world was no longer scary. She breathed in the fresh morning and kicked through dewy grass.

Coffee? Even before Kate opened the kitchen door she smelled it. Inside, Mother and Father were speaking quietly as if they had a secret. When Kate entered, they stopped abruptly and pulled away from each other. Yes, they were drinking coffee!

"Would you like a cup?" Charlotte asked. "And there's cream and sugar."

"Yes, please!" Kate scooted her chair up to the table.

Charlotte served plates of scrambled eggs with grapefruit slices and pastry.

Thomas took a bite. "Little Mother. How do you do it?"

Charlotte smiled and held up the pot. "More coffee?"

"Ah, yes." After another sip, he said, "I'm going to have the PWs start spraying today. I found aphids in the trees on the far side of the orchard."

Charlotte touched Kate's hand. "Mind that you stay upwind of the poison."

Kate knew well enough. Breathing in the pesticide tasted awful and burned her lungs.

"I'm going to try something new. I got a letter from Dr. Michaels down at the university. He told me that a simple soap mixture could do as well as the lead-arsenic. Safer, less expensive too."

Charlotte shook her head. "Of all the years, this isn't the time to try anything new. We could lose the whole crop—"

"I'll test it on a small sample. If the aphids return, I can always follow with the poison. Right, Kate?"

She nodded. *Why is Mother always so negative?*

"He sent me the recipe." Thomas wiped his mouth with a napkin. "I'll have Karl help me mix the solution in the barn."

"You'll have a guard with you, of course."

"Karl and I will be fine—"

Charlotte held her fork in the air. "You can't trust any of those prisoners—"

"What do you expect him to do, Char? Steal a chicken?"

"I'm thinking of the butchering tools."

"So maybe he'll butcher a chicken?" Thomas patted her hand, chuckling.

"He's younger and . . . and maybe stronger than you." She stood and cleared the plates from the table.

Thomas picked up his pipe, paused. "I've spent time with Karl, off away from the others. He has some interesting thoughts about Thomas Mann. In *Magic Mountain*, Karl sees allusions to irrational forces within the human psyche. I'm going to read it again."

Irrational forces within the human psyche? "I'd like to read it too," Kate said, rising to help.

"Excellent. Then we'll discuss it, you and I. And Karl."

Charlotte turned from the sink. "Kate discussing things with prisoners? No. Never." She banged the cast-iron skillet on the wooden countertop. "Those prisoners come into the orchard with guards and leave with guards and so be it. We'll have our harvest and that's the end of it."

Recalling the eyes of that crazy Nazi Fritz, Kate for once sided with her mother.

Thomas shook his head. "Karl is an intellectual. He'd like to read more American authors." He sucked on his empty pipe, then after a moment, added, "I told him I'd lend him some of my books."

"Lending personal items to prisoners?"

"What's the harm?" He put his pipe on the table.

Charlotte rinsed dishes in silence, handing them to Kate to dry. Then she wiped her hands on her apron. "Well, if you're going to be sharing things with him, you might ask for something in return."

"I enjoy his conversation."

"The canteen truck comes every week. He has Army scrip to buy anything they bring. Why not trade the loan of your books for some pipe tobacco? I know how you miss it."

"I never thought of that, Char." He stared at the empty bowl of his pipe. "Sure would be nice to have tobacco again."

"I don't believe this!" Kate broke in. "Ben's buddies are being blown apart over there."

Father put down the pipe. "Where do you get such ideas?"

"It's his letters to that girl, isn't it?" Mother crossed her arms.

"Yes," Kate heard herself whisper.

"Please don't keep information about Ben from us, Kate," Father said.

"The letters have lines blacked out. We're just guessing what's behind the marks." Oh, she should have kept her mouth shut. "If Josie found out that I told you, she wouldn't show me anything else."

Thomas cleared his throat. "We certainly don't want you to lie to your friend. You don't have to tell us anything personal Ben writes to her, just the news of what's happening. That's all. Is that reasonable?"

Kate nodded and wiped her hands on her overalls. "I have to wash and change for school."

"Yes, and you'd better work on your math," Thomas said. "Otherwise, you'll be taking remedial classes at the university instead of doing the work you want."

Math, ugh. Kate expected to get all A's on her report card again this semester, except in math.

"Say, what would you think . . ." Thomas began. "Our Kate here needs help with mathematics, a tutor."

Kate waited for more.

"Karl's a math professor—"

"What!" Charlotte spun around.

"I've asked Karl many probing questions about his background and sympathies. He wasn't one of Hitler's men." He paused a moment. "I'd be right here with him."

"I don't like it," Charlotte said.

Thomas leaned forward. "Believe me, I see most of those PWs as the enemy. And I don't want them near my home. But Karl . . . I think we can trust him."

"*Think?*" Charlotte balled her fists. "You *think* we can trust him?"

"I'll come in with him when we're done with our work in the orchard. He can tutor Kate after supper."

"Are you suggesting we invite him for supper?"

"I wasn't proposing that, but it would be good for us to get to know him over a meal." Thomas sucked on his empty pipe.

"And how do you expect me to add another plate to the table?" Charlotte put her hands on her hips. "I have enough for us today and tomorrow, but I'll be damned if I'm going to share our food with some prisoner who gets all he needs from the Army." Charlotte wiped her hands on her apron. "If Kate's math isn't good enough for the university, so be it. She can attend one of the state normal schools and teach until she gets married."

"I don't want to go to a state normal school." *And I may never get married, either. Professor Fleming isn't married.*

Charlotte untied her apron and threw it on the counter. "If you insist on such foolishness, I want to meet this man. Yes. Bring him here for supper. Station a guard at the door. But it's up to you to get the fixings. I have nothing to offer."

Kate thought of the play, the girls in the dorm. She'd do anything to get away and make it on her own. She hesitated, then whispered, "I'm willing to give up one of my rabbits—"

Mother's eyes widened.

"Not to eat," Kate said quickly, "but to trade. After all, what are my rabbits worth if I can't make it at the university?"

CHAPTER EIGHT

CHARLOTTE PUT THREE QUARTS of goat's milk into the front wicker basket of her bicycle and two butchered rabbits into the back and then peddled down Orchard Lane, fat tires bumping along the gravel. The lane led through rows and rows of cherry trees, fragrant now with pink and white blossoms and buzzing with bees. Within two months, blossoms would turn to fruit, and as long as God didn't damn them with pestilence, flood, drought, disease, or frost, Charlotte would be making cherry pies by the end of July. Drought was unlikely at this point, but the others remained real possibilities. At the end of the lane Charlotte veered onto County Trunk Q, north toward town.

In summers past, this road hummed with traffic, families heading for orchards and beaches, merchant trucks delivering supplies. But there were few tourists now. And with tires and gasoline in short supply, the only vehicles Charlotte passed were occasional farm trucks hauling feed or animals.

But here was crazy Walter, sitting proud on the seat of his hay cart filled with junk, tapping the hind end of his ancient mule. With his long gray hair and beard, he could be Jesus's own grandfather. He waved and gave a toothless grin. Charlotte waved back.

When Charlotte reached Turtle Bay, the early sun was slanting across the paved road, touching the town with golden light. She rode past the Farmers' Co-op, Ginny's Dress Shoppe, the credit union, and the barbershop where Old Man Berger's yellow mutt lay sleeping. Down the street she breathed in the yeasty warm fragrance wafting from the open door of the bakery. And there was Ellie Jensen, putting up a sign on the window of her dry goods store.

"Morning, Charlotte."

"Morning, Ellie."

Charlotte parked her bicycle in front of Zwicky's Market. Inside the clean, orderly shop, Catherine Zwicky readily accepted the goat's milk in trade for a pound of potatoes, a quarter-pound of flour, a tin of salt, a cup of Crisco, and a small jar of applesauce.

Charlotte put her bundles into the baskets and pushed her bicycle down the block to the butcher shop. Through the plate-glass window she watched the butcher's widow arranging fresh cuts of meat in the cooler, then opened the door, setting the bell jangling. "Morning, Olga." She gave the old woman the warmest smile she could muster.

Olga wiped her hands on her bloodstained apron and pushed strands of gray hair back into a tidy bun. "Mornin', Charlotte."

Charlotte placed the package on the counter. "Two of Kate's young rabbits. Dressed, ready for stewing."

Olga's eyebrows went up. She untied the string around the newspaper wrapping, a bit of a smile playing on her lips. "What would you like?"

"I need a roast for dinner. Something special. Enough for four."

"Four? Is Ben home?"

Charlotte was startled with the possibility, then regained her composure. "I wish he were." But no, men and boys didn't return from war unless they were wounded. "I mean, I wish this war would end and they'd all come home." She caught sight of the photograph of Olga's son, Martin, hanging behind the counter. Thirty-seven years old, Charlotte's very age, missing in action somewhere in Asia. Shortly after Olga and her husband received the telegram, the butcher had a heart attack. Now Olga was alone.

The widow blinked fast for a moment, wiped her cheek with the back of her hand.

Peering into the meat cooler, Charlotte's eyes flashed on a pink pork tenderloin, large enough to stretch for two days. It was worth more than the rabbits, Charlotte knew, but that was what she wanted. "The pork, is it fresh?"

"Just this mornin'." Olga nodded. "Eric Engel, ya know, does business with hog farmers downstate, brought in a good haul. I got so much in the storage freezer, gonna make sausage tonight."

Ah, so that was why she was letting it go so easily. "I'll take it then."

Olga smiled as she wrapped the beautiful roast in white butcher paper.

As Charlotte left the shop she noted that Olga was placing Kate's rabbits prominently in the cooler.

HEAT LIGHTNING COURSED THROUGH THE HUMID SKY. A coming storm.

It was late in the afternoon when Charlotte lit the kitchen stove. For two nights now they'd had the lightkeeper's fish for dinner. Tonight would be a roast. She hummed as she pulled the roasting pan from the cupboard. So long since she had used it! She oiled the roast and set it in the pan and salted it.

That was when she saw them, Thomas and that Becker fellow walking toward the barn. And there was Kate, riding into the yard. Charlotte watched as Thomas motioned Kate over and brought her into their conversation.

She didn't like it, this prisoner coming into her home, Thomas expecting his wife to serve a killer. Charlotte stared at the beautiful roast. Becker could have eaten his prison rations with the rest of them. She stood for a moment, watching the three of them. Maybe she should cancel the whole thing—the invitation, Kate's lessons. No good could come of it.

When Charlotte opened the oven door, heat pulsed out like anger. She slid the roast in and slammed the door shut.

Holding to the countertop, she took a deep breath to calm herself. No, if this man was to tutor Kate, Charlotte wanted to meet him, decide for herself before any lessons began. If she didn't like him, she'd end it. In the meantime, they'd have a hearty meal.

Kate came through the door, smiling. "I'll be down in a minute to help with supper." She hurried toward the stairs.

The enthusiasm in Kate's voice worried Charlotte, and only grew when Kate returned to the kitchen dressed in a flattering skirt and a pretty blouse with ruffles.

"You're so fancy for kitchen work." Charlotte tried to sound nonchalant. She herself wore a simple housedress, as she did every day. "It's not as if we're having company. This man's a prisoner."

"Mr. Becker is a teacher." Kate took an apron off the hook, pulled the neckband over her head, and tied the waist straps. "Besides, if Ben were taken prisoner, we would want the Germans to show respect."

Charlotte tensed. "Ben is fighting for freedom and justice." She looked into her daughter's soft blue eyes. "Maybe this man can teach you math, but he fights on the side of evil."

THE KITCHEN WAS WARM and moist with humidity. Charlotte was stirring the pork gravy when she saw the two men approach the back door, dark clouds gathering behind them. She wiped perspiration from her forehead and glanced toward the cupboard drawer where she kept the revolver.

The German was not tall like Thomas, but broad in the shoulders. He moved easily in a strong fit body. Must be about thirty.

As they entered, Charlotte kept her back to them, ostensibly checking on the potatoes Kate was mashing.

"Char," Thomas said, "this here's Karl Becker."

When Charlotte turned to look at him, a wild animal lurched inside her chest. She had expected a penitent prisoner, but this man exuded self-confidence, control.

He had close-cut hair like the rest of them, but it was growing out a bit, dark, neatly oiled and combed. His mouth was a straight line, serious. He had a hard jaw and blue-gray eyes that made her stare. Not the warm blue of Ben's eyes, she was glad of that. No, these were icy eyes, wolf eyes, reflecting rather than inviting. She shuddered.

"My wife, Mrs. Christiansen," Thomas said.

"Mrs. Christiansen." Becker stood at attention, gave a slight bow. She was relieved he didn't click his heels.

Why had she agreed to this? This Nazi in her home? She wiped her hands on her apron to steady herself, then faced him, eye-to-eye, unsmiling. "You'll join us for supper." Not a question, not requesting an answer, not even a howdy-do. No, it had been decided for him. She would go through with this tonight, and that would be the end of it. She need never see him again.

"*Danke.*" He breathed in deeply through flared nostrils, as if Charlotte's words had entitled him to the sensual pleasures of her kitchen. She felt perversely exposed.

"Such an aroma I have not enjoyed in so long." The edges of his mouth curved up gently, a deceptively innocent smile. And dimples! Evil people weren't supposed to have dimples. She must have been staring because he raised an eyebrow, and his eyes grew warm, open, intimate, as if seeking some deep secret within her. Her cheeks burned.

The breeze through the window carried Becker's musky scent to her. She had to get away from him.

"Thomas, please show Mr. Becker to the parlor."

When the two men had left, Kate was at Charlotte's side. "Mother, are you all right? Everything's ready to serve."

Charlotte had forgotten her daughter, forgotten everything except the visceral presence of that man in her kitchen. "Just give me a minute." She hurried out through the door and ran until she reached a budding cherry tree. She put her hand against the solid trunk and inhaled the earthiness of the fertile soil. Thomas had told her that Becker was intellectual, but she sensed something else, something more physical—this man lived in his body.

A wind from the west cooled her cheeks and brought the taste of coming rain. Lightning coursed across the sky, followed by a long rolling thunder. Another flash. She breathed it in, then walked slowly back to the kitchen.

THE SMALL DINING ROOM TABLE SEATED FOUR. There were leaves somewhere but they hadn't been used for years. After they were settled, Charlotte realized that Becker was sitting at Ben's place, and she resented him for that.

He ate in a peculiar way, keeping the fork tongs upside down in his left hand, pushing things with the knife in his right. His English had a formal accent to it, British perhaps, but he had a pleasant tenor voice, melodious almost, and she disliked him for that too.

He was asking Kate questions about how she spent her days. Kate told him about riding her bicycle to Turtle Bay, caring for her rabbits, visiting Josie at the lighthouse. Was he fishing for enemy information? Charlotte thought of Marta's warning and changed the focus of the conversation. "How do you find the work in the orchard?"

"I enjoy to work in your orchard, to get my hands dirty."

"Well, then, you need to know that Mr. Christiansen is the number-one cherry grower in all of Door County."

"My congratulations." Becker held up his glass of water to Thomas as if to toast.

"He brings in the best yields year after year," Charlotte said. "He went to the university and specialized in . . . what's that subject?" She looked to her husband.

"Agronomy. But I didn't quite finish."

"You would have if it weren't for the fire." Charlotte turned to Becker. "He's an expert on yields and pests and diseases, and everyone asks for his help and he always gives it."

Thomas nodded. "I like helping the other growers. It's good for all of us."

Becker took a bite of pork roast, swallowed, then glanced back and forth from Thomas to Charlotte. "Did you both grow up in this area, may I ask?"

Thomas patted his mouth with his napkin. "Mrs. Christiansen grew up on a dairy farm downstate." He grinned. "When I tasted her pies, I knew she was the one."

"Just because of my pies?" Charlotte tossed her hair and laughed.

He winked toward Becker. "I asked her to make me a cherry pie, and she said she would if she had the cherries. She wanted an orchard and I wanted a cherry pie. So we had to get married."

Kate laughed. "Oh Father, that's silly."

"All right. That wasn't all. Char—Mrs. Christiansen—is one of the best businesswomen I've ever met, smart as any man I know." He paused, serious. "She runs this farm like a well-oiled engine."

"You've got to taste Mother's cherry pie." Kate looked so pretty. She sat up tall and straight and proper, her long blond hair pulled aside with a bobby pin, wide blue eyes trained on this man Charlotte feared. Charlotte watched Becker's response. Any sign of interest would be the end of the lessons.

"I feel blessed to be on your farm," he said to Thomas. "You are all kind. You treat us as if we belong."

"We feel blessed as well," Thomas said. "It was actually Mrs. Christiansen's idea for you to work in the orchard." He scooped up a forkful of mashed potatoes.

"Thank you, Mrs. Christiansen," Becker said. "I grew up on a small farm. I like helping to grow things. Cabbages, potatoes, turnips, greens. And flowers. My *Mutter,* she loves flowers." Becker's dimples deepened. "You must love flowers as well, Mrs. Christiansen."

Flowers, yes, she did love flowers, but she didn't have room in her garden for such extravagance.

"You grew up on a farm but decided to leave, to teach?" Thomas asked. "Same as me. Whaddya know."

"No. I wanted to stay on the farm. My brother, he will inherit it. He is married with children. His family lives there with *Mutter.*"

"You'd rather be on the farm? Well, that's ironic." Thomas said, almost to himself.

Karl nodded. "These potatoes and gravy, very delicious. This meal, it reminds me of home."

Yes, Charlotte had made a substantial meal. Not only for Becker, of course, but it was gratifying to hear a stranger compliment her cooking. Thomas was always generous with praise, but that was because he was a good husband. Becker recognized the art of Charlotte's gravy, the tiniest measure of flour and water mixed into the drippings slowly and carefully until it was creamy and rich and you wanted to pour it on everything.

"You miss your home," she said.

"I do." He stared off into space.

"Well, let's hope this war's over soon so you can go back."

In the silence that followed, Charlotte realized how rude that had sounded. "I didn't mean to . . . Are you comfortable here in the camp?" Why did she ask that? She didn't care whether he was comfortable or not.

"Until the war is over, I want to stay here in your camp more than return to Deutschland."

"You'd rather stay in prison than go home?" Kate said, eyes wide.

"Back home, I would be sent to the Russian front. That would be the final end." He stared straight ahead. "The Russians, they are not Americans."

"I hope you're still here when Ben comes home," Kate said. "I know you'd like him."

"That would be *gut.*" Karl nodded.

"What town are you from, Karl?" Thomas asked.

"Dresden. My family is safe there. The enemy—excuse me," he cast about, "the Allied forces—they would never get that far . . ." His words drifted off. He looked down.

Of course they will! Charlotte didn't say it out loud. She watched this presumptuous man who expected that Hitler would hold Europe and then attack America from the Atlantic as the Japanese had from the Pacific. They were already out there, Ole had said, German submarines lurking. Her mind flashed on the daily radio broadcasts from London, Edward R. Murrow, and behind his voice, air raid sirens, swooping planes, pops and blasts. No, that can't happen here.

A stormy gust shook the windowpanes. No one spoke for some time, until Kate broke the silence. "Did you want to be a soldier, Mr. Becker?"

Becker put down his fork and knife. "All the boys went to *der Hitler-Jugend,* like your Boy Scouts. We played games, marched with rifles. Learned to shoot. All in fun. Until the war began."

"So you didn't want to go?" Kate asked.

"We grew up with the pledge to fight for the *Vaterland.* Fight against *die Übeltäter.*"

"*Ubel . . .* ?" Kate tried to say. "What's that?"

Karl paused and swallowed hard. "I am sorry . . . it means . . . evildoers."

All was quiet except for the wind.

Karl picked up his napkin and touched his lips. "During the fight, so much is going on, being shot and . . . one does not have the time to think."

"In the heat of the battle," Thomas said. "And now that you've had time to think?"

"Here, American people are *gut*." He took a drink of water. "But not Americans I saw over there."

"That's not true. Our Ben—" Charlotte blurted.

Thomas put up a hand. "Karl hasn't met Ben."

After a pause, Karl said, "Germans are *gut* too."

"Hitler?" Charlotte challenged. "You think Hitler is good?"

Becker went pale.

Thomas gave Charlotte a stern look.

Maybe Thomas was right. Over there the only Americans Karl saw were shooting at him. She watched this man, so solemn now, and chastised herself for trying to shame him here in her own home.

Becker took a bite of pork. "Very tender, Mrs. Christiansen."

"Yes," Thomas said. "Mrs. Christiansen lays out a fine table, even in the hardest of times." He patted Charlotte's hand.

Becker put down his utensils. "Most prisoners are not true Nazis. Hitler sent to the front those who were opposing him. To be first killed or captured. But . . ." he hesitated. "Some are not to trust." He paused. "What I tell you, I would not say this to the others." He motioned in the direction of the migrant camp, then spoke quietly, conspiratorially, scanning the faces around the table. "I feel safe to tell you here."

This man was saying exactly what Big Mike feared, what the county officials feared, what Charlotte herself feared.

Kate squinted. "That crazy one . . ."

Becker swirled gravy through his potatoes.

After some silence, Kate said softly, "Have you ever killed anyone?"

"Kate," Thomas held up a hand.

Charlotte held her fork in the air, waiting.

Becker hesitated, then took another bite of roast, his eyes fixed firmly on his plate.

WHEN KATE ROSE TO CLEAR THE DINING TABLE, Charlotte stood. "I'll take care of this. Why don't you and . . ." she couldn't bring herself to say his name. "How about if you work on your lessons in the kitchen?"

At the kitchen table, Charlotte motioned for Becker to sit facing the parlor, away from the sink and stove where she would be working. As she washed the dishes, Charlotte took in the breadth of Becker's shoulders, the thickness of his dark hair, the skin on his neck pink from the sun, the sweat stains on his collar. She wondered if he had a woman in Dresden, a sweetheart, a wife perhaps. Someone to wash his shirts and rub those shoulders and put salve on the burn. Someone lying in bed right now, longing for him.

Lightning crackled outside and thunder rattled the house.

Becker handed Thomas a pouch of tobacco. "I would like for you to enjoy this."

Thomas put the pouch to his nose and breathed it in. He picked up his pipe and filled the bowl, struck a match. *Puff puff puff.* That old familiar sound. Once the tobacco caught, he drew it in. "Ah. Thank you, Karl."

Charlotte had always associated Thomas with that fragrance. Now she realized how she had missed it.

"You are most welcome."

"I have my trigonometry book." Kate offered Becker the textbook from her senior math class.

"First, Miss Kate, I have a present for you." Becker reached into his pocket. He brought out a piece of paper folded like an envelope and opened it on the table. "Cocoa with sugar." He opened another pouch. "And here is the powdered milk to add."

Chocolate! How long it had been since Charlotte had tasted chocolate. A sweet after supper. Hot cocoa. And yet . . . No! He's not entitled to . . . to be so familiar. She came around to face Becker. "You will not bribe my daughter."

"Mother!" Kate's eyebrows rose.

Thomas put down his pipe. "Charlotte, Karl was only offering a gift in gratitude for your generous meal. Isn't that right, Karl?"

"I didn't want to . . ."

Charlotte wiped her hands on her apron. "If it's in return for the meal, well . . ." She accepted the envelopes from him.

Thomas took the pipe from his mouth. "I'm enjoying my tobacco. You two gals share the hot chocolate."

As Charlotte added water and steamed the cocoa, her mind raced. Why was the Army giving this treat to prisoners? These murderers were enjoying better provisions than tax-paying citizens. Her hand shook as she poured half the cocoa into a cup. She should have waited until Becker left before making it so he wouldn't see how they enjoyed it. No, she wouldn't have hers now. She wouldn't have any at all. She wasn't going to accept any gifts from this man who shouldn't be in the position of giving.

But oh, the steamy aroma! She breathed it in. She glanced toward the table to make sure he wasn't watching and breathed in again. That was all she needed.

She put a cup of steaming cocoa on the table and Kate picked it up and blew on it and took a sip. "Mmm."

Just then, hailstones pelted the windows. Thomas rose and hurried to the back porch.

Charlotte followed, her hand to her mouth. "The cherries . . ."

Thomas put an arm around her waist. "The new buds should be hardy enough to hold up. Thank God the trees haven't blossomed yet."

When the hail turned to rain, Charlotte realized they had left Kate alone with the prisoner. "Kate!" She rushed back into the kitchen.

The two sat across from each other at the round table, just as they had before. Karl had already begun the lesson. He spoke with his hands, large capable hands that made shapes in the air. Where Thomas's hands were long and delicate, Karl's were square and thick, a farmer's hands, designed to work the land.

When she was done with the dishes, Charlotte didn't want to leave the room. She needed to keep her eye on this man. The wind had abated, but the rain continued, fast and hard. She pulled a log from out of the wood box, added it to the stove, and poked the fire. She heated water and mixed in vinegar and began washing counter-tops and cupboard doors, inside and out.

"This room. How would you figure the height?" Karl asked.

Kate laughed. "With a ladder and a ruler."

Becker cleared his throat. "Let us take something more difficult. The lighthouse. How far is it from here?"

Charlotte froze. Marta had warned her that the PWs would try to set up communications with Nazi submarines.

"Half a mile maybe?" Kate looked to Thomas.

"About that," Thomas said.

"To learn how high the tower is—"

Charlotte swung around the table to face the prisoner. "Why do you want to know about the lighthouse?"

The three of them stared up at her. "Mother?" Kate said.

Heavy rain fell in a shimmering curtain outside the window, insulating the little kitchen from the rest of the world. Anything could happen. No one would know.

Becker hesitated before he spoke. "It might be of interest for Miss Kate to know how high is she when she sits with her friend."

"Not the lighthouse. Choose something else." Charlotte turned back to the cupboards, heat rushing through her veins.

After a pause, Thomas said, "The silo. Kate's not about to mea-sure the silo."

"Yes," Charlotte put a hand on Thomas's shoulder. "Find the

height of the silo." She felt jangled. Was she reading too much into these questions? Or not enough?

"Miss Kate, my assignment to you is to find three solutions to the height of the silo. Algebra, geometry, trigonometry." He went on a bit longer, giving Kate details to guide her.

Kate took notes, then asked, "When are you coming again, Karl?"

Karl? She's calling him Karl?

"When you are finished, do you have a place to post up your lessons, out of the rain?" he said.

Charlotte stiffened at the thought of personal messages between this man and her daughter. But before she could respond, Kate said, "In the barn. I'll tack my homework to the rabbit hutch."

Thomas nodded.

Charlotte's blood pulsed hard near the surface. Thomas was giving this prisoner permission to enter the barn at will. The butchering tools! "Thomas?"

Lightning flashed, exposing rain like silver needles.

Thomas put down his pipe. "Best I walk you back to the camp."

The men stood. Thomas gave Karl a rain slicker to wear—Ben's slicker!—and the two of them went out the door. Charlotte stood on the porch, hugging herself, as she watched them disappear into the storm. This Nazi war criminal, this charming man-boy, had put them all under his spell. *Be careful, husband.*

Back in the kitchen, Charlotte noted the excitement in Kate's face.

"Mother, what do you think?"

"I think we don't want to get too close."

"Too close?"

"He may be a good teacher. But he's the enemy. And don't you forget it."

CHAPTER NINE

PROPPED AGAINST BED PILLOWS, Kate turned the page, regretting the novel's end: "So we beat on, boats against the current, borne back ceaselessly into the past."

She gazed out at the lake and imagined herself in West Egg at one of Gatsby's enchanted parties, "among the whispering and the champagne and the stars," where guests mingled in witty conversation and "yellow cocktail music." If there were ever to be a motion picture, Kate would want Katharine Hepburn to play Daisy Buchanan.

Kate used to go to the picture show nearly every Saturday afternoon, a nickel for the matinee. She marveled over Hepburn's characters in *Morning Glory* and *Alice Adams* and *The Philadelphia Story*. She memorized Hepburn's best lines and sometimes stood in front of the mirror, mimicking her snappy repartee.

A shaft of light swept across the ceiling. Gusty winds rattled her bedroom window. She closed the book and waited.

The radio down in the parlor resonated with the top-of-the-hour newscaster's familiar voice, and soon after, the big-band sound came on. Mother would be mending or knitting, Father reading a book.

Soon they would switch off the Philco, take turns in the outhouse, wash up at the kitchen pump. Kate had learned to be patient.

Finally, she heard them climbing the stairs.

Mother peeked through Kate's open door. "Better get to sleep."

"I will. Good night, Mother."

She waited longer, until the light went out in the bedroom across the landing, until she could hear Mother's sleep-breathing, Father's soft snore. She closed her door and stepped into overalls and pulled two woolen sweaters over her cotton blouse. She would have liked to put on her wool jacket, but she didn't want to risk going down the squeaky stairs. She opened the window.

The rain clouds had cleared and the sky was filled with stars, but a gusty wind whipped through the dark night and trees creaked in warning. She reached for the thick oak branch.

Down onshore, waves crashed up hard and loud. The path was flooded, so Kate left her bicycle in the barn and set off on foot, winds from the south pushing her forward through ankle-deep water.

When she finally reached the channel, the black water between the mainland and the island churned with whitecaps. She didn't bother rolling up her pant legs because they were already soaked. She grabbed for the safety rope secured to the fallen bridge and started across. Within a few feet, a wave rose up and slapped her. She held fast, pulling herself hand over hand, to the opposite shore. Once on the island, Kate struggled from the water, fighting against her weighty clothes, and made her way along the path through the woods to the lightkeeper's house.

Only minutes after Kate had thrown the stone, Josie opened the door and pulled Kate in. "You're soaked. You must be freezing."

Trembling, Kate followed Josie up the circular stairs. At the top of the tower, Josie took her father's thick storm jacket from a hook— "take off those wet sweaters"—then opened the door to the gallery. They moved around to the north side, away from the wind. Kate pulled her sweaters off and snuggled into the warmth of the jacket, which smelled of black tea and kerosene. She pushed up the collar and stuffed her hands deep into the pockets. After the two friends settled on the cast-iron floor, Josie lit a cigarette and handed it to Kate, then lit one for herself. Kate drew the fiery smoke deep into her lungs and watched the shaft of light beaming out from above them reveal the world in circular bursts of dark sky, angry water.

"It's as wild as the Atlantic," Josie said, recalling her time in Boston. "You wouldn't have come out in this storm unless you wanted to tell me something important."

Kate realized the folly of her trip. Yes, she had wanted to tell Josie something important, but now she was too cold and tired to explain it all, to convince Josie that Karl wasn't a Nazi, just a math professor. No, she would stay a bit to get warm and go home, come back when the sun was out. She put up a hand to ward off any questions, then took a drag on her cigarette and closed her eyes.

"Well, I have some news."

For once Kate was grateful for Josie's self-absorption.

Josie took a folded paper from the jacket she wore over flannel pajamas. "I have a letter from Ben, in Italy."

"I've always thought of Italy as romantic," Kate whispered.

"Romantic?" Josie gave a sarcastic laugh. "He's in the mountains, freezing."

Kate shivered from within the big coat. She was freezing too, but her warm bed was only half a mile away.

Josie held the lantern to the pages and read about hiking up an icy trail. That was followed by a blacked-out section. "You can imagine what the Army doesn't want us to know. The strategic positions, the danger, boys dying."

"Poor Ben!" Kate longed for her brother to be home.

"See here, where the black pen smooched—'. . . buddy . . . lost . . . crippled . . .' He can't even tell us how he's suffering over there. Does that sound romantic?"

Then she read aloud the part that wasn't blacked out, about Ben loving Josie, wanting her. "I'll never forget our last night at the cottage—" Josie brought the pages to her lips.

Kate leaned in. "What night?" She stared at Josie's face and saw a secret reflected behind those dark eyes. *They've done it!*

Josie put her arm through Kate's. "I like to think of you as my sister."

"What did you do in the cottage?" Kate was both fascinated and fearful. After all, this was her brother. She didn't want to think of him like that.

"You'll know one day. You'll find someone. Then you'll know how beautiful it is to love." Josie closed her eyes, her face pointing toward the stars.

Kate saw tears running down her friend's cheeks. "He'll be back soon," Kate said. "That's what Mother says. She senses things, things that come true."

Josie sucked in on her cigarette before she spoke. "Ben's so popular. He must have had a lot of girlfriends before I came to town."

"Girls were interested in him, sure, but Ben didn't pay much attention." When the school bell rang after the last class, Ben would go right home. "He had chores to do."

"But when he met me . . . did he ever say why he chose me?"

Kate recalled the potluck supper that had welcomed the new lighthouse keeper and his family to the community that summer, the square dance at the armory. Josie's flirtatious eyes and the way her body moved in a snug tease of a dress that promised something exotic, mysterious. She didn't know how to square dance, so Ben took her into a corner and taught her the steps. She stayed with him all evening, even through the slow dances. Other boys cut in, but when the band played the final number, she was with Ben.

Then came the August hayride. Boys and girls piled into the wagon, enveloped together in a dusty fragrance of hay and autumn leaves. When the driver gave a whistle, the horses clip-clopped down the road. The glow from the full moon edged every tree with silver.

One of the boys strummed a guitar. Josie snuggled in next to Ben against the breezy night air, and soon his arm was around her shoulders, their heads close.

At the beach, the football captain lit the bonfire. After the cheers died down, the fellow with the guitar played and everyone sang along—"Fools Rush In," "When You Wish Upon a Star," and other favorites from the Hit Parade. Though Kate sat with them, Ben and Josie sang to each other as if they were alone, Ben's strong tenor harmonizing with Josie's husky alto. Ben put an arm around Josie's waist and drew her to him, his eyes shining in the firelight.

The next day, Josie arrived at the Christiansens' dock in her father's motorboat. Kate ran down to meet her.

"Ben told me you like to read," Josie said, handing Kate a dog-eared pocketbook.

"*Fanny Hill?* What's it about?"

"It's filled with secrets," Josie whispered conspiratorially. Before she could say more, Ben came strolling down the dock, smiling. Josie motioned for Kate to hide it. "Go and read it now."

Kate put it into her sweater pocket and left the two of them alone.

Yes, it was full of secrets, and the beginning of a friendship. A loner by choice, Kate trusted Josie to advise her about intimate things she didn't dare ask anyone else, and Kate reciprocated with information Josie sought about Ben. Now, since Ben's departure, the two friends had become even closer.

"Kate!" Josie gave her a poke, bringing her back to the present. "So what attracted him to me?"

The lighthouse beam swung out across the lake.

Kate flicked her cigarette butt over the rail. "Maybe he was intrigued with your ways."

"What ways?"

"I don't know, Josie. You'll have to ask him." Kate didn't want to think about what might attract Ben.

After a short silence, Josie continued. "Does he ever say any-thing about me, in his letters?"

Josie had asked this so many times, Kate merely shook her head.

"You said he likes chocolate. Brownies or chocolate chip cook-ies? Which do you think?"

"Cookies." Katie closed her eyes. *Oh, to have a chocolate chip cookie!*

"Let's make them together. Come for lunch tomorrow."

Kate didn't want to think about tomorrow. She just wanted to be warm in her bed.

Josie gave Kate another poke. "You came out in this storm for a reason. You have something to tell me."

A raw wind blew around the lighthouse.

"I don't think this is a good time . . ." Kate hesitated. "I should get home."

"But why did you come?"

Might as well say it. She'd tell her eventually. "I have a math tutor, that's all."

"A new tutor? There must be more. Are you in love?"

"No! It's not like that at all!" Kate laughed. "I just wanted to talk with you because"—she swallowed, then whispered—"he's a PW."

"In your house?" Josie jerked away. "You must be joking. How could your parents ever—"

"It's all right," Kate said wearily. "He likes America now—"

"Of course he'd say that. My father said that those Nazis are from Rommel's panzer troops. Don't you get it? That's who Ben's fighting." She was shouting, her face contorted. "They're profes-sional murderers!" She jumped up. "I'm not allowed to go to your house because of those Nazis. Did you know that? Not as long as they're on your property."

So that was why Josie hadn't been over to visit.

A light went on in the house below. Kate's heart caught. Josie's parents would tell Kate's parents, and that would be the end of that.

Josie's eyes were wild. "Go now!"

Kate threw off the lightkeeper's jacket and grabbed her sodden sweaters. She ducked through the passageway and hurried down the winding steps, teeth chattering. *She doesn't understand. I have to make her understand.* Kate feared losing her friend.

Out in the yard, after pulling on the wet sweaters, she ran along the path to the channel, tears raging down her cheeks. *I'll introduce them. Yes, that's what I'll do. When she meets Karl, she'll see. I have to find a way.*

Teeth chattering, Kate stepped into the cold water. A blast of wind nearly knocked her down. She grabbed for the rope with both hands. The wind would be against her all the way home. About halfway across the channel, a volley of hard waves swept up and caught her by surprise, pulling her off her feet. Though she held tightly to the rope, her body floated on the fast current, feet pointing northward, icy hands simply holding on now, not advancing, just holding on. She squinted toward the mainland. Not so far away, not so far.

She would have to move forward on the rope, hand over hand. The only way. One hand had to let go. Let go! She opened her left hand and reached out, but spray and rain blinded her and a wave tugged her away, and when she grabbed forward again her right hand slipped and the lake swallowed her whole.

She went under and up and under and up, gulping for air, trying to keep her head above the choppy swells. She was a strong swimmer, but the waves were stronger. They pulled her down and forward and under and tossed her up again. She flailed her arms but the current had her. The deep black lake was in charge. She screamed into the darkness but there was no one to hear. Water over her head, in her ears, her nose. Ben's voice coming to her, singing for her to wake up, floating away, Mother scolding about broken eggs, Miss Fleming beckoning—*Yes, I can swim. I can make it! Miss Fleming is waiting. The girls in the dorm. Father!*

A wave tossed Kate toward shore. She grabbed for an overhanging branch and held on but the lake ripped her away, the rough bark burning her hand. Ben! She strained to envision his face as she gulped air and then gulped water and floundered toward the surface, muscles aching. *This is what it feels like to drown. I'm going to drown!* The shore was near but rushing quickly past, farther and farther from home, and the sky was bright with stars so far away that Kate watched herself as if from above, tiny in the huge lake, as insignificant as a water bug. Arms and legs heavy, leaden, barely moving.

Let go, I could just let go and float up to the stars. Easy, so easy.

CHAPTER TEN

CHARLOTTE WOKE FROM A DREAM of Karl climbing through her open window, his dark thick hair, wolf eyes, bare chest, spicy body slick with sweat . . .

She sat up, breathing hard, oddly aroused. Thomas stirred beside her.

"Thomas," she whispered. "There's somebody out there. I heard something in the trees."

She moved to get out of bed but Thomas pulled her back. "Just the wind."

She lay next to him, listening. His arm was around her and he kissed her cheek and moved his large palm across her nightgown until he found her breasts. She quivered, then relaxed under his touch. She sighed as his warm hand moved down her flat stomach, down to her muff, which he held like a ball, moving a finger around her wetness, into her wetness, breathing against her ear. When he drew her hand onto his erect penis, she caught her breath. She loved him for that, the way his body wanted hers. She moved her hand slowly up and down the strong length of it until he crawled on top of her and rocked into her, gently at first, rubbing against the walls of her wanting, then harder, in rhythm with her breathing, his breathing, her tongue teasing at his nipples, his face in her hair, her hands on his buttocks, pushing with him, together, rocking together, her body taking over her mind until she shook and he moaned and flowed into her and lay panting, the two of them panting.

After he finally rolled away, she lay in the dark, listening to his sleeping breath. She closed her eyes and slowly fell back to a dreamy state where Karl waited for her just beyond the window.

CHAPTER ELEVEN

KATE'S OUTSTRETCHED ARM bumped against something solid, and her icy fingers grabbed hold. A ladder? She hung on against the current. Her wet clothes weighed her down as she tried to pull herself up. At the top she collapsed on a platform, chest heaving. The lake churned in her stomach, burning up through her throat. She turned on her side, gagging.

After some time, she pushed up, sitting, bent over. She was on a dock that jutted out into the wild lake on the northern point of a bay. Far to the south the lighthouse blinked. Miles away, she thought, and home even farther. When an owl hooted, Kate looked behind her, a dense forest. Wild water in front of her, forest behind her. Wind icy around her. She couldn't stop shaking.

Looking up the beach, she saw a rowboat overturned on the shore. She couldn't take it tonight. She wasn't strong enough to fight the current rushing in the opposite direction. But she could crawl under it until the storm broke. She staggered to her feet, muscles weak and aching, teeth chattering.

What was that? A wolf racing toward her, barking. She stared down at the choppy lake. If she jumped in again, she would surely drown. But to be torn apart by a wolf . . . !

The animal came to the edge of the dock, snarling, teeth bared.

Kate took a step back. The wolf put a foot on the dock, growling, guarding the edge, barring her way. Not a wolf, but a burly German shepherd kind of dog. Fierce and menacing.

"Jake!" A man's voice called out. "Here, Jake."

At the sound of the man's voice, the dog stopped growling, but stood its ground.

"Who is it?" the man called as he approached, white jacket gleaming in the starlight.

Kate's lips were too cold to form an answer.

"Good boy," he said, coming closer, petting the dog, close enough to see Kate. "What's happened to you? You're soaking wet!" He took off his jacket and fixed it across her shoulders. "C'mon, let's get you into the house. You could freeze to death out here!"

The jacket was warm with body heat and smelled vaguely of vanilla. Kate pulled it close around her. "I n——. . . n——. . . need to g——. . . g——. . . go home," she finally managed to say.

"First we'll get you thawed out." He put an arm around her waist and half-carried her down the dock and across a wide expanse of lawn toward a house set far back from shore, away from the wind. It was a sprawling house filled with light. As they got closer, she heard bits of music, laughter. Stumbling alongside this warm strong man, Kate tried to focus. On the other side of the bright windows, people were dancing. *Am I dreaming?*

Orange and purple paper lanterns showed the way. A tall Negro wearing a white apron stood in the yard poking at something that hung over a fire pit. Kate sucked in the aroma of roasting meat. *Supper so late? Or is it tomorrow?*

A shorter man approached the cook and said, "William, the guests are getting stewed. We need to feed them."

"Yes, sir." William was working to unhitch what appeared to be a whole pig on a spit.

"Where's our host?" He turned and saw them. "Ah, Clayton, there you are," the short man slurred, coming forward, ice cubes clinking in a drink in his hand. "What's this, some flotsam you picked up on the beach?"

Flotsom?

"Shut up, Ronny. Let's get her in through the back."

"You're not taking her to your room, buddy—"

"Christ, Ronny. She needs dry clothes. Help me find Peggy. This girl's taller, but about Peggy's size."

When they came under a porch light, he let go of her waist and gave a quick bow. "Clayton Wesley Sullivan, at your service."

He had a strong jaw, bright blue eyes, and a boyish nose splashed with freckles. When he bowed, his curly dark hair dipped onto his forehead. "Call me Clay."

She couldn't possibly manage her whole name. "Kate," she said through quivering lips. "Kate Christiansen."

He opened the back door and drew her in. Two girls stood in the hallway. They wore silky gowns and jewels and ribbons in their hair and had arched eyebrows, rouged cheeks, laughing lipstick mouths. When they saw Kate, they stopped their chatter and stared, eyes wide.

"Please excuse us," Clay said.

The girls stepped aside, whispering, about her no doubt.

But Clayton was leading Kate away from them, up a back staircase, down a hall, and into a bedroom, a feminine room with pink and green pillows and satiny striped curtains, calm and inviting.

A fluffy white cat glanced up from a green divan, then returned to licking its paws, unconcerned.

Kate caught sight of herself in a full-length oval mirror. *Oh!* Her blond hair was plastered to her head, her face was a deathly white, her clothes stuck to her tall, thin form. "I'm dripping on your floor," she said through chattering teeth, staring down at a celery green wool rug decorated with vines of pink and plum roses.

"We'll have you fixed up in no time," Clay assured her.

A slim girl about Kate's age floated into the room, her flouncy silk dress the color of strawberry ice cream. Her dark curls were pulled into a ribbon, accentuating high cheekbones and full soft lips. She was fresh and rich like someone out of a Fitzgerald novel, pretty in the way Clay was handsome. When she saw Kate, her eyebrows lifted in alarm.

"Ah, Peggy," Clay said. "This sweet mermaid has washed ashore and needs a bath and clean clothes."

"Of course. Come in. I'll start the water."

Kate took a ragged breath, finally safe.

After Clay left, Peggy introduced herself as Clay's younger sister and led Kate to a pink bathroom large enough to live in. It had marble counters and tiles and polished brass fixtures, and it smelled like flowers. Unlike the tin tub at home, which sat behind a curtain in an alcove off the kitchen, this tub was white porcelain, long enough to lie in. Peggy turned a brass handle and steamy water poured from a spout. She tossed in a handful of salts perfumed with lilac. Kate moved toward the heat and held out her hands.

"You must get out of those cold things." Peggy hung a white terrycloth robe on a hook, put a thick bath towel on the counter, and handed Kate a washcloth and a bar of soap. "Can I bring you anything else?"

Kate shook her head, because that's all she could do.

As Kate stepped into the hot water, her frozen legs burned, but she forced herself to sink in. Soon her blood warmed, and she closed her eyes and lay back to luxuriate in the sensuality of the scented water, so unlike anything on the farm.

Did I fall asleep? Kate sat up with a start. The water had cooled. Rising from the bath, she slipped into the terrycloth robe and toweled her hair nearly dry, then returned to Peggy's bedroom.

Soon there came a knock on the door. "Kate?" Peggy's voice.

"Please come in!"

Peggy held out her hands for Kate. "Oh, you must feel so much better!" She opened a closet and pulled out a dress that looked like pink cotton candy. "How's this?" She held it up to Kate but didn't wait for a response. "No, I think blue." She rummaged in her closet and came out with another. "The color of your eyes. Do you like it?"

Like it! It was a rich blue silk with a low neckline, cinched-in waist, and full skirt. Kate had only seen such luxury in magazines. She touched it. "It's too pretty for me. I just need something to wear home. Do you have any trousers?"

"You're not staying for the party?" Peggy looked disappointed.

An invitation? Kate's heart surged with renewed energy. Oh yes! She wanted to stay with this generous girl and her princely brother and the music and dancing and fancy people and everything she had never known. "I would love to stay."

"Well, then, let's get started." Peggy instructed Kate to sit in front of a dressing table mirror. Peggy put Kate's hair into bobby pins and then used a handheld contraption to dry her hair. Kate's hair had always been straight, but when Peggy took out the pins, she had waves of shiny blond curls. Peggy opened a drawer of ribbons, pulled out a thick blue velvet one, and tied it in Kate's hair. "Oh, how that brings out your big blue eyes!"

Kate stared at her reflection in disbelief, glowing in the mirror.

"I have makeup." Peggy examined Kate's face. "But your skin is so clear and fresh, you're better off without it." She opened a drawer. "Perhaps a touch of pink lipstick."

Kate put up her lips as Peggy dabbed on the pink.

"You are so beautiful!" Peggy said, opening the door. "I'll leave you to dress. Just come downstairs when you're ready."

Under the watchful eye of the fluffy cat, Kate stepped into the dress. In the mirror, her cheeks flushed from the hot bath, her eyes had never looked bluer. Her white-blond curls gleamed in the light.

In spite of her small breasts, the fitted tailoring accentuated her narrow waist and gave her body a sensual shape. When Kate twirled, the cat looked up and stared. Kate laughed and twirled again, the full skirt flying up around her thighs. Finally, she stepped into the peep-toe party sandals Peggy had left on the floor.

This was a Gatsby party come to life. *No one knows me, so I can be anything I want.* Tonight she would be Daisy Buchanan. She recalled Fitzgerald's description: "There was an excitement to her voice . . . a promise that . . . there were gay exciting things hovering in the next hour." Yes, gay exciting things hovering.

She held up her head and moved gracefully down a grand circular staircase into the music and easy banter swirling below.

The boys were dressed in dinner jackets. The girls flitted about like exotic birds in lavender and almond and apricot fabrics that gleamed, dresses with full skirts nipped in at the waist like the one Kate wore. And there was Clay. As if he sensed her approach, he turned away from the laughing conversation and his eyes sparkled up toward her. At the bottom of the stairs, he held out his hand. "You look so sweet, you ought to be rationed."

Kate smiled, challenging herself to speak slowly, enunciating her words, as Daisy would certainly do. "You saved my life, really."

He bowed and picked up a glass of champagne from a roving waiter. "I should have given this to you earlier, to enjoy in your bath."

Kate blushed at the thought of this beautiful boy picturing her in the tub. When she took a sip, sparkling bubbles ticked her nose.

"I thought you might have fallen off a ship, but seeing you now, I expect you fell from a star."

These partygoers all appeared as if they had come from stars. Kate's eyes landed on a sophisticated girl who stood with one foot delicately in front of the other, like a ballerina, and moved her own well-planted feet into the more feminine stance. "I was at the lighthouse down the coast and got swept up in the current."

"The lighthouse?" He raised an eyebrow. "Imprisoned in the

tower, no doubt." He opened a silver case and offered her a cigarette.

Kate scanned the room. Yes, other girls were smoking, holding cigarettes with a casual elegance, as if they were part of their costumes. She chose one and held it near her lips, ready for a light. Clay flicked open a chrome-encased lighter that glowed with a ready blue flame. Watching his eyes, she drew in the smoke, thankful that Josie had taught her how to inhale without coughing. She took another sip of champagne as if she did this every day.

"I've never been in a lighthouse." He grinned. "Maybe you'll show me one day."

Something *he's* never done, how ironic. "Perhaps." She gazed at him from under her lashes, as she had seen starlets do.

At five-foot-eight, Kate had always been the tallest girl in her class, and she seemed to be the tallest girl at the party as well. In heels, she was almost as tall as Clay, but not quite.

A tinkling bell rang out and guests swept off toward another room, the dining room. People stared at Kate as she entered on Clay's arm. She heard whispers. *Who is she?*

In the center of the buffet was the roast pig, the whole thing, with an apple in its mouth. It was surrounded by roasted vegetables and plates of cheeses, fruits, and breads. Another table held cakes and pies and cookies.

"Gee whiz!" she said, immediately embarrassed for giving herself away.

Clay picked up a plate. "What would you like? Caviar, oysters, lobster . . ."

Kate had never tasted any of those things. "Oh yes . . . that . . . and that . . ." They moved around the table.

"My, my." A female voice approached. "Quite an appetite."

Over her shoulder, Kate spied a petite girl with a pretty face, green eyes, and lush red hair curled under into a pageboy. She wore a striking silvery dress, and she was staring at Kate's plate. Glancing about, Kate noted that other plates held tiny bits. Hers was heaping.

"Oh Lizzie, give us a break," Clay said. "Our little mermaid has just swum up from the sea. Wouldn't you be hungry?"

The girl regarded Kate, settling on Kate's rough hands, ragged nails, and a bruise Kate hadn't noticed on her arm where she had bumped against the dock ladder. "Ah, well, I don't know much about mermaids, but I suppose they need to grab their fill before they're back to the bottom."

Lizzie's nails were sculpted and polished, little white crescent moons at the base of each one. Kate closed her hands to hide her own fingers. She had always been proud of her upbringing—her family was well respected in the community—but now, in the face of Lizzie's disdain, Kate was dismayed.

"You're on my dance card for this one," Lizzie said to Clay, motioning toward the dance floor.

"My dear Lizzie," he said, "I do believe you need another glass of champagne."

Lizzie frowned. When she shifted away, Clay whispered to Kate, "Let's not invite her back."

Kate was the one who didn't belong. "Maybe I should go—"

"Please don't let her spoil the party for us." Clay guided Kate to a chaise away from the crowd and sat beside her. "Tell me, Miss Kate, what do you do for fun when you're not swimming the wild seas?"

Relieved at Clay's acceptance of her as she was, she spoke the truth. "I like reading, mostly novels."

"How perfectly romantic."

She wanted to gobble up everything on her plate, but instead she took a tiny bite of cheese. She longed to take some of this home to share, but that would give away too much.

The jazz trio in the foyer was playing "String of Pearls." Clay held out his hand. "Let's dance."

Kate took his hand, soft but strong. His nails were clipped and clean. His skin smelled warm like vanilla. He escorted her to the

dance floor and led her gracefully. She was Ginger Rogers in the arms
of Fred Astaire. She gladly followed him through the next dance and
the next, feeling other guests peel away as she and Clay swept around
the ballroom, eyes locked together.

Clay breathed in her ear, "You're so fresh and unspoiled. That's
what I like about you, Kate."

When they finally returned to their seats, a buxom brunette in
a low-cut red dress came forward. "Introduce me," she said to Clay.

"Eva, please meet Kate. Kate Christiansen." Then to Kate, "Eva
Gordon."

Eva took a puff from a cigarette in a long silver holder. "Pleased
to meet you."

A man in a butler's uniform came up to Clay. "Your father has
arrived."

"Please excuse me," Clay said.

Kate panicked. She wasn't up to conversation with any of these
sophisticated girls with perfect nails. She'd surely give herself away.
She glanced about for Peggy but didn't see her.

"I thought I knew all Clay's friends," Eva said.

A waiter hovered near, and when Eva took a glass of champagne,
Kate did as well.

"I'm not a friend—"

"Oh come now. Everyone wants to be Clay's friend."

Kate took a sip of champagne. The alcohol helped her feel more
confident in her new role. "I'm Clay's secret lover." She peered from
under her lashes in a way she hoped would convey as much.

Eva choked out cigarette smoke and gave Kate a once-over.
"Really!"

After a pause, Kate asked, "How do *you* know him?"

Eva stood up straight. "We're neighbors. Lake Forest." She blew
smoke out the side of her mouth.

Lake Forest? Kate had never heard of it.

"Senator," someone called. The room quieted.

"Oh, there's Clay's father," Eva said.

"He's a senator?"

Eva laughed. "You have no idea, do you?" After a pause, she said. "Senator Sullivan."

The name sounded familiar, but he wasn't a Wisconsin senator, Kate knew that much. She wished she had paid more attention to the news. "Come on." Eva moved off in a crowd that pushed toward the senator. Amid the applause, Kate heard him say, "War is good." It was followed by words of encouragement from others.

Kate shook her head. *I couldn't have heard that right. He must have said, "This is a good war."* She was suddenly tired, so tired.

Clay returned to her side and offered her another glass of champagne.

Kate put up her hand to stop him. "What time is it?"

"Nearly two. You must be exhausted." He took her hands.

Kate nodded.

"We have guest rooms upstairs. I'll be making my signature eggs Benedict for breakfast, but not until around ten or eleven. We sleep late here." He squeezed her hands.

"If only I could!" She had to get home before her parents noticed she was gone. She had to milk Mia and clean the barn before sunrise. She dreaded the walk through the woods, it must be miles, with the cold wind against her and prowling animals all about. "I'm sorry, but I have to go."

Clay's smile faded. "Of course, I understand. I'll drive you."

"Oh, thank you!" Kate wanted to throw her arms around Clay, but that would be too forward.

"I'll have Peggy bring your clothes."

Soon Peggy came with a satchel. "Your wet things are in here."

"But I couldn't wear your beautiful dress home . . ."

Peggy put a hand on Kate's arm. "You can return it after you've had a good night's sleep."

Clay excused himself from the party and led Kate outside. When he pulled open the garage door, Kate beheld the most magnificent automobile she had ever seen—a shiny red convertible.

"It's a Duesy," he said, following her eyes. "A 1924 Duesenberg." He opened the passenger door and she slid onto the leather bench seat.

The top was down, the wind merely a breeze now. Clay maneuvered the car along a woodsy drive, his arm around her shoulders, headlights glancing off piney trees, a skunk ambling off, a deer freezing in place.

When they reached County Trunk Q, Kate pointed south. She worried that the orchard would give her away. Maybe she should direct him to the road that ended at the causeway leading to the lighthouse and walk home from there. She had to tell him. "I don't actually live in a lighthouse," she said quickly.

"Oh?" He grinned as if he had never believed her anyway.

"I live in an enchanted orchard filled with magical cherry trees."

"Ah. So that explains it."

"Explains what?" *That I'm a simple farm girl?*

"How you bewitched me." He took her hand. "And when will your cherries be ripe?" His voice came low and seductive.

"Soon," she said, relieved. "I will make you a pie. A fantastical cherry pie."

He laughed out loud. "Oh Kate, Kate. I like you, Kate." He pulled her close. Her skin tingled at his touch.

"And I like you."

Clay gave her a squeeze.

"I like your sister too. Peggy's a swell girl."

"She is." Clay pulled back his arm to change gears, and when he gunned the engine the car accelerated so quickly that Kate's body pressed against the seat. She reached out and grabbed the door handle.

"Don't worry. This baby was made to go fast." He had to shout over the racing motor.

"Is it . . . safe?"

"When *I'm* driving, it is." He slowed and pulled her to him again. "But I don't want to scare you."

She was shaken. "I've never gone that fast."

"Wait until you're up in an airplane. You'll love it."

An airplane! What made him think she would ever go up in an airplane?

"I'll be back at Northwestern in the fall. Would you like to come for a visit?" He glanced her way. "You and me, we'll have a grand time."

Kate's mind raced with anticipation. She'd be mingling with the kind of people she had met at the university, discussing literature and art, and she'd have this exciting boy as her companion. "I'll be going to the UW in Madison in the fall." She was proud to say it.

"Splendid." His white teeth gleamed.

"I'm going to write stories. And maybe you'll be in one of them."

"I'd like that." He smiled her way. "Will you show me one of your stories . . . next time?" Clay's fingers lightly stroked her bare shoulder.

Next time!

With the night air blowing through her hair, a million stars sparkling above, and the most charming boy she had ever met at her side, Kate felt beautiful.

"Do you have parties often?" she asked, then worried that he might think she was fishing for an invitation. Well, maybe she was.

"In the summers mostly."

They rode in silence for a while until she came up with something else to ask. "Are you planning to go into politics, as your father did?"

Clay frowned. "No."

Kate waited, and when Clay didn't add to that, she said, "So what do you want to do?"

"Fly airplanes. I'm taking lessons."

"Really!" She couldn't imagine going up in an airplane, and here was Clay, learning to fly, as if it were as commonplace as riding a bicycle. What different worlds they lived in. "What's it like?"

He looked her way, then back to the road. "Climbing up and up until you lose all connection with the world below and live only in the moment."

"It sounds so freeing."

"Free and 'pierced with beauty and danger.' That's what Lindbergh said."

"Charles Lindbergh?"

"Yes, I met him after one of his public appearances, told him I wanted to be an aviator."

"But what about the danger?"

"That's the most exciting part."

Kate wasn't too excited about that part, Clay pierced with danger.

"When Lindbergh was my age, he quit college and hired out as a barnstormer—wing walking, parachuting, flying barrel rolls, spins, dives—"

"But you wouldn't do that!"

Clay grabbed Kate's hand and laughed. "Lindbergh's wife said she was glad she didn't know him then."

"You met his wife?"

"Sure. She's a writer, did you know?" He didn't wait for her response. "Lindbergh taught her to fly."

"Gee whiz!" Kate couldn't conceive of it, learning to fly. And Lindbergh . . . "They say he's a Nazi sympathizer."

Clay frowned. "It's his flying I'm interested in, not his politics."

Her mind drifted back to the party, and she recalled the words the senator had spoken. "Did I hear your father say, 'War is good'? Did he mean 'This war is a good war'—everybody says that—or was he talking about war in general?"

Clay pulled his arm back to hold to the wheel. "It's not about this war or that war, it's about business. War is good for the economy."

"I don't understand . . ."

"We were in a depression until the war machine geared up. And now we're all fat and happy. Simple economics."

Kate thought of telling him that her family wasn't fat and happy, but decided against it. "I don't know anything about economics, but all I can see is that everything is going to the war, including men and boys, and things are coming apart."

"Coming apart? No, no, no." He shook his head. "The government is buying tanks, ships, fuel, clothing, parachutes, bullets, guns, airplanes, food, you name it. And paying the salaries for all the fighting men. No more unemployment." He shot her a glance. "Even the women are making money now."

"So you agree with your father? That war is good?"

"From a business standpoint, yes." Clay paused. "And this war . . . we're fighting to keep our country safe and free."

"We?" It suddenly occurred to her that the boys at the party were certainly old enough to enlist. Could they all be 4-F, like Frank Sinatra with his punctured eardrum? She backed away and stared at Clay. "What's wrong with all of you that you're not serving?"

He looked startled. "I'm in the Naval Reserve Officers Training Corps."

"Reserve? Reserved for what?"

Clay's jaw clenched. "We have . . . deferments."

A surge of anger rose in Kate's chest. How unfair!

"I want to join up, but . . . my father has threatened . . ." His voice trailed off.

"Threatened?" It was none of her business, but yes, it was. She didn't like that she was attracted to someone who let other people do the hard work.

"I have a lot to lose," he finally said.

"Not any more than any other boy. It's their lives they're risking. My own brother is fighting in Italy."

After a tense silence, Clay said, "You must be proud of him. I hope I can meet him one day."

Well, if you sit out the war, he won't want to meet you! She didn't say it out loud because it didn't matter anymore. The magical evening was ruined. She'd never see Clay again. And maybe she didn't want to.

They were quiet until Kate directed him onto Orchard Lane. She asked Clay to stop some distance from the house so her parents wouldn't hear the car.

He switched off the motor and turned to her. "You've given me a lot to think about, Kate."

"What? What are you going to think about?"

"My father . . ." But he didn't say anything more.

Kate thought of her own father. She wouldn't do anything to cross him. But she never had to—he always supported her decisions.

Clay reached toward her and put a hand on her cheek. "You're a different kind of girl, Kate."

She hesitated, not sure whether she wanted to know what he meant. "Different how?"

"I don't know how to explain it." He paused. "You're so . . . so real."

Real? She touched the warm hand on her face. Then she realized what she was wearing. "Peggy's dress—"

"You can give it to me next time."

Next time? There it was again.

"May I call you?"

"We don't have a telephone."

He sat back, and the surprise on his face reminded her what different worlds they lived in. No, she would never hear from him again.

He pulled forward and kissed her nose. "Then we'll have to find another way." He got out of the car and came around to her side. She had already opened the door, and he laughed when he saw she was about to step out. "You can't walk on this gravel in those flimsy shoes. You'll trip and break an ankle." He bent forward. "Let me carry you—"

Kate slipped off the shoes and swung her legs around and stood on the gravel. "I'm more comfortable barefoot."

He put his hands on her waist. "You're a spunky gal, Miss Kate Christiansen."

Before she could say another word, Clay gently kissed her cheek, then her mouth. Then he picked her up. "I just bet you'd like to go flying too."

CHAPTER TWELVE

WHEN MORNING BIRDS CALLED, Kate pulled the covers over her ears and tried to slip back into the dream. She breathed in floral bath salts and opened her eyes, and there was the dress. Peggy's dress. It wasn't a dream at all. Clay was real. He had kissed her. He had kissed her and invited her to visit him at school. Her heart fluttered in her chest like a bird taking wing. Fly away with Clay.

She fluffed up her pillow, thoughts racing. When she was done with her chores, she would ride her bicycle up County Trunk Q and search for the road to his house. It must be one of those small roads branching off through the woods. Oh, she wished she had paid more attention. And the dress! That would be her entrée, an excuse to visit. She'd wrap it in tissue paper and put it into her bicycle basket. She'd ring her bicycle bell. Special delivery! She snuggled into the covers.

But what if Clay wasn't home? What if Peggy answered and thanked Kate for returning the dress and that was the end of that? No, she wouldn't take the dress, she'd simply ride by. If he happened to be in the yard, she'd wave and stop, as if she rode that way often. And if he wasn't in the yard?

A woodpecker drilled into the oak outside her window.

Let him come to me. He knows where I live.

Kate was through with classes, done with school. She could stay home all day waiting for Clay's arrival. After her chores, she would wash away the stench of the barn and put on a summer dress. She'd sit at the picnic table in the yard, work on her math problems, or read that new book Professor Fleming had sent, *To the Lighthouse:* "Dear Kate, I believe you'll appreciate Virginia Woolf's introspective voice." Yes, that was how Clay would find her. Introspecting.

She rose from bed and picked up the dress and twirled with it, laughing. Mother rarely came into Kate's room, but just in case, she hid the dress in the back of her closet.

"We sleep late," he had said. She had plenty of time. She stepped into her overalls.

SITTING AT THE PICNIC TABLE, Kate found it difficult to concentrate on math. Images of the party flickered through her mind—the graceful home, the music, the food, the way Clay's friends were so easy with each other, Peggy so sweet and generous, Clay dancing her around the room. Oh! She could hardly wait for him to find her again.

It was a fine spring morning. The storm had chased the clouds away, and now pink and white cherry blossoms fluttered in a fragrant breeze. A Baltimore oriole sang from the reedy meadow.

Lucky for her, Father had taken the PWs to work the far side of the orchard, out of sight. It was perfect, so perfect. She couldn't help but look up at every sound, eager to see Clay's red convertible. She would ask him not to say anything to Mother or Father about last night. "We met at the library," she'd whisper. He'd wink knowingly.

By the time Mother called her in for lunch, Kate had finished two of the math problems Karl had given her. When she entered the kitchen, Father put down his pipe. "You're all prettied up, Kate."

Mother's eyes fixed on Kate. "Why are you sitting out there, so . . . so dressed up?"

Kate's cheeks went hot. "It's a pretty day, and I wanted to be pretty with it."

"And pretty you are," Father said.

Mother scowled and picked up her spoon. The silence that followed was punctuated only by the slurping of soup, the scraping of bowls.

Kate finally changed the subject. "I finished the problem about the volume of the silo with algebra and geometry." She explained how she had solved it each way.

"Only trigonometry left," he said.

Kate groaned. "That's the hardest."

Mother touched a napkin to her lips. "Kate, I need help in the garden. After all the rain we've had . . . you'll need to change into your work clothes."

Kate's heart fell. She didn't want Clay to find her working in the dirt. "I've got a hunch how to solve the last problem—"

"Charlotte," Father said, "perhaps the weeds can wait until tomorrow. The weather should hold for a day or two. Kate has her lessons."

Mother frowned.

CHAPTER THIRTEEN

THE MORNING SUN FELL golden across Charlotte's garden. It was the first of June, and early sprouts were just emerging. But weeds were sprouting as well, creeping in daily, stealing sun and water and nutrients and choking off Charlotte's tender seedlings. The trick was to catch the weeds when they were no more than thin white threads peeking out from the soil, before they had a chance to take hold. Charlotte used a hoe to scrape off weeds between the beds, but she babied her seedlings, picking off invaders by hand.

A spiderweb, suspended between two tomato leaves, glistened with drops of morning dew. Spiders were a gardener's friends, eating the pests. She left them alone.

After finishing the first row, Charlotte stood and stretched. She gazed at the scene before her. Off in the orchard, trees were bursting with blossoms. It would be a fruitful year. Thomas had the PWs hoeing around the trunks while he himself manned the tractor, dragging for weeds between rows. As she watched, the tractor sputtered and stopped. Thomas walked to where the prisoners were working and brought that bad one with the scar, the mechanical one, Vehlmer, over to look at the contraption.

Three years ago, before gas rationing, Thomas sold their good plow horses for this thing that needed fixing at every turn. Charlotte had cared for those horses from the time they were colts. All they needed was a bit of feed, an occasional brushing, and they would do anything. Now feed was much easier to come by than gasoline. When the tractor rattled to life, a whiff of exhaust blew toward the garden. Charlotte turned back to her plants.

The cherry harvest was only six weeks away. Charlotte envisioned going to town with a purse full of money. She'd pay the butcher's wife what she owed. Then she'd buy butter and flour and sugar and bake for days. Thomas sent most of the cherries to local canneries for shipment all across the country, but first Charlotte would take her share for pies. Stores up and down the peninsula carried her blue-ribbon cherry pies. When the money came in, she'd buy gifts for her family. Chocolate for Ben, fabric for Kate—she'd want to make new clothes for college. A sturdy pair of work boots for Thomas. She might even splurge on perfumed soap. Jasmine. She'd touched her wrist to it last week in Ellie's Dry Goods and had enjoyed the scent for hours.

It wasn't quite noon when Charlotte put away her gardening tools. She had to get the laundry hung while the sun was still warm.

In the kitchen, she pumped cold water into a big pot and put it on the stove. She bent down and opened the wood box. Only a few bits of kindling remained. From the window she could see that the woodshed was nearly empty too, save for the newly pruned branches, too green to burn. Ben had always kept the shed full, going into the woods with an ax to chop up fallen trees. He kept the kitchen wood box full as well.

Off beyond the barn, a maple tree struck by lightning the previous year lay on the ground. That was what she needed. Solid, aged wood.

Charlotte went into the barn and found Ben's leather gloves, stiff in the shape of his big hands. She held them a moment, then slid her smaller hands inside.

She took down the ax—it was heavier than she'd expected—from where it hung on the wall. As she approached the fallen maple, a chipmunk flashed out from an undergrowth of leaves. Charlotte felt a tic of guilt that this little thing would have to find another home for her family. Then she brought down the ax.

She first tackled the smaller branches, chopping them for kindling. But when she struck at a stout limb, the ax merely bounced against the hardwood, jarring Charlotte's hands. She whacked it again and again until it finally broke apart. Her arms and shoulders ached. She dropped the ax and pushed a loose strand of hair from her forehead.

"Mrs. Christiansen." She turned to see his solid silhouette against the late morning sun.

Karl. That was what she called him now. It had been nearly three weeks since that first lesson, that awkward supper. He came every few days to tutor Kate, but Charlotte hadn't invited him back for a meal.

"Thomas sent me to help you."

Charlotte looked out toward the orchard. Thomas waved to her, she waved back.

When Karl moved forward, his face came into the light—that hard jaw, those eyes, the dimples. She stared. Too long, she realized.

She pulled off Ben's gloves. Before yielding them to Karl, she hesitated. But he didn't. His big hands pushed into them, filling them, changing their shape.

He picked up the ax, and with a few sure strokes, he chopped a thick branch into pieces small enough for the stove. He loaded the wheelbarrow and followed Charlotte to the house.

The wood box opened from two sides—the outside door was for stocking the wood, and the door in the kitchen was for removing it.

Karl began loading from the outside while Charlotte went in and opened the interior door. Karl's hands pushed the thick logs toward her, filling the kitchen with the earthy fragrance of fresh-cut maple.

When he had finished unloading, he returned to the fallen tree and continued chopping, piling logs neatly in the woodshed. She watched through the window as he brought the ax down again and again in a strong, graceful tempo. After some time, he went into the barn and returned with Thomas's bow saw and began sawing the trunk into thick rounds—back and forth, back and forth—before taking up the ax again to split them. All the while Charlotte stared, mesmerized by the rhythm of his body.

Steam rose from the pot on the stove and beaded on Charlotte's face. She pushed herself away from the window and filled the deep wash sink, pumping in more cold water until the temperature was not too hot for her hands.

Her mind wandered as she scrubbed one of Thomas's grass-stained shirts against the washboard. Once the harvest came, she'd make a special supper to celebrate the abundance. It had been years since she'd made ice cream. Warm cherry pie with vanilla ice cream melting on top. She'd take a rack of pies down to Mettler's dairy and trade them for fresh cream.

"Mrs. Christiansen."

She dropped the shirt and swung around toward the voice. Karl's face peered in through the screen like a priest's in a confessional. How long had he been watching her?

"May I help you to do more things?"

She wiped her hands on her apron. "The garden fence needs mending." Her mind began ticking off all the things Karl could fix. "I'll show you where we keep the wire."

The air in the barn was close with dark, feral odors. In the dim light, Charlotte saw that Karl had hung up the saw and ax alongside the heavy shovels and sharp picks and spike-toothed animal traps and shiny butchering tools. Charlotte feared being alone with this man. Not because he would do her physical harm. No, it was that dream, the dream of him climbing through her bedroom window. And now, when she caught the musk of his body, blood raced hot beneath her skin. She swayed involuntarily toward him.

"*Das* wire?"

"Oh, yes." She stepped back. "This way."

Approaching the rabbit hutch, Charlotte stopped and put her hand to her throat. A note was tacked to the roof. Karl's name written clearly in Kate's handwriting. "What's this!" She tugged it off, anger rising, recalling Kate dressed in her best, obviously waiting for someone's attention. The girl had never shown any desire to date the boys at school. No, she thought herself literary, sophisticated. And here was an older man, an educated man, a man of foreign intrigue. Of course Kate would be attracted to him.

"I will not tolerate secret messages between you and my daughter." She opened Kate's note and tried to make out the odd figures. A code? "What does this mean?" she demanded, holding the note before him.

Karl studied the page. "Your daughter is a smart girl. She solved her lessons."

Embarrassment clouded Charlotte's mind. She let out a breath. "I'm sorry if . . ." She couldn't finish. She didn't want him to know. Know what? She rubbed her clammy palms down her apron.

"If you like, Kate could give her papers to Thomas—"

"No," Charlotte didn't trust Thomas to notice signs. "She will give her completed assignments to me."

"How will I—"

"You will come to my kitchen window every afternoon." With that, Charlotte grabbed the wire from a shelf, handed it to Karl, and left him alone.

From the cover of her kitchen, Charlotte spied through the window, watching Karl search for holes in the fence, watching him cut the wire and make neat repairs. *What must he think of me after that outburst, that accusation?* She breathed deeply, trying to regain her composure.

Damn! I don't care what he thinks. I don't care I don't care I don't care!

She pushed Thomas's shirt into the sink, but the water had gone cold.

CHAPTER FOURTEEN

DID HE FORGET WHERE I LIVE?

It had been nearly a week since the party, and Kate could sit still no longer. She went to the barn and rolled her bicycle onto the path. She had to talk to Josie.

The lake was calm, the channel low. Kate set her bicycle against the birch tree and kicked off her shoes and held up the hem of her summer dress and waded across to the island.

As she approached the yard, Kate heard Josie singing "Boogie Woogie Bugle Boy of Company B" in her strong alto. Around the corner of the cookhouse, there she was, hanging wash on the line, swinging her hips in rhythm, "A-toot, a-toot, a-toot-diddelyada-toot . . . he blows eight-to-the-bar . . . in boogie rhythm . . ."

Kate ran forward, clapping.

"Kate! Where have you been?"

"Oh, Josie, I'm in love!" Kate twirled.

Josie dropped the blouse she was holding. "Not with that Nazi!"

"No, no." Kate picked up the blouse and secured it on the line with wooden clothespins. "With a new boy."

"A new boy?" Josie wanted to know more.

"Remember the last time I was with you in the lighthouse, the night of the storm?" Kate raced through the story of being swept up the shore to the big house. "And we danced. Oh, Josie, we danced and danced! It was magical!" Kate put her arms into dance position and swirled around the lawn.

"Well, he can't be as good a dancer as Ben."

"But oh, to be in Clay's arms . . . !"

"Sounds like you've written yourself into one of your romantic stories." Josie clipped a pair of cotton shorts to the line.

"I have his sister's silk party dress to prove it."

"You stole a dress?"

"I didn't steal it. Peggy lent it to me. She's the most generous girl. Oh, I do hope she wants to be friends with me."

Josie made a sour face.

"You too, Josie. The three of us."

"I want to see the dress."

"Yes, but I'll need to take it back soon . . ." *What if I keep it for a while? For months, years maybe, and Peggy will say, "Oh I wondered where that old thing went."*

Kate pulled a pair of lacy panties from the basket. She had never seen anything so sexy. "Are these your mother's?"

Josie snatched them from her. "For my trousseau." She giggled. "But I couldn't wait to wear them."

A trousseau for working on the farm?

"How old is this new boyfriend of yours?"

"Older than me. He's in college. A sophomore."

"College?" Josie flicked a pillowcase. "Why isn't he overseas fighting with Ben and the other boys? There must be something wrong with him."

"No." Kate hesitated. She picked up a smock that belonged to Josie's younger sister and hung it on the line. "He has one of those college deferments. But he's in the Naval Reserve Officers Training Corps."

Josie put her hands on her hips. "He's a coward, then. The war will be over before he even graduates."

"He's not like that . . ." Kate stopped herself from defending him. He had told her things in confidence.

"Then what *is* he like?"

Kate closed her eyes and recalled Clay's strong arm around her, leading her out of the storm. His eyes smiling up from the bottom of the staircase, welcoming her to his party. "He's got a great smile. And he's smart and well-spoken." His kiss, the way he held her. Kate stifled a sigh and told Josie about the invitation to visit him at school. "I'll have to make new clothes." She thought of the stylish girls at the university.

"Well, *I* think he's a coward."

"Josie, no. He wants to go, but . . ." How could she explain without explaining too much? She put up her chin and changed the subject. "We talked about our ambitions—he wants to be a pilot, I told him I wanted to write stories—"

Josie rolled her eyes. "How boring! Boys like girls who are fun."

Kate pondered this. Maybe that was why she hadn't heard from him. "Oh, Josie, I just *have* to see him. I'm thinking of riding my bicycle up there."

Josie picked up a man's nightshirt and two clothespins, then stopped and dropped them into the basket. "Say, how about if we go right now? Father's off in the motorboat, but we could take the rowboat."

"Yes!" Kate thrilled at the plan.

As the two friends headed to the boathouse, Josie began singing, "I got a crush on you, Sweetie Pie . . ." She sang sweetly, then she paused and belted out the last of it in a slow, growling, hip-gyrating, " 'cause I got a crush, oooo oh my baby, on youuuuuu!"

Yes, fun. That's what Kate liked best about Josie. She was different from the other girls. She didn't care what people thought. She just sang it out.

IN TRYING TO DIRECT THE ROWBOAT away from the dock, Josie made a show of being clumsy.

"Let me do it," Kate said.

"You're so much stronger than I am." Josie settled in like a princess.

Kate feathered the oars and gave Josie a quick spray.

"You did that on purpose!"

Kate laughed and guided the boat north.

"That's it!" She slowed at the sight of the house set far back from the shore.

"Wow, that's some place."

Kate pulled up the oars and let the boat bob on soft waves.

"C'mon. Let's go up."

Kate noted her cotton housedress and dirty bare feet. Her tangled hair needed brushing. "No. I look like a ragamuffin."

"Well, why did we come then? If he's your boyfriend, he'll want to see you no matter what."

"I didn't say he was my boyfriend—"

"You said you were in love! What else could that mean?"

"Oh, all right. But he has a nasty dog, so if you get bitten, don't blame me." Hoping the dog would remember her, Kate maneuvered the boat to shore, stepped out, and pulled it up onto the marshy beach.

On this bright sunny day, Kate saw the property in a different light. At night she hadn't noticed the grand sweep of lawns and gardens.

At the house, they walked up the porch steps and Kate rang the doorbell. No one came. No dog barked.

She peered through the window. "This is where we danced." She recalled the jazz trio, the sugary dresses, Clay leading her around the room, everyone's eyes on them . . .

"Well? Where are they?" Josie demanded.

Just then, William—the man who had roasted the pig at the

party—came around the corner of the house, pushing a lawn mower. He stopped at the edge of the porch and squinted up toward them. "Nobody home."

"When will they be back?" Kate said.

"Won't know till they 'rive."

"But . . . when did they leave?"

"Last week." He wiped an arm across his forehead.

"Last week?" *Right after the party?*

"If he cared, he would have told you," Josie said.

Kate tried to hide her embarrassment. "It must have been a last-minute decision."

ONCE THEY'D RETURNED TO LOON ISLAND, Kate waded back to the mainland and rode her bicycle to the Turtle Bay branch library. There she learned that Senator Sullivan was from Illinois.

In answer to Kate's questions, the librarian—the perpetually unsmiling one—directed her to the editorial pages of a recent copy of the *Chicago Tribune*. "He's a war profiteer," the woman said.

"War profiteer?"

"He's involved with a company that sold munitions to the Germans."

"But that must have been before we went to war."

"At the time, Germany was fighting our allies in Europe—"

"Oh!" Kate's cheeks went hot. "Well, I will write to him about how disappointed I am to hear that."

"I'm sure that will change everything," the woman chortled.

"Could you please help me find his address?"

The librarian opened a file cabinet and brought out a folder. "Here it is."

Kate copied down his address at the Senate Office Building, Washington, DC.

On the way out, Kate noticed a display of new books. She picked up a fat one with a picture of a woman in a low-cut dress from an earlier century and scanned a few pages. *Forever Amber.* It looked like something Josie would like. When she took it to the checkout desk, the librarian said, "This is not meant for a young lady. Let's find something more appropriate."

"I'd like this one, thank you." Kate ignored the librarian's grumbling as she checked it out.

Riding home, Kate wondered what Clay thought about his father's business, about supplying the Germans. He had said he didn't agree with his father, but what did that mean?

Kate had a box of fine pink stationery she had never used, not even to write to Professor Fleming. A birthday present from Ben, she'd been saving it for just the right occasion . . . and this was it. Sitting at her bedroom desk, she opened the box and pulled out a page. She dipped the tip of her fountain pen into the ink jar and filled it.

Dear Clay,

Thank you for saving my life! What an enchanting evening. I wonder when you and Peggy might be coming back to Door County so I can return Peggy's party dress.
I do hope you and your family are having a swell summer.

Sincerely,
Kate Christiansen

It was getting dark when Kate rode back to town, to the barbershop, which also served as the local post office. Was the letter too forward? She recalled the touch of Clay's fingers on her shoulder, his invitation to Northwestern, his disappointment in hearing she didn't have a phone number. *If I don't write to him, I may never hear from him again.* Before she could change her mind, she marched up the steps and put the letter into the mailbox.

After dinner, Kate sat on the porch swing facing the lake, her notebook in front of her. She began a story about a man and a woman from different worlds who fall in love. It came to her quickly—his way of thinking totally at odds with hers. What drew them together also held them apart.

But then she was stuck.

She gazed out over the wide lake, stars brightening against the darkening sky. How would the story end?

CHAPTER FIFTEEN

CHARLOTTE NOTICED A NEW MOODINESS she had never seen in her daughter. The girl was distracted, even more so than usual, pushing vegetables around on her plate. Karl would be coming tonight for another lesson. Was that it?

After supper, as Kate cleared the table, she dropped a plate on the floor.

Charlotte jumped at the crash. "Pay attention!"

"I'm sorry," Kate bent to pick up the pieces.

"Char," Thomas said, "calm yourself. We have plenty of dishes."

"Not to throw away!" Charlotte felt nervous, on edge.

"Good evening," Karl called through the screen door.

"Come on in," Thomas said.

Once Karl was seated, his back to Charlotte, she was free to watch him, watch Kate, watch for signs. Hands, eyes, it should be obvious. But they remained respectful of each other, sitting well apart, focused on the lessons.

Charlotte finished up the dishes as quickly as possible and left the room. Thomas would stay with them, chaperoning, puffing on his pipe.

She went to the parlor and sat on the couch to nurse memories of her outburst in the barn. *Stay away from him!*

Bingo jumped up, mewing for attention. Charlotte ran her fingers through the cat's fur, trying to hush the inner voices, breathing more evenly now. Once the cat settled, Charlotte picked up her sewing basket and shuffled among the projects. Three of Thomas's socks needed darning. She pulled a strand of wool through her darning needle and began the methodical task that left her mind free to roam.

Tomorrow she would trade goat's milk for a soup bone and a bit of rice and make a broth with early vegetables. She hummed along with Billie Holiday. She should take advantage of the good weather to start the spring cleaning—hang the rugs on the back porch and give them a thorough beating, wash the windows, air out pillows and mattresses . . .

The music stopped abruptly. An announcer introduced the president. Soon Roosevelt began in that sonorous voice: "My friends. Yesterday, on June fourth, 1944, Rome fell to American and Allied troops. The first of the Axis capitals is now in our hands. One up and two to go!"

Charlotte pushed the cat to the floor and ran to the kitchen. "Thomas, come listen!"

Thomas hurried into the parlor, with Kate and Karl right behind.

"We've taken Rome!" Charlotte was laughing, crying.

Roosevelt went on: "The Italians too, forswearing a partnership in the Axis which they never desired, have sent their troops to join us in our battles against the German trespassers on their soil."

"The Italians surrendered?" Thomas took the pipe from his mouth and stared at the radio.

Charlotte held a hand to her mouth, tears streaming down her cheeks.

"For this quarter-century, the Italian people were enslaved. They were degraded by the rule of Mussolini from Rome. They will mark its liberation with deep emotion. In the north of Italy, the people are still dominated and threatened by the Nazi overlords and their Fascist puppets . . . Our victory comes at an excellent time, while our Allied forces are poised for another strike at Western Europe—and while the armies of other Nazi soldiers nervously await our assault. And in the meantime our gallant Russian allies continue to make their power felt more and more."

"Get 'em," Thomas interjected, pumping a fist in the air.

When the cat jumped back into her lap, Charlotte cuddled it closely. "That's General Mark Clark's Army. That's Ben's unit," she said to the cat. "No wonder he hasn't had time to write." It had been weeks now since they'd had a letter from Ben. When she looked up, she saw Karl's face, pale and sickly. Well, what did he expect? Of course good would win over evil.

Roosevelt continued: "Germany has not yet been driven to surrender . . . Therefore, the victory still lies some distance ahead. That distance will be covered in due time—have no fear of that. But it will be tough and it will be costly, as I have told you many, many times."

When the address ended, Vera Lynn's soaring voice sang out, "There'll be bluebirds over the White Cliffs of Dover . . ." Charlotte let tears fall freely.

Thomas cleared his throat and turned to Karl. "What do you think of this?"

Head down, Karl was focused on the large hands sitting limp in his lap. He didn't respond.

" 'There'll be love and laughter, and peace ever after . . .' "

"Karl, are you all right?" Charlotte said.

He raised his eyes to her. "It is difficult to listen to how your president tells of our people." He took a breath. "You are good people, here on this farm, but we are good people too." He stood.

Kate stood and moved toward him. "We're not against *you*, Karl . . ."

"We are done with our lesson." He gave a bow and left.

Charlotte wanted to follow him. Instead, she sat rigid.

"I feel sorry for Karl's family . . ." Kate smeared the backside of a hand across her teary face. "But I want Ben to come home."

Charlotte stared at the War Mother's Flag hanging in the window. She didn't want to think of what Ben must have endured to get this far.

CHAPTER SIXTEEN

RAIN BEAT AGAINST THE HOOD of Kate's yellow slicker as she steered her bicycle along the slippery pavement. A wash of green meadow to her left, deep woods to her right. She passed the ice cream stand, the Moravian church, the weathered wooden sign leading down to the boat launch. Up ahead was Turtle Bay. Not quite noon. It had been three weeks since she'd mailed her letter to Clay.

When she arrived at the candy-cane pole in front of the barbershop, Kate set her bicycle against the white clapboard building and hurried up the steps to the covered porch. Inside, she threw back her hood and headed to the woodstove where Roger, a yellow Labrador sort of mongrel, lay warming himself.

Holding her cold hands over the center of warmth, Kate closed her eyes and let the fragrance of cedar envelop her. Then she bent to pet Roger. He lay back at her approach and exposed his tummy for her to rub. "You silly mutt," she said, scratching his tummy.

Old Man Berger looked up from behind the big chair where he was clipping Mr. Beal's thinning hair. "Howdy, Missy Kate."

The barber was a certified postal officer, and his shop was the town's gathering place. A familiar group of old men sat about in cracked leather chairs, smoking pipes, rustling pages of the *Door County Advocate* and the *Green Bay Press Gazette*. The RCA played in the background, a swing number. They nodded her way. "Morning, Kate." For weeks they'd been celebrating the capture of Rome, then the landing at Normandy. Today they were talking about Assisi.

Kate came to check for mail nearly every day now, embarrassed in front of these men at the lack of response, as if they knew why she was here. A jilted lover. Was that what she was?

"How's your mother?" Mr. Krause asked.

"Fine, thank you."

"You know," he continued, addressing the others, "I think this girl is looking more and more like Charlotte every day."

Kate winced as eyes fixed on her, men smiling, exchanging glances. Kate caught the sharp scent of aftershave Mr. Berger was patting onto Mr. Beal's cheeks.

"Got a couple of letters for you, Missy," the barber said, wiping his doughy hands on the white cotton apron stretched over his round belly.

Kate's heart leapt, but then she had to wait. She waited while Old Man Berger unsnapped his customer's smock, while Mr. Beal fiddled in his pocket for a few coins, while the barber went behind the counter, opened the cash register, and dropped coins into their proper compartments.

Mr. Mueller stood and climbed into the big barber's throne. "Just a shave today."

"My letters?" Kate was nearly breathless.

"Ah." Old Man Berger opened a cupboard drawer to retrieve two envelopes. "One's for your mother"—he handed her an envelope that looked like so many others Ben had sent—"but this here, this one's mighty fancy." He gave her a wink.

It was a cream-colored, linen-textured envelope with a fine blue script addressed to Miss Kate Christiansen. The postmark was

Washington, DC. *Clay!* Kate slipped her finger under the flap and gently, slowly, moved it along the edge—the very edge Clay must have licked—down to the rounded point and back up the other side. She opened the flap and slid out the folded page.

The men were watching her. She ducked out to the covered porch.

Dear Kate,

Your most welcome note has made its way from my father's office to our residence here in Georgetown.

I apologize for leaving without a word, but politics called my father away, all of us away, no time to say good-bye. Please know that I have thought often of our evening together, how lovely you looked and, even more, how genuine you are, rare and unique. Unafraid. You inspired me to face up to my own challenge. I'll explain when I see you.

I will be returning to Door County to host a Fourth of July wingding. I would be delighted if you could join us. It will be a casual day of games. Bring a swimsuit. I see us gliding in a canoe in the moonlight.

Yours truly,
Clay

Kate spun around. "Rare" . . . "unique" . . . "lovely" . . . oh! And he could have written "sincerely," but instead he wrote "yours truly"!

That was when she noticed the second letter. The envelope was addressed to Mrs. Christiansen. That was odd. Ben typically sent letters to all three of them—Mother, Father, and Kate. What secret does he have for Mother? Resisting the temptation to open it, she slipped it into her slicker pocket along with the letter from Clay. *Clay!*

The rain had stopped and the world smelled fresh and clean. A fragment of rainbow crossed the sky, pointing right to Clay's house. She danced down the steps and breathed in the spring air. Feeling like the leading lady, she sang out, "Oh, what a beautiful morning, oh, what a beautiful day . . ." She pushed her bicycle past the feed store and the shuttered Dew Drop Inn and the fragrant bakery and the butcher shop. She began forming a response. *"I was thrilled to receive . . ." No, no, no. Let him know I'm interested, but not too interested.* "Imply other options," Josie would say.

Kate's mind drifted to Gatsby parties on the lawn, picturing herself among elegant people, elegant conversation, elegant clothes. She stopped. *What will I wear?* The other girls would surely be showing off the latest chic styles.

Kate pushed her bicycle across the street to Schwarz's Drug Store and peered through the window at the magazine rack. *Vogue.* She had a few coins in her pocket, not enough to buy a magazine, but enough for a cherry soda. Inside, she picked up a copy of *Vogue* and sat at the counter and ordered a soda. It was the big summer issue, introducing the latest designs in linen skirts and slacks and pedal pushers and midi-blouses and . . . *yes!* She stared at a photo of Ginger Rogers in short tap pants, cinched in at the waist, cut and flared at the thigh. *That's it! Josie tells me I have nice legs. Mrs. J will help me.* Kate cast a guilty glimpse around the room—no one was watching—then tore the photo from the magazine and tucked it into her pocket.

"Mrs. J" was Ellie Jensen, owner of the dry goods store. Kate left her slicker outside on her bicycle and brushed herself off before entering.

"Good morning, Charlotte. Oh, I'm sorry. Kate! You certainly take after your mother!"

"Hello, Mrs. J." Kate sauntered over to the fabric corner.

"Are you planning a sewing project?"

"I'm thinking of shorts and a blouse—"

"I have some lovely polished cotton. You'd be good in baby blue, pink—"

"Is there any chance . . . do you know where I might find silk?"

"Silk is for parachutes, Kate. You know that."

"Yes, I just thought—"

Mrs. J put a finger to her lips. "A special event?" She whispered conspiratorially, though there was no one to hear.

Kate nodded.

"Well, then, if you don't mind a used fabric, a woman brought in silk brocade draperies yesterday to trade for wool crepe. She should have turned it in, but . . ." She led Kate to the back room and opened a trunk and pulled out yards of forest green brocade. She laid out the silk on a long cutting table. Kate ran her hand across the rich fabric.

Next, Mrs. J unfolded drapery sheers of celadon green, a fine complement to the darker fabric. "The color is light and young." She pulled a corner of fabric across Kate's arm. "Perfect against your pale skin. Just the thing for the blouse . . ."

"But it's nearly transparent!"

"Of course you'll wear a camisole underneath."

"Of course." Kate's heart raced. She could see it too.

"A new boyfriend?"

Kate cheeks went hot.

"I can keep a secret."

Kate did want Mrs. J's advice. "I would like to be in style for a party. Yes, maybe a new boy. I don't know yet."

"Hmm . . . well, you'll need a matching skirt, or—"

"Tap pants." Kate pulled out the photo of Ginger Rogers.

"Tap pants! Quite risqué," she said, a serious look. "These would be fabulous on you, but . . . well, I wouldn't have expected—"

"Maybe I've changed." Kate grinned.

"Ah." Mrs. J smiled. "The dark green silk brocade would be becoming with your complexion. Is it an afternoon party, or evening?"

"Afternoon and evening both."

"Dancing?"

Kate nodded.

"Well, then, you'll need a dancing skirt too."

"A dancing skirt. Yes, that's just what I need!"

Mrs. J looked Kate up and down. "How about a knee-length swing skirt? It'll flip up when you dance to show off your long legs." She gave a wink. "You'll be the envy of the county."

The bell above the door jangled. Mrs. Schmidt came into the store. Mrs. J threw a piece of muslin over the drapes, put a finger to her lips, and went out to greet the other woman. Mrs. Schmidt bought a spool of thread and soon left.

Mrs. J came back. "If you're going to be outside, a sweater would be nice."

A sweater would be perfect, but Kate didn't have time to knit a matching sweater before the party. "That would take too long."

"How about a short jacket?"

"Yes, I could make a jacket."

Mrs. J pulled the fabric across the cutting table, measuring it between brass tacks. One yard, two yards, three yards. "Nearly eight yards. Certainly enough to make whatever you'd like." She turned away from the table. "Let's take a look at the patterns."

Leading Kate down the aisle, Mrs. J said, "Tell me about this boy. Would I know him? Is he from one of the farms?"

Kate lowered her voice, as if there were others to hear. "His family has a summer home just up the lake from us."

"An out-of-towner?"

Kate nodded.

Mrs. J stopped, mid-aisle. Her face suddenly serious. "You have a good head on your shoulders, Kate. I trust you'll be careful. A local boy is one thing, but these out-of-town boys, they're often fishing for a summer fling. And then they leave you alone, or worse. You know what I mean?" She patted her tummy.

"He's not like that." Kate felt the blush coming. "Besides, there will be lots of other guests. You don't have to worry about me."

"I hope not."

At the pattern counter, Mrs. J rifled through drawers and pulled patterns out for Kate to examine—blouses, camisoles, skirts, jackets. She fiddled with the groupings. "How about this combination? I'll have to special-order the pattern for tap pants. Not something I get much call for."

Kate scanned the pattern covers, imagining how glamorous she would look. Patterns, fabric, buttons, zippers, thread. She bit her lip. "How much will all this be?"

"Hmm." Mrs. J appeared to be thinking. "Can you spare two of your rabbits?"

Two rabbits! Maybe she should bargain for only part of it, just enough fabric for the shorts and blouse and camisole, and leave the rest.

"And you'll need some pink nail polish, lipstick, a light perfume. I can have those for you as well." After a pause, Mrs. J added, "And perhaps a pair of peep-toe wedge sandals? I'll see if I can order them in a forest green."

Matching sandals and pink toenails! "I'll bring the rabbits tomorrow. But . . ." she hesitated. "Please don't tell anyone."

"Of course your mother knows."

"Not yet. I . . . I'm going to surprise her with my outfit. I want to tell her myself."

Mrs. J winked. "It's our secret."

RIDING HOME THROUGH THE ORCHARD was like entering an enchanted fairyland. The clouds had broken and the late-afternoon sun glistened on the green fruit, sparkling like emeralds. Off through the trees, Kate spied Father working with the men, weeding, preparing for the harvest. Her heart swelled with happiness. When Father looked her way, she waved, and he waved back.

And there was Mother in the garden. "Letter from Ben," Kate called.

Inside, she set Ben's letter on the kitchen table and hurried up
to her room. After reading Clay's letter three more times—*I have to
show Josie!*—she raced downstairs.

Mother stood in the kitchen, Ben's letter in hand. Something was
wrong.

"Mother?"

Mother stared at Kate, pain in her eyes. "I don't understand."

Ben! Kate's scalp bristled with fear. "What happened?"

"It's about the prisoners. Did you write to him about the prisoners? And Karl—"

"What about Karl?"

"Coming into the house to tutor you. Did you tell him?"

"No, I haven't written anything about the prisoners. What is it?"

Mother put a hand over her mouth and handed the letter to
Kate.

"Mother," it began. Not "Dear Mother" or "Dearest Mother."
Just "Mother."

> *I've learned you have BLACKED OUT working in*
> *the orchard, and worse, you've let them into the house.*
> *Did you forget that I'm fighting these BLACKED OUT?*
> *I have spared you details, but BLACKED OUT. These*
> *are dangerous men and I am afraid for you and Kate, and*
> *Father too. If I were there, this would not happen. Please*
> *write and tell me it isn't true.*
>
> *Ben*

"Josie," Kate whispered. "I told her about Karl."

"Josie! Of course." Mother's anger filled the air. "She's trying to
pull him away from us, don't you see? That cunning little—"

"I don't think that Josie—"

"No. You don't think. That's the problem with you, Kate. You live in a make-believe world. Well, this is real." Her voice rose. "This is your brother, fighting for us. Needing to know that we support him. Needing to know that we're safe. Now he'll worry. He'll be distracted . . ."

KATE FOUND JOSIE SITTING on the end of the dock, a fishing pole in her hand. Josie turned at Kate's approach.

"Why?" Kate shouted, walking forward.

Josie set her pole down and stood. "Why what?"

"Why did you tell Ben about the prisoners?"

"He needed to know. Why didn't your mother tell him?"

"Mother didn't want him to worry. She wanted to protect him. And besides, it's none of your business."

"My daddy says it *is* our business. It's bad enough that there are war criminals outside with guards, but letting them into your house, encouraging them to get so close, it can put us all in danger . . ."

"But why tell Ben?"

"Your mother listens to him."

Not anymore, Kate thought. "You don't know Karl. He would never . . . and Mother, you can't imagine how this has upset her." Kate's eyes watered. *My fault.*

"Ben and I tell each other everything."

"You don't have to tell him what's none of your business. None of your damn business!"

"Don't swear at me," Josie said softly.

"Oh, so now I suppose you're going to tell Ben I swore at you." Kate turned her back on her friend and stomped off the dock. She remembered the letter in her pocket. No, Josie would tell Ben about Clay's party, and he'd tell Mother. No, I can't tell her anything, ever again.

"Kate . . ." Josie called. "Kate, don't leave! I didn't do anything wrong . . ."

Eyes stinging, Kate ignored Josie, running across the lawn and through the woods to the channel.

APPROACHING THE CLEARING in front of the house, Kate froze at the sight of Mother standing with the twelve-gauge shotgun at her shoulder, pointed toward the woods. *A prisoner?* Kate's eyes followed to where it aimed.

Bam!

A flock of grouse scattered, save one unfortunate bird that plopped onto the grass.

"Good shot, Mother!" Kate hoped this would be a happy distraction from Ben's letter.

But Mother merely glanced her way, then walked to the edge of the woods and picked up the bird by its feet. A big one, bigger than a chicken.

Following Mother into the kitchen, Kate longed to turn her mood around. "Can I help?"

Her back to Kate, Mother lit the stove and put a pot of water on the burner to soften the bird's skin and loosen its feathers.

Kate found yesterday's newspaper and opened it across the table. She put a kitchen towel on top to absorb the water.

Mother was silent until she pulled the bird from the pot and laid it on the towel. "Ben has no idea how bad things are. I've kept it from him so he wouldn't worry. And now—"

"I'm sorry . . ." Kate braced for what would come.

"For starters, you give up your math lessons. Karl will no longer come to the house. And you'll tell Josie so she tells Ben. Understand?" She began tugging feathers from the bird's breast.

Kate put her head back to keep the tears from falling. "But I need Karl's help to . . ."

Mother leveled her eyes at Kate. "That's more important than Ben's life?"

"Let's write to Ben. We'll do it together," Kate said. "We'll tell him what it was like before but we don't have to worry any longer because of the PWs. He'll understand. He'll understand if it comes from both of us. Okay?"

Kate cringed as Mother yanked away another handful of feathers. Then another. After some time, Mother looked up and wiped her forehead with her arm. "Get a pencil and paper and we'll see what we can do."

Kate hurried off, relieved that Mother was including her in the response.

CHAPTER SEVENTEEN

ONCE THE BIRD WAS IN THE OVEN, Charlotte sharpened a pencil and opened a box of stationery. Kate sat across from her, drumming her fingers on the kitchen table, drumming on Charlotte's nerves. Charlotte wished she hadn't agreed to a joint letter.

Kate began, "Maybe we should start with—"

"I think I need to do this myself," Charlotte said. "If you don't mind."

Kate looked hurt.

Charlotte put a hand on her daughter's arm. "We could each write a letter. Our argument would be stronger if he heard from us separately, don't you think?"

"I guess." Kate stood.

"How about if you go to the garden and choose vegetables for supper?"

Once Kate had left, Charlotte could think more clearly. She gazed at the kitchen window, imagining Ben walking up to the back porch just as he had thousands of times before. What would she say to him if he were sitting across from her now?

Dear Ben,

    I'm sorry you had to find out about the German prisoners from someone else. I didn't want to worry you.

    I have not told you how things are here at home, but since the war began the migrant workers have found better jobs than picking fruit. For a year we've been living off the goodness of the community. With the prisoners, we can have a harvest and finally pay off our debts.

    About that PW who tutors Kate—

Charlotte held the pencil in the air, poised to write the name. *Karl.* No, Ben would think that too familiar. Because it *was* too familiar.

She stood and picked up a paring knife and sharpened her pencil. How odd to be defending a prisoner.

A tap on the window frame startled her. Karl peering in through the screen, deep dimples in his smiling cheeks. He held up a bunch of violets. "I found them near to the forest."

Charlotte was beginning to find his guttural accent endearing. She went to the back hall and opened the door. When she accepted the flowers, his hand touched hers. A fleeting touch, but the tingling lingered.

"Thank you," she murmured.

"Does Miss Kate have papers for me?"

"No" was all she could say.

"I'll come tomorrow."

Surely he must smell the bird roasting in the oven. Maybe she should invite him to supper.

"Yes. Yes, come tomorrow."

He gave a slight bow. Charlotte watched him walk away, his broad shoulders, confident stride.

Charlotte put the violets into a small vase and placed it in front of her on the table. She touched her hand where he had touched it. She should have invited him for supper.

After some time, she picked up the pencil.

> He doesn't support Hitler. He's a good man, a
> gentleman, a math professor, educated in England, you can
> hear it in his voice. You know how important it is for Kate
> to go to the university.

The university! How foolish that sounded in the face of what Ben must be going through. What could she say that would make him accept all this when she herself had a hard time accepting it?

Kate came in with a basket of garden greens. "It smells so good in here!" She put the greens on the counter. "Where did the violets come from?"

Charlotte quickly wrote a last line and signed the letter, folded it, and slipped it into an envelope. She hadn't written anything Kate didn't already know. And yet . . . "Could you please take this to the barbershop for tomorrow's mail?"

Kate held out her hand. "What did you tell him?"

"I told him the truth."

Kate hesitated, as if waiting for more, but when Charlotte stood and turned to the stove, Kate left with the letter.

THOMAS MARVELED at the homey aroma of roasting game. After washing at the sink, he stood over the butcher block and carved the bird.

Once they were seated, Thomas noticed the violets. "Nice touch, Kate."

"I didn't pick them."

"Karl brought them," Charlotte said.

"Karl?" Thomas's eyes focused hard on hers.

"To celebrate summer," she added. "For us."

"Ah, yes." He took up his pipe. "I recall Karl said that his mother loved flowers. And he thought you would too."

His mother! Charlotte stiffened. But when she touched that place on her hand again, it felt like a burn.

CHAPTER EIGHTEEN

KATE PULLED THE FABRIC from the bottom of her closet and snuck it down the hall. The day was warm, and the sewing room was musty from being closed off for so long. Dead bugs lay along the windowsills, and when Kate pulled up the blinds, dust motes floated in the yellow afternoon light. She sneezed and opened the windows to let in the fresh summer air.

The cutting table was strewn with pieces of floral-printed flour sack from Mother's last project, a square dancing skirt. Kate recalled Mother's pleasure in creating new outfits, back before the war, when there were potlucks and square dances, charity events for the school and the hospital. But now she wore the same old housedresses— cotton in summer, wool in winter—day after day.

Kate opened a drawer and hid her bundles under a pile of fabric scraps Mother had once collected for making a quilt. She grabbed some odd ends and dusted the cutting table, the windowsills, the full-length mirror that rocked in its oak stand, the dressmaker form, the cabinet filled with patterns, and finally, the Singer itself.

Mother had taught Kate to sew, and Mrs. J had encouraged her from an early age with fun projects—puppets and dolls, then doll clothes, and finally patterns that Kate could use for designing her own outfits. It was a creative endeavor that took Kate away from tedious chores. That was what she liked about it. Whenever Kate sat with a book, Mother would find something practical for her to do. "Idle hands . . ." she'd say. But when Kate was sewing, Mother left her alone. With only the friendly hum of the Singer, Kate's mind could roam into her own fantasy world.

Kate slid onto the cane-back chair and rocked her foot on the treadle, testing it. When the needle buzzed up and down, the table thrummed against the floor. Would they hear it in the parlor below? Kate couldn't take that chance.

Through the window, Kate saw Mother carrying a basket of wash to the clothesline in the side yard. "Hello, Mother," she called down. "Do you have anything that needs mending?"

Mother looked up, smiling. "Why, yes, I do. Check my sewing basket in the parlor."

Within an hour, Kate had sewn patches on the elbows of two of Father's work shirts, mended the hem of one of Mother's dresses, fixed the torn seam of a blouse, and patched a bedsheet. To keep up the pretense, she left a few things in the basket to work on later.

Then she closed the door to the hall, closing herself in the sewing room, and lifted one of her bundles from its hiding place—a fine cotton fabric the color of her skin—and smoothed it out on the cutting table. She opened the Butterick pattern for the camisole and pinned tissue pieces to the cloth.

The adjustable dressmaker form was set to her mother's proportions. Kate measured it before changing it to her own measurements, then pinned the pieces around it. Once she had sewn them together and added a lacy edging, she took off her blouse and bra and pulled on the spaghetti-strap camisole.

Turning this way and that, the girl in the mirror looked quite alluring. Kate swayed and swooned before her reflection, trying out poses for Clay. She laughed and hurried to her room to hang the camisole in the back of the closet, next to Peggy's party dress.

Kate wished she could share her feelings about Clay with Josie, but she never wanted to see that girl again. Such a blabbermouth! Peggy would be a better friend. Kate had planned to return Peggy's dress to her at the party, but now she thought of a better idea. She would arrange a separate meeting, where she could ask Peggy about Clay. Peggy would be her new confidante.

Kate hadn't given *Forever Amber* to Josie after all. Instead, she was reading it herself, eagerly opening the library book each night to pore over daring love scenes. "She was warm and drowsy, marvelously content, and glad with every fibre of her being that it had happened. It seemed that until this moment she had been only half alive."

If only she could experience that with Clay! She trembled at the thought. Where she may once have been fearful of sex, Kate couldn't help but long for the thrilling intimacy that Amber enjoyed. *But no, how could she do that! But yes, if only!*

OVER THE ENSUING WEEK, Kate made the sheer celadon blouse, the silk brocade tap pants, and a dancing skirt that spun up on her thighs when she twirled, showing off the silk lining that matched her blouse. She was starting on the jacket, the most difficult of the pieces, when she heard the door opening. She turned, hiding the fabric behind her.

"Well, you're a busy girl," Mother said. "What have you got there?" She came into the room and spied the brocade.

"I felt like sewing . . . and I wanted to surprise you."

"Oh?" Mother raised an eyebrow.

"I've nearly finished the mending." Kate indicated the things folded on the cutting table. "I can come down and iron . . ."

"I like seeing you interested in homemaking." Mother stood in the doorway as if wanting a conversation.

"I forgot how much fun it is to sew." Kate kept her fingers on her work so Mother would see she wanted to keep going.

"I'll leave you, then."

Now Kate would have to make something for Mother. At least there was plenty of drapery fabric.

As she pumped the foot treadle and pushed the brocade through the Singer, Kate wondered if she should tell Mother and Father about Clay, about the party. No, they'd want to meet him, meet his family. Impossible.

The party was to start at four in the afternoon and would surely go late into the evening. She'd need an excuse to be out so late.

KATE FOUND JOSIE SITTING on the dock in the shade of the light-house reading one of those tell-all magazines. It had been more than a week since their argument about the letter.

"Josie," Kate called out as she approached, waving.

Josie jumped to her feet and hugged Kate. "I'm so so glad you came back. I missed you. I really really did."

Josie looked pretty in a blue summer dress. She had pulled her dark hair into pigtails, a look that emphasized her heart-shaped face and wide eyes. *She's going to be my sister-in-law. We need to trust each other.*

"You wanted to show me those pictures of wedding dresses?"

"Oh yes! Wait here." Josie ran toward the house.

It was a hot day, bugs buzzing lazy in the air, the lake glassy calm. Waiting, Kate sat on the edge of the dock and dangled her bare feet in the water. A dragonfly glittered before her, alighted on the dock for a moment, then floated off into the sky. A slight breeze ruffled the surface of the lake. Three water beetles the size of black beans circled a wooden dock post. A small fish swam into view. Kate kicked her feet. "You better watch out, little beans."

Josie returned carrying a stack of *The Bride's Magazine*s and sat next to Kate. She had dog-eared the pages with dresses she liked most. Slinky silks, frothy chiffons, formal satins.

"Look at this!" Josie cooed, then read the caption: " 'The Forget-Me-Not Bride, designed by Kathryn Kuhn.' Oh! 'Snowy pure silk marquisette, lightly traced with embroidered blue forget-me-nots. To be treasured for generations. Made to order. Bridal Salon.' " Her eyes shone. "I want this one!"

Kate peered at the ordering information. Josie would have to send her measurements to the Jay Thorpe Gown Showroom at 24 West 57th Street in Manhattan. "But look at that price!" Kate poked the page. "Six hundred and fifty dollars!" That was enough to pay for four years of tuition and books and room and board . . . and maybe a house too!

"I don't care. I want it."

"For just one day? That's a shameful waste of money!"

Josie continued to read: " 'The bride's diamond necklace, by Cartier.' "

"Oh, Josie!" Kate reached over and turned the page.

Josie turned a few more pages until Kate stopped her. "How about this one?" She pointed to a dress with a sleeveless shirred silk bodice and a slender floor-length skirt with layers of ribbony silk like silver feathers that trailed on the floor behind. So elegant! Kate imagined herself in that very dress, Clay at her side . . .

"That would be hard to dance in," Josie said. "I want to *dance* at my wedding." She turned the page and sighed. "I want the Forget-Me-Not dress." She flipped back to the dog-eared page and gazed fixedly at the dress as though staring hard enough might make it appear.

"It's so expensive, Josie—"

Josie looked up with a sudden smile and clapped her hands. "Kate, *you* know how to sew. You can help me make the one I want. We could send to New York for the pattern. We'll do it together. After all, we're going to be sisters!" Josie put an arm through Kate's and looked into her eyes. "Would you be my bridesmaid?"

Kate gave Josie's arm a squeeze. "I would be honored."

"You'll help me with the dress?"

"Of course," Kate said.

The two friends sat silent for a while, gazing out over the big lake. Bits of white clouds floated overhead. A freighter slid into view, slipping slowly along the horizon.

Kate splashed her feet in the water, waiting long enough before speaking. "I'd like you to help me with something as well."

"Oh yes. I want to."

"It's a secret."

Josie's eyes lit up. "I promise I won't tell."

"Especially Ben."

"Cross my heart."

WHILE MOTHER SCRAMBLED EGGS with parsley fresh from the garden, Kate set the table for supper.

"Josie's having a Fourth of July party," Kate said, as casually as she could manage.

"I don't like that girl. Writing to Ben . . ."

"She didn't know you hadn't told him about the prisoners. You and Ben are so close, she assumed . . . She's so sorry." Kate searched for something to say in Josie's favor, but she came up short. "It will be in the afternoon, and into the evening. It's a Tuesday." That didn't matter, but it was something to say.

"Is it a family event? Parents included? I'm really not interested in visiting those people—"

"You don't have to go. Only Josie's friends."

"Just girls, then. Of course, all the boys her age are away," Mother mused. "Who else is she inviting?"

Kate picked up the wooden spoon and stirred the mushroom soup. "It would be rude to ask, don't you think?" After a pause, she added, "I think we shouldn't tell anyone else. Other girls might feel left out. Where did you find these mushrooms?"

"Under the crabapple trees in the woods—you know the place."
Mother wiped her hands on her apron. "Can you taste the herbs? I
put basil and dill in the broth. What do you think?"

"Mmm. Delicious." After a pause, Kate said. "So I can go to
Josie's party?"

"Well, I suppose your father could take you to the island in the
boat. How long will it go on? You know he likes to be in bed by nine."

Kate's heart beat fast. She certainly wouldn't want to leave the
party before nine, and how would she get back to the island anyway?
"That won't be necessary. Josie will pick me up and bring me back in
her father's motorboat."

"You'll need to be home before dark."

Before dark! Kate hadn't thought that far ahead. Would Clay
drive her home? Was she Clay's date, or merely one of the guests?
She'd have to figure that out later. "Josie has it all arranged."

Mother frowned. "What does she have arranged?"

This wasn't going well. Kate took another taste of the mushroom
soup. "Oh, this is so good!"

"Kate." Mother faced her, hands on hips. "I don't want you two
girls out on the lake alone in the dark."

"Josie's father will be there. You don't need to worry."

Mother spooned eggs onto the dinner plates. "I'll speak with
your father about this."

"I need to let Josie know by tomorrow so she can plan."

"Tomorrow?" Mother laughed. "If she must know tomorrow,
then tell her no. If she can wait, your father and I will decide."

Kate suppressed a groan. She would have to make something
extra special for Mother.

ONCE KATE HAD FINISHED making her jacket, she changed the
form back to Mother's size and rifled through the drawers of patterns. She found one for a slim, sleeveless sheath dress. It wouldn't

be difficult. Within a few days, Kate had tailored the dress from the leftover green silk brocade and lined it with the sheerer celadon.

When Mother was out in the garden, Kate gathered her new things—shorts, blouse, skirt, camisole, jacket—and Mother's dress, and scurried down to the kitchen. She heated the flatiron on the stove, keeping an eye on Mother through the window as she ironed each item. Once the garments were free of wrinkles, she put them on hangers and ran upstairs to hide them in her closet.

THE EVENING BEFORE THE PARTY, a fresh sweet evening, Kate followed the scent of cherry tobacco to the parlor. Father sat in the green wingback chair with his pipe, reading a book. Mother sat on the couch, feet tucked beneath her, darning a sock. Bing Crosby was crooning from the radio, "Moonlight becomes you, it goes with your hair . . ."

Father glanced up. "Whatcha got there, Kate?"

She held up the dress. "I made it for Mother."

He took his pipe from his lips. "You made this, for your mother? What a perfect color for you, Char."

"It's silk," Kate said, walking across the room to the couch.

"Silk?" Mother touched the fabric. "Where in the world did you find silk? I hope you didn't sacrifice any of your rabbits for this . . ."

"No . . . I stopped at the dry goods store . . . to say hello to Mrs. J." Kate's mind sought a believable story. "Someone had just brought in a set of silk drapes, in trade. Mrs. J was going to send them to the government, but . . . I asked if I could have a piece . . . I told her I wanted to make something special . . . for you." She paused, smiling. "The fabric for your dress, it didn't cost anything." It didn't really, Kate reasoned. She had traded rabbits for her own outfit. The dress fabric was simply left over.

Mother put down her darning and stood to hold the dress to her body. "It's lovely, Kate. But I don't know where I'll wear it."

"Wear it for me, Char," Father said, winking in Kate's direction. "Put it on. I want to see it on you."

Mother smiled and left the room. Kate noted that her step was a bit lighter than usual.

Father took a pull on his pipe. "That was quite generous of you, Kate. You've made your mother happy. I like to see her happy."

Kate didn't feel generous at all. She squirmed under Father's gaze. It was easier to lie to Mother. "It was nothing," she whispered.

After a few more puffs, Father continued. "Karl says you're doing well with your lessons."

Kate relaxed at the change of topic. "He's a good teacher."

"Yes, he is. And you've a good chance now to pass that test. I'm proud of you."

She was about to respond when Father looked beyond her and took his pipe from his mouth. "Ah, here's my lovely."

Kate turned to see Mother approach the parlor. The dress skimmed her figure gracefully. She had brushed her hair and put on pink lipstick. Her cheeks were pink as well, but that was natural when she was excited.

A sultry voice came from the radio, Helen Forrest: "I'm wild again, beguiled again, a simpering, whimpering child again . . ."

Father stood and bowed to Mother. "May I have this dance?" He took her hand and the two of them circled the room in a waltz, Father in his socks, Mother barefoot.

"You dance well together," Kate said. Receiving no response, she added, "I'm going upstairs to get a good night's sleep." She faked a yawn. "I'll be out late tomorrow night, remember? Josie's party . . ."

Mother looked as if she was about to say something, but Father spoke first. "Have fun." He pulled Mother closer.

Kate went up to her room to paint her toenails.

CHAPTER NINETEEN

FOUR O'CLOCK, FOURTH OF JULY.

Kate slipped out the front door and hurried down to the dock where Josie waited. The day was hot but breezy, the sky a friendly blue.

"Wow," Josie said. "You look like one of those sassy Vargas Girls!"

Laughing, Kate stepped into the boat.

"And your hair, it shines like gold in the sunlight. I'll go slowly so I don't muss it."

Kate had curled her hair into rippling waves and added a green brocade ribbon. But she was eager to get to the party. She thought of Katharine Hepburn. "Go fast."

Josie motored north and slowed in front of the big house. "Wow. It's like that barbecue scene in *Gone with the Wind*."

Guests clustered in the dappled sunlight and strolled on the wide lawn. This wasn't the romantic light of the nighttime party. Here Kate would be fully exposed, an outsider.

Sitting in the boat, Josie held to the dock. "Well, go on."

"Maybe I should come back later, after dark."

Josie gave her a shove. "What's wrong with you? I wish I could go."

Kate stepped out of the boat and stood on the dock and smoothed her hair.

"You're gorgeous," Josie said. "Come see me tomorrow. I can't wait to hear all about it."

Kate lifted her chin, smiled boldly, and moved slowly up the walkway into the laughter that floated across the green along with the rhythmic bounce of a tennis ball and the clink of horseshoes.

Clay's burly dog came dashing toward her, but this time Kate wasn't frightened. "Jake," she said sternly. "Sit."

Jake did as he was told, tongue lolling.

"Good boy." She pushed her pretty pink nails through his fur.

"Kate!" Clay was hurrying her way.

Sauntering toward him as casually as she could, Kate was aware of her sleeveless silk blouse that showed off the form-fitting cami-sole beneath, her tap pants snug across her flat tummy, her long bare legs, and her peep-toe sandals that made her even taller than she was. She liked being tall. On her shoulder she carried a matching brocade satchel, which held the rest of her outfit, for later.

"You are a vision." Clay reached for her hands and kissed her lightly on the cheek, his vanilla-scented skin brushing her own.

She took in his blue smiling eyes, his dark hair neatly brushed and oiled, his boyish freckles. He wore navy shorts and a white short-sleeved button-down shirt, open at the top, showing off a bit of curly hair on his chest.

"Lucky for you I had an opening on my dance card," she said.

"I want the whole thing." Clay gave her a sideways hug, his large hand caressing her bare shoulders. He offered her his elbow, and they strolled together up the stone walk.

The other girls wore swingy summer dresses or neat linen trou-sers. A few wore shorts, but not sexy tap pants like Kate's. She rec-ognized girls from the previous party, girls who now stared her way. Lizzie, Eva. This time she wasn't going to let them rattle her.

She heard a whistle from one of the boys, then another. She ignored the attention and glided forward, as Katharine Hepburn would do.

A jazzy tune drifted from the covered porch where a three-piece ensemble played—saxophone, drum, bass. Smoky scents wafted from a long grill.

"C'mon, let's get you a beer." Clay steered her to a canvas awning that sheltered buffet tables from the sun. He picked up a beer glass and tilted it before the spout on a keg, filling the air with a malty aroma. Kate had tried beer once before and disliked its bitter taste. But this was different, refreshingly cold. She licked the foam off her upper lip. "Where's Peggy?" She gazed out across the lawn.

"Oh, these are just my school chums. She's too young for . . ." He stopped.

Too young for what? Peggy couldn't be any younger than me.

"You're just in time for croquet," he quickly added. "What's your favorite color?"

"Blue." Kate gave him a sly grin. She knew well enough that blue went first. She followed Clay across the lawn.

Including Kate, there were three girls and three boys in the game. Clay chose yellow.

Kate handed him her beer and walked to the starting position. She took the blue-striped mallet from the rack and rolled the blue ball forward with her right foot, conscious of eyes on her. When she bent at the waist to swing, she realized she must be exposing more of her upper thighs than she was comfortable with, along with the curve of her bottom. But if she straightened up, she would jeopardize her shot. She wanted to win. Just as she pulled back on the mallet, a low whistle stopped her.

"Hey," Clay shouted, scowling toward the sound.

Kate's cheeks went hot. She stared at the ball, trying to focus.

When she struck, blue rolled nicely through the first wicket and stopped short of the second, earning a point and another turn. With her next swing, Kate tapped through the second wicket, landing just outside the third.

Next up was Lizzie. She looked fresh and cool in a belted seer-sucker dress. The afternoon sun showed off purple highlights in her wavy, shoulder-length red hair. She was really quite striking. She stepped into position and kicked off her white sandals. Before she lifted her mallet, she glanced back at Clay. *What kind of a look was that?*

Kate noticed Lizzie's thin, spindly arms. Glancing about, she noted that nearly all the girls had skinny arms. In comparison, Kate's arms and shoulders were muscled from lifting and hauling and shoveling. She should have put sleeves on her blouse to hide them.

Lizzie bent over her ball and tapped it at an odd angle, launching it backward. She giggled and stepped aside for Ronny, who slammed through two wickets and took the lead. When it was Clay's turn, he drove his yellow through the first two wickets and hit Kate's blue, sending it a bit off course.

"I saw that!" Kate gave Clay a mock pout.

"So sorry." There was fun in his eyes.

Eva was next. Her dark brown hair was piled in curls around her plump face. She wore a pink polka dot dress with a low neckline, and when she bent to swing her mallet, the tops of her breasts jiggled for all to see. "Owww!" she cried when the mallet hit her foot. It must not have hurt terribly because she tittered and peeped around to see who was watching.

When Kate was up again, she managed to angle her ball through the third wicket, hitting Lizzie's red. That gave her two turns. She picked up her ball and took it to where Clay's yellow sat in the lead.

"No!" Clay cried out with a laugh.

Kate placed her ball next to his and put a sandaled foot on blue to hold it in place. She raised her mallet and gave blue a whack, driving yellow clear across the yard. "Touché!"

"Why, you little minx!" Clay rushed toward her and tickled her around the waist until she doubled over and finally fell to the grass, giddy with laughter.

Guests from across the lawn drifted over to see what the commotion was all about.

"My turn," Lizzie called, claiming attention.

For the remainder of the game, they had an audience: boys and girls who had wandered over from other games, cheering every stroke. In the end, Kate won.

"To the victor, another beer!" Clay declared, taking Kate's hand.

Hot and thirsty, Kate drank greedily.

A petite brunette came up to her. "You're Kate, I hear."

Clay introduced them. Her name was Sylvia. "You really showed Clay what's what," she said with a giggle.

"He started it." Kate laughed.

Clay shook his head.

"Boys like to win, you know," Sylvia said. "Lucky for you Clay's such a good sport."

"That I am." Clay bowed.

"Hey, Clay," a boy called. "Let's see if you win when you're not playing with girls."

"Excuse me," Clay said, leaving the two girls together.

"We're just starting a tennis match," Sylvia said. "Do you play?"

Kate knew nothing about tennis except that it was an elite sport, something that Gatsby's guests would play, but she didn't want Sylvia to know that. "Thank you, but I'm a bit worn out from croquet. I'll just sit here and catch my breath."

"I so wanted you to be my partner," Sylvia pouted. "Next time, then."

After Sylvia left for the tennis court, Kate roamed down the lawn. The breeze from the lake cooled the afternoon. The late sun gave everyone's skin a tawny glow.

Clay was across the yard now, tossing a football with a few of his pals. Other boys sat on the porch playing a noisy game of poker, girls crowding around, egging them on.

Off under a grove of maples, a group of girls sat on a blanket.

One of them looked up, shading her eyes against the low sun. "Want to join us?" She moved to make room. "I'm Beth."

Kate sat next to her, grateful for the invitation. Beth offered Kate a bottle of Jitterbug insect repellent. It smelled nasty. Kate declined. Bug bites didn't bother her much—they were such a part of living on a farm that she barely noticed them.

The others introduced themselves. They were mostly from Chicago's northwest suburbs—Highland Park, Lake Forest, Evanston. They had gone to the same private schools, their families belonged to the same clubs. Now they attended a variety of small colleges and finishing schools. A world away from Kate's life.

Colored balloons floated about. When a yellow balloon approached the blanket, Eva stood and squealed and batted it on to the next group. She drank from a flask and passed it around. Kate took a whiff and decided against it.

After Lizzie took a long sip, she touched Kate's shorts. "We have to know. Where did you get your outfit?"

Beth reached forward as well. "Silk?"

Were they making fun of her? Pushing her to confess she was too poor to buy things?

Kate thought of Katharine Hepburn in *Alice Adams* and spoke slowly. "I was paging through *Vogue,* and when I saw this, I just knew I had to have it."

They looked impressed, as if they believed she had ordered it from New York or Paris or Milan.

"Where do you go to school?" Lizzie asked.

"Madison," Kate said matter-of-factly. "I'll be starting at the U. Majoring in English."

"Starting?"

Will the challenges never end? To deflect the question, she added, "It's my father's alma mater."

"What business is your family in?" Lizzie said.

Kate took a sip of beer before answering. She didn't like all these questions. "Property." Then, after a pause, "We have people working the land. Mostly cherries now."

Beth leaned forward. "Which sorority do you plan to pledge?"

The thought of joining a sorority had never occurred to Kate. It probably cost something, something she couldn't afford. But she liked Beth. Beth was nicer than Lizzie and Eva. "I haven't decided."

"I'm in Kappa Kappa Gamma, at Loyola," Beth said. "We have a chapter in Madison. I'd love for you to come down to meet my sorority sisters before pledge week so you can see for yourself."

Another girl bent forward. "At Northwestern, we—"

"I don't know what's so special about sororities," Lizzie snapped.

The conversation came to a halt. Apparently Lizzie was not someone to cross.

Kate sipped her beer, thinking it might be better to ask the questions than to answer them. She squinted toward Lizzie, whose face was in shadow, the sun low behind her. "Where do you go to school?"

Lizzie threw back her head. "Miss Pamela's Modeling School." She said it as if Kate should know it. She lit herself a cigarette, then picked a bit of tobacco off her tongue.

"That sounds so glamorous. Which magazine do you want to work for?" Kate asked.

Lizzie gave a laugh. "Models are not *employed* by magazines. They have agents."

"Well, you'd make a great model, I'm sure."

"I'm not interested in *working*." She stared at Kate. "I'm interested in culture, stylish dress, deportment." After a pause, she added, "Why, I could give *you* some tips." Lizzie reached over and ran her fingers through Kate's hair. "It's awfully fine. You need a proper cut. Short. I'd cut it short. Hmm? What do you think, Eva?"

"That's a great idea," Eva said. "Lizzie did my hair."

"Let's do it tomorrow," Lizzie said.

"You're staying until tomorrow?" Kate said it too quickly.

"You're not?" Lizzie smirked.

Kate caught Lizzie and Eva exchanging a smile. Kate wanted Clay's friends to like her, but she was off-balance here, unsure of her footing.

A cowbell rang out. "Come and get it," Ronny shouted from the porch.

William was crossing the lawn with a tray of barbecued meats.

Guests rose and made their way to the buffet tables laden with trays of grilled hamburgers and bratwurst, fruits, salads, baked beans, breads, cakes and cookies. A fat watermelon sat with a vodka bottle nose down, draining into it. There were bottles of other liquors as well.

Some began filling plates. Others stood about, drinking, talking.

When a heavyset boy she knew approached her, Kate smiled, wanting to be friendly. "Hello, Bradley."

"Hey there, little girl." He came close and put an arm around her waist. "I've got a blanket over there by the woods."

His body reeked of meaty sweat, his breath of booze. She felt the closeness, the lumbering heaviness. She pulled away. "Thank you, but I'm Clay's guest."

"Sir Clay?" He laughed. "We all are." He took a drag on a cigar. "Especially Lizzie." He paused. "Since you're not one of us, I thought you might want to know."

Clay and Lizzie? So that's what the interrogations are all about. And if Clay's with her, what am I doing here?

But there he was, walking her way. Clay came forward and took Kate's arm and steered her toward an empty blanket on the lawn.

Biting into her hamburger, Kate forced herself to eat slowly. "This is so so good!"

Clay leaned forward and dabbed her chin with a napkin.

Behind him, the sky was a wash of pink and purple pastels. An evening breeze came soft from the lake. The trio was playing sweet tunes—"Stardust," "Polka Dots and Moonbeams," "You Stepped Out of a Dream."

Once they'd finished dinner, Kate and Clay moved toward the porch where others stood against walls or sat on chairs, smoking, drinking, listening to the trio. With an attentive audience, the musicians began showing off, jazzing up the standards.

Someone passed a flask to Clay and he handed it to Kate. "Brandy." His eyes on her.

It burned as it went down.

When he nodded for her to take another sip, she handed it back. "It makes me feel dizzy."

"That's the point," he whispered.

She shook her head, laughing, and put up her hand to ward it off.

The sky held that gentle gray-blue light that comes just after sunset, mysterious, romantic. Paper lanterns swayed, softly orange. Fireflies flitted like tiny stars, on and off.

When Ronny and Sylvia danced to the center of the porch, the trio upped the tempo and played an energetic swing. Kate thought of changing into her dancing skirt, but there was Lizzie, watching from outside the circle of light. Kate didn't want to leave Clay now.

He lit a cigarette and handed it to her, then another for himself.

Sylvia's party dress swung up around her thighs. Ronny held her out and then slid her down on the floor between his open legs. He pulled her up and put his hands on her waist and lifted her in the air, revealing her red panties. After that little show, he slid her down close along his body, their eyes locked together.

Kate clapped along with the others. "They dance like they're in love," she whispered to Clay.

"More like in heat. They like to show off."

The trio slowed it down. "I'll Never Smile Again."

Standing next to Clay, Kate swayed, wanting him to ask her to dance.

"Clay!" It was Lizzie, holding out a hand.

Clay looked toward Kate with an apologetic shrug and moved with Lizzie to the dance floor.

The trio played it slow and bluesy, the bass player singing, "I'll never love again . . . I'm so in love with you . . ."

Lizzie moved into Clay, or was he moving into her? So close, so so close. Her arms reaching about his neck, his arms moving down around her waist.

Ronny and Sylvia were up there again, challenging with sexy moves. The trio worked it, playing along, keeping up the competition. Girls squealed. Boys hooted.

In a slow turn, Clay's eyes caught Kate's. He pushed away from Lizzie. Lizzie fell back just then, so he had to catch her. She moved her hands to Clay's chest, her torso so close, her hips pushed in.

Enough! Kate walked out of the light, over to the buffet tables. She should have brought flat shoes for walking home.

Jake ambled over as if he knew she needed comfort. Kate put her hand on his head and stroked his fur. "Why did I ever think I could fit in with this crowd?" He nosed into her hand. She was woozy. How much had she drunk? She recalled what Mrs. J had said, a summer fling.

"Kate?" It was Clay.

She stood up straight. Katharine Hepburn. "You naughty boy," she said with a mock pout.

He laughed and took her hand. "Come dance with me."

Did she want to be on display with Clay? Everyone watching? She didn't dance sexy like Sylvia and Lizzie. But when Clay held out his hand, she took it.

It was a slow one. "Fools rush in, where angels fear to tread . . ." Clay held her at a respectable distance, elbows out. As the song progressed, he brought her toward him until they were close, and closer still. She watched his eyes watching hers. They swirled in rhythm to the music, her body following his every move. The trio played to them, matching their rhythm.

A high voice whooped from the front door, spoiling the moment.

Eva stood under the porch light in a swimsuit. "Catch me if you can!" She ran down the lawn to the lake.

Lizzie followed, dashing from the house.

"Did you bring a swimming suit?" Clay asked.

Kate nodded.

After changing upstairs with the other girls, Kate hurried down to the lake. A slim moon hung amid a million sparkling stars. The water was calm, lapping gently on the fine brown-sugary sand.

Some of the guests sat on the dock, smoking and drinking. Others waded in the shallows. That was where Clay was. Kate walked past them all and dove outward into the water, chilly against the warm night. She swam in a strong crawl, out to where the water was deeper, colder. Sobering cold. That was what she needed.

On the way back, she felt a tug on her ankle. "Where are you going, little mermaid?" Clay swam up alongside. She turned toward him and snapped into a sidekick, slicing through the water like a knife. Swimming in rhythm. When they came to a sandbar, he helped her to her feet and they stood in waist-deep water. Feeling momentarily disoriented, she put her hand on Clay's chest to steady herself. She kept it there, fingered the dark curly hair, thick from nipple to nipple, diving in a dark V toward his swim shorts. She lost her footing, and he caught her and brought her close, and when he kissed her lips her insides tightened.

"Your lips are sweet as cherry pie." His arms were warm and firm around her, his eyes watching hers. They closed as his tongue plunged in.

Her body was fluid, open. He pressed her to him and she felt a thickness against her pelvis, hard against her, moving against her but with her because she was moving too. Rubbing together. His breathing faster, her breathing faster, her skin tingling. He was panting. She knew about breeding—rabbits, chickens, goats—frantic matings, then off to munch on greener grasses.

When she attempted to push away, he held her tight. "Shh, I won't do anything to hurt you, my love."

My love!

She couldn't help it. Moving in rhythm, underwater, with the lapping of the waves. She should swim from the dream, but the energy, gathering, gushing, pulsed through her body and she couldn't turn it off. She didn't want to turn it off. Her body quivered against his, her hips moved toward his, his passion hard against her, his hands on her bottom, his mouth on her bathing suit where her nipples stood hard. And down there, rubbing and rubbing and rubbing . . .

"Clay, I—"

"Kate!" He called close in her ear. He grabbed her hard, pressing against her, his body rigid. The thickness hard against her. Then it was gone. He shuddered and moaned.

What just happened? What did she miss?

He opened his eyes and whispered, "Oh, Kate, I'm sorry."

Though still in their swimsuits, Kate felt as if they had been naked together, so close!

Sorry for what? She didn't feel sorry for anything. "I feel beautiful in your arms."

"Ah." He breathed slowly. Then after a pause, he whispered, "Beautiful. Yes you are. Innocent beauty. Pure and good." He kissed her face. "That's what I like about you."

She wanted to stay in his arms forever, listen to the sound of his deep whisper in her ear.

"Kate, I—"

A scream startled them apart. She turned to see Eva in the water, waving something over her head.

"Look what I have . . ." Eva called.

Her bathing suit!

"Oh lord," Clay sighed.

One of the boys swam toward Eva and snatched the suit from her. "Come and get it," he called to her.

Eva shrieked and swam after him toward shore.

"Okay, everybody," Clay called. "Time for fireworks."

"Time to hit the blankets!" a boy yelled.

Kate worried about what might come next. Recalling what Lizzie had said, Kate asked Clay, "Is everyone sleeping here tonight?"

He smiled and hugged her. "Well, sure."

"But . . . I can't. I need to . . ." What could she say?

"You can't stay? I should have made it clear in the invitation."

"I'm sorry, but—" She didn't want to tell the truth. That she wasn't allowed to stay out late. That she had animals to care for in the morning. Instead, she peeked at him from under her lashes and said, "I didn't bring my pajamas."

He laughed and kissed her cheeks. "Let's go watch the fireworks."

Kate went inside to change into her skirt and blouse. When she came out, Clay was waiting on the porch. He handed her a sparkler.

"Aren't fireworks illegal, with the war?"

Clay mussed her hair. "Don't worry. We've got boys watching for the Coast Guard down by the shore."

Kate laughed and kicked off her sandals and ran barefoot down the lawn with the others, writing sparkling messages across the dark sky.

When their sparklers fizzled, Clay led her to a blanket on the grass, just the two of them. Roman candles bursting from shore sent sprays of sparks high into the sky. Noisy things popped, and Kate ducked into Clay's arms to escape the sounds.

"Be right back." Clay scrambled to his feet and left Kate alone.

Scanning the lawn, Kate spied Lizzie, sitting on a blanket with a group of girls in pajamas, watching her.

Clay returned with ice cream cones dribbling with a rich sauce that smelled of liquor. Flasks of fiery drinks made their way from blanket to blanket—brandy, whiskey, scotch. Fireworks blurred.

. . . .

KATE WOKE IN THE DARK to the pulse of crickets in the night. Clay's arm lay across her stomach and she realized where she was. She sat up in a panic. *What time is it?*

Her skirt was skewed, crimping her waist. She had to pee. She slipped from under Clay's arm and stepped carefully around couples lying on blankets across the lawn, some sleeping, others whispering. She used the bathroom, found her satchel, and returned to Clay.

"I have to go."

He moaned.

"Clay?"

"Kate. Oh." His voice was flat. "Can't you stay until morning?" He reached up to pull her back.

She shook away. "I can't."

He sat up and rubbed his eyes. "I'll drive you, then."

Clay was silent most of the ride, his eyes on the road. Kate didn't want to distract him. He was tired, maybe drunk. Kate's own brain fizzed and her head bobbed sleepy on the seat, scenes of the party floating through her mind. That thing that happened in the lake. Would Josie know what that meant? No, Kate wasn't going to ask. It was too private, intimate. Maybe that's what love is, secret things you don't share with anyone else.

So drowsy. She startled awake with the thought of Lizzie. Would he go to her blanket and lie with her?

"You're quite the little athlete," Clay said, breaking into her thoughts. "I could hardly keep up with you swimming." He glanced her way. "And you shamed me in croquet."

"I'm just strong . . ." She hesitated. He was used to dainty debutantes who went to charm school. He wouldn't want to think he might lose to a girl who built up her strength lugging pails of milk and shoveling slop every morning.

"Not just strong, but . . ." He paused. "You win because you're smart about it. And you're fun."

"Sylvia said that boys don't like girls to win," Kate ventured. Ben had always cheered for Kate when she made a goal in broom hockey on the frozen pond, or when she hit the softball in a direction he couldn't catch. "Is it true? Are college boys so fragile?"

Clay laughed and reached out to grab her hand. "That's what I like about you, Kate. You're not afraid to say and do whatever you want."

He swung onto Orchard Lane, slowed to a stop, and turned off the headlights. He slid from behind the wheel and put his warm arm around her shoulders and kissed her hair.

She pulled back. "What about Lizzie? The way you danced together—"

"Lizzie?" He sighed. "We were childhood sweethearts, and sure, we dated for a while, but it's long over."

Could she trust him?

"I need to tell you something, Kate. I've waited until we're alone." He paused.

He's going to tell me he loves me . . .

"I joined up. I'm in the Navy." His white teeth gleamed in the moonlight.

Her heart nearly stopped. "You're leaving? Going to war?"

"It was you who knocked me out of my complacency." He looked so proud. "Oh, Kate, after our talk, I realized this is what I want to do. What I *have* to do. I'm a commissioned officer. I'm going to flight school first, then—"

Kate sat stunned. "But you haven't finished college." She grasped at random thoughts. "My father never graduated, and he regrets it to this day. Why don't you finish first and—"

"I haven't told my father yet. Not anyone. You're the first." Clay frowned. "He'll be furious, of course, and would probably agree with you, but there's nothing he can do about it now."

Kate could feel tears starting to spill down her cheeks. "It's so dangerous, torpedoes and mines and—" It was all her fault. She wished she had kept her opinions to herself.

His body bent toward her, his wide shoulders and vanilla scent. He gently dropped kisses on her face, then he pulled her close.

"You don't have to do this for me," she said, breathless from his kisses.

"Not just for you, Kate. I did it for me, my duty to our country. How can I sit here while others are over there . . ." He paused. "Besides, I'm eager to fly for real—" He was kissing her neck, opening her blouse, a hand on her camisole, brushing her nipples, the other under her skirt, moving up her thigh, making her dizzy. "My beautiful Kate."

"Clay . . ." She gripped his arm. "When do you leave?"

"I'm driving home tomorrow to pack and make arrangements."

Tomorrow!

"I'll come back to see you before I ship out."

"Will you?" His hand on her leg left her limp as a ragdoll.

He pulled her to him. "I will, Kate."

His mouth found hers again. When his hand swept across her breasts, she didn't stop him. Instead, she lay back, drawing her arms tight around him, wanting more.

"Oh, Kate." He sighed. "I better stop before we do something we'll both regret."

He sat up and pulled away. Kate shivered with the loss of his warmth.

CHAPTER TWENTY

FEARING THAT MOTHER WOULD BE WAITING UP, Kate declined Clay's offer to walk her to the door. She hurried along the path through the dark orchard, wary of the prisoners in the bunkhouse on the far side of the property. Approaching the house, she saw a glow coming from the parlor window. Heart racing, she crept forward through shadows and peeked in. Mother was lying on the couch under a quilt.

Kate slipped around to the front of the house and climbed the oak tree to her bedroom window. After changing into a nightgown, she stole quietly down the stairs. She washed up in the kitchen, then tiptoed to the parlor and knelt next to the couch. "Mother," she touched her shoulder.

Mother startled. "Oh. Kate." She rubbed her eyes. "I guess I fell asleep. What time is it?"

"Time to go to bed," Kate whispered. "I didn't want to wake you when I came in earlier. You looked so peaceful."

Yawning, Mother pushed herself from the couch. "Did you have a good time?"

"Oh yes."

CHAPTER TWENTY-ONE

CHARLOTTE PUT A QUART OF GOAT'S MILK into her bicycle basket, rode into Turtle Bay, and parked in front of the dry goods store. Inside, Ellie Jensen was organizing soaps on a shelf in the sundries aisle. When she saw Charlotte, she hurried to the front. "Charlotte, how lovely to see you. Of course you've heard the news."

Yes, Charlotte had heard. The Allies had taken Caen. "Your Philip, we're all so proud of him." Ellie's husband was fighting in France.

"And your Ben in Italy." Ellie grabbed Charlotte's arms. "They've got the Germans on the run. Our boys will be coming home soon, victorious. Just you wait!"

Charlotte had imagined the scene many times, Ben arriving on the train, waving his cap, strong and sure. He'd run to her and they'd hold each other, crying, laughing.

"Came by in case you could use a quart of Mia's milk. Sweet from the summer grass." She took the bottle from her satchel.

"Why, I do believe I could. Thank you. And what can I do for you?"

"A box of my favorite stationery. And three pencils, please."

"Of course." Ellie went to the stationery department and returned with the supplies.

Charlotte picked out a pink barrette from a basket of notions on the counter.

"That'll be mighty pretty in your blond hair."

"I was thinking of Kate."

"Ah, yes. Take it then."

"I'd like to thank you for encouraging her in sewing."

Ellie smiled. "If I had a daughter, I'd want her to be just like your Kate." Yes, she had told Charlotte many times how she enjoyed spending time with Kate. "What did you think of her outfit?"

"The dress is lovely. Just lovely. It was kind of you to give her the fabric. Thank you."

Ellie's eyebrows dipped into a question. "She decided to make a dress? I thought—"

"Yes. She made me a beautiful dress."

"Oh."

Charlotte saw something odd in Ellie's expression. "What did you think she was going to make?"

"I don't know." Ellie fiddled with the receipt. "I thought she was going to make something for herself. Something special."

"Special for what?"

"Her new boyfriend. I thought—"

"Boyfriend?" Charlotte's scalp bristled. *Karl!*

"She was going to tell you—"

Charlotte blanched. Did everyone know but her? "Oh, that's right," she said as calmly as she could. "So hard to keep up with all that's been going on, the war news. Dear me. Now I've even forgotten his name."

Ellie pursed her lips in a way that made Charlotte wonder what she might be hiding. "Kate didn't mention a name."

CHARLOTTE TUCKED THE STATIONERY into her satchel. *I knew it! I just knew it!* Her head throbbed with a growing ache. She would go right up to Kate's room and confront her. Or if she saw Karl first . . . Karl and his precious violets! *Oh! What a fool I've been, to think that . . .* She shook impossible thoughts from her head.

Riding down Orchard Lane, Charlotte saw Thomas on the tractor off across the property. I must tell him. If Karl is encouraging Kate in this ridiculous affair, he needs to be sent back to a prison camp. "We won't miss him!" She said it out loud to tamp down the other feelings that bubbled below the surface.

But if Karl was sent back, the whole county would hear about it. Big Mike and the rest of them. It would be just as they predicted— Nazis luring innocent girls. They'd demand that all the prisoners be sent back. That would mean no harvest. Another year without income. How would they survive it? Charlotte went cold at the thought. No, Thomas mustn't know. It was up to her to nip this in the bud.

Kate's bicycle wasn't in the barn. "Where is that girl!" With that bad influence Josie, no doubt. Josie probably knew all about Karl.

Charlotte heard a floorboard squeak on the other side of the barn. "Kate?"

She waited, listening. All was silent.

Ginger Cat jumped from out of the shadows.

"Oh, so it's you. What were you chasing over there?"

The cat skittered past her and out the door.

On the way to the house, Charlotte fumed. Where do they meet, those two? Thomas had given Karl privileges, allowing him to roam the property without a guard. Charlotte had never been one to monitor her children. As long as they got their chores done and were home in time for supper, she trusted them on their own. During the school year, Kate spent her spare time at the library. Once the harvest came, she handled the sales at the roadside fruit stand. But in the meantime, Kate had far too much time on her hands. The devil's workshop. Well, there was plenty of work she could give Kate to keep those idle hands busy.

Charlotte boiled water and made a cup of mint tea to calm herself, but it was no use. Looking toward the garden, she decided to take out her anxiety on the weeds. She rinsed her cup and returned to the barn.

The garden tools hung on the far wall. As she reached for a hoe, she heard scuffling behind her. Heavy steps thudding toward her. A thick sweaty hand clapped over her mouth. Hot breath on her neck.

She bit down on the salty palm and tasted blood. A grunt. A knee banged against the back of her own knee, knocking her to the floor.

In front of her now, squatting over her, was that crazy-eyed Nazi, the lurid scar purple across his cheek.

"No! No!" She caught his beefy arms, digging her fingernails into his flesh, flailing her body from side to side, thrashing her legs. She reached for his face to poke thumbs into his eyes. He seized her arms and pinned them to the floor above her head, holding them in a meaty paw. With the other hand, he pushed up her dress and tore at her underpants, ripping them apart. He put a knee between her legs, his thick body looming over her. He fumbled one-handed with the buttons on his trousers, muttering words that sounded like a curse.

The more Charlotte struggled, the firmer he held her. There was no way he was going to let go unless . . . She lay still and calmed her breathing. He let her hands loose to focus on his buttons. When he pulled out his bloated penis, she found her moment and shoved her right knee hard into his balls. He moaned and clutched at his groin.

She rolled away and screamed and pushed herself from the floor. She stumbled toward the wall and grabbed a butcher knife.

A hand caught her ankle and jerked her down. Her shoulder banged against the floor, then her head. Ears ringing, she swung the knife at him. He tried to seize it but caught it by the blade. She jerked it forward, slicing through flesh, blood dripping. He cried out and let go.

She scooted away and tried to regain her footing, still holding the knife.

He lurched toward her, and she swung again, missing his throat but gashing his chest, sending blood spurting across her face and dress.

He howled. His hand pulled back, and she watched, slow motion, the solid fist coming. Her head jerked sideways with the punch.

Through blurred vision, she saw a hand reach for the knife. Not Vehlmer's meaty paw. No, this large square hand she knew.

The two men struggled over the knife. Karl lurched forward. His eyes cold, his face distorted in rage. "*Umkommen!*" he yelled, slicing the knife across Vehlmer's throat.

"MRS. CHRISTIANSEN. *AUFWACHEN!* WAKE UP!"

She opened her eyes. Karl knelt over her, his face and clothes splattered with blood.

She screamed and pushed away. Her breath came in gulps. Her head throbbed. Her right cheek pulsed with pain.

"Shh." He sat on the floor and pulled her gently into his lap, rocking her. "It's over. You are now safe."

She glanced around, wary.

"You were so brave," he said.

"There!" She pointed, trembling. Vehlmer's eyes crazy open, throat slashed, brown trousers caught around his ankles. Blood oozed and puddled beneath him on the wooden floor. And next to the body, the butcher knife, smeared red.

"Get Thomas!" she cried. "Thomas!"

"He cannot hear you. He is on that tractor."

"Go get him. Get a guard. Now!" she demanded, struggling to push herself to a sitting position.

"Shh. Mrs. Christiansen, you need to calm."

"Calm?" Why was Karl here? Was he in on this? Karl and Vehlmer together? "Go!"

"*Bitte!*" His eyes pleaded. "Do you want for me to hang for that murder of a man who was to rape and kill you?"

"What?" She shook her head. "You're not guilty. You saved me!"

"But your Army . . . they will hang me."

"I'll tell them I did it."

"Blood is on my clothes. I am not now with the others. They will know." He breathed heavily. "You must hide me."

"Hide you?" Her mind spun with questions, her head spun with pain. "If you hide they will know it was you. They will find you."

Karl's eyes widened, his mouth opened and closed. He stared at the dead man. "We have to get rid of it."

Her heart raced. "Getting rid of the body . . . that's as much as admitting guilt."

"If they see him, they will stop your harvest."

Karl was right. The county would take all the prisoners away. They were so close, so close. She couldn't lose the harvest now. And Karl . . . would they really hang him?

She grabbed his shirt. "Do it then."

"I will take him to the woods—"

"No." She sat up, her head heavy. "Dump him into the lake. Take the motorboat. The lake drops off about twenty yards beyond the dock. Dump him over and let the fish eat him."

"The lake, it drops off. *Gut.*"

"No." She caught his arm. "Go north with the current so he won't come up around here. Let them find him in Escanaba or Marionette."

Karl nodded.

"But bring the boat back. Promise me." She searched his eyes. "If you run, they'll suspect you." She let go of his arm.

Karl brought the wheelbarrow to where Vehlmer lay. Charlotte found an old horse blanket to wrap around the body so it wouldn't trail blood. She peeked out the barn door, scanned the yard, then hurried to the boathouse and turned the winch to lower the motorboat into the water.

Standing on the dock, Karl dumped the body into the boat and stepped in. He eased out the choke and pulled the cord. Rainbows of oily gasoline floated across the placid surface.

Charlotte shuddered and pushed the wheelbarrow back to the barn. She opened the supply cabinet and took out a bucket and filled it with water. She lathered the hand brush with soap and got down on her knees and scrubbed at the stain on the dark wood floor. She poured bleach into the water to clean the butcher knife. She doused the wheelbarrow.

Finally, she plunged her hands into the bucket. But how could she ever feel clean again?

CHAPTER TWENTY-TWO

JOSIE AND KATE SAT CROSSED-LEGGED facing each other on the warm south side of the lighthouse balcony. The two girls had grown closer now that Clay would be fighting the enemy too.

Josie held a cigarette aloft. "I was worried he was a coward." She blew smoke through her nose. "The war's nearly over, at least in Europe. But he's finally doing the right thing."

Kate was still hoping he wouldn't have to go. But she didn't say it.

A white gull glided close and landed on the railing. Josie flung her arm out. The bird screeched at her and flew away.

Off in the distance an open barge floated southward, to Milwaukee or Chicago perhaps, or all the way to New Orleans. Closer in, a small boat caught Kate's eye, motoring slowly forward.

"Now you will understand the pain of being apart from your love," Josie was saying.

It was a blue wooden motorboat, her father's boat. But the man steering wasn't Father. *Who is that?* The late afternoon sun filled Kate's eyes, blotting out details.

"The Coast Guard supply boat is coming in a few days. Want me to put in a library request for you? Maybe a romance novel or two?"

"Romance novels?" Kate shook her head. "No thank you. But there are some others . . ."

The man below stood and hefted what appeared to be an awkward, weighty bundle. The boat listed sideways as he rolled the bundle overboard. Something wrapped in a blanket.

"What others?" Josie said. "What are you looking at?" She peered toward the scene below.

"Could I have a cigarette?"

Josie picked up her pack of Chesterfields and shook one out. Kate took the cigarette and bent toward her friend for the light, all the while keeping an eye on the water.

The heavy thing flopped out of the blanket and floated just below the surface. Kate put a hand to her mouth and leaned forward, watching it slowly disappear.

"What is it?" Josie said.

Kate quickly turned back to Josie. "What would I like to order? Let's see . . . Tillie Olsen, Dorothy Parker, Edna O'Brien . . ." She tried to remember the other authors Miss Fleming had recommended.

"Tillie . . . you'll have to write these down."

The man at the tiller turned and Kate saw who it was. She stood. "I have to go."

CHAPTER TWENTY-THREE

CHARLOTTE CLIMBED THE LADDER to the loft and forked hay down to the barn floor to mask the scent of bleach, the scent of blood, the scent of evil. Her hair and face were damp with sweat and fear. Her dress clung to her body.

What was that?

She stopped and listened. The ladder scraped on the wood floor below, someone coming up. Her breath caught in her throat. She ducked behind a stack of bales.

"Mrs. Christiansen?"

"Karl!" She came out from her hiding place and stared at him across an expanse of hay.

He was splattered with blood. "It's done," he whispered.

When he stepped forward, she stepped back, her mind reeling with the chilling excitement in his eyes as he put the knife to Vehlmer's throat.

He reached toward her. "Mrs. Christiansen, your face, it is swelling."

She ducked from his touch. "What were you doing here?"

He backed off, startled. "I came to pick up the tools. A lopper and a rake."

Lopper and rake? Was it true? She turned away. What would have happened if he hadn't come? She would have been raped, killed. She hugged herself, shivering with the thought of it.

The tractor growled in the distance. Karl glanced toward the window. "I must now go."

"But the blood on your clothes . . . how will you explain?"

He looked down at his shirt. "You butchered an animal. I helped you."

"I don't have an animal to butcher!"

"Your goat."

"No! Not my last goat!"

"A chicken then."

"A chicken? All that from a chicken?" She almost laughed. "You're pretty sloppy, Karl."

He didn't laugh. "You cut off the head. It ran in circles and I caught it."

"So I'm the sloppy one."

She had so few chickens left, but there was no other explanation. After the harvest she would replenish her flock. "Yes, a chicken."

That's when she heard it. Kate's voice, coming toward the barn. "Mother! Where are you?"

Charlotte's heart whirred. "Stay here," she whispered to Karl, a finger to her lips. Hurrying down the ladder, she reached the floor just as Kate pushed the barn door open.

"What's going on?" Kate rushed across the dim expanse. "Mother?" As she got closer, she stopped. "What happened to you?"

Charlotte realized what she must look like—her face bruised and swollen, her clothes bloodstained and torn.

Kate's eyes were wide. "You weren't in the house . . . I was afraid . . ."

"Afraid . . . ?"

"I saw Karl in the boat. He dumped something overboard . . ."

Charlotte froze.

"It looked like a body."

"Kate, it's . . ."

"It's what?"

Charlotte stared at her daughter.

"Mother! What's happened?"

If Charlotte told her, Kate would be implicated. "It was a dog. A rabid dog. Karl killed it for me."

"I don't believe it," Kate said. "Why would anyone dump a dead dog into the lake? I saw it. It was a man."

Kate knew too much. Charlotte would have to take a chance. "It was Vehlmer. The bad one. He was hiding in the barn when I—"

Kate's hands flew to her mouth. "What did he do?"

"I fought him. I fought him off." She sucked in her breath, bile rising in her throat.

"Mother?" Kate's eyes were huge, terrified.

Charlotte worked to control herself. Big slow breaths. A lesson. Let's turn this into a lesson. She took Kate's shoulders. "When someone comes after you, you need to keep your head. I did. I kept him away until Karl came and—"

"And what?"

"Karl saved me . . . he killed Vehlmer."

"Oh, Mother!" Kate grabbed Charlotte into a hug.

"It's all right, Kate. He didn't hurt me." She wasn't used to hugging her daughter, but now she held her close.

"I'll get Father."

"No!" Charlotte pulled away, holding Kate at arm's length. "He can't know."

Kate's eyebrows arched in surprise. "Why not?"

Charlotte was conscious of Karl in the loft. Kate had keen senses like Thomas. If Karl were to move, sneeze, cough, Kate would hear, she'd ask him about it, and who knew what he would say. Charlotte would lose control of the story. She had to stay in control. Her mind recalled Ellie's words. If Kate cared about Karl, she would want to protect him.

"If the Army finds out, Karl will be taken away. They'll all be taken away." She grabbed Kate's shoulders and whispered, "He may be hanged!"

"No one will care that the crazy Nazi is gone. He could have killed you! He deserved to die!"

Some distant part of Charlotte's mind registered that Kate didn't seem to care about Karl's fate at all.

"We got rid of the body," Charlotte whispered. "It's too late to be honest now."

"But that's a crime!" Kate blurted, tears running down her cheeks.

"That's why you can tell no one." Charlotte held her daughter's shoulders. "No one! Understand?"

"No! No, I don't understand!" Kate twisted away, horror in her eyes.

CHAPTER TWENTY-FOUR

CHARLOTTE BUTCHERED one of her beautiful chickens. With shaking hands, she scalded and plucked the bird, seasoned it with fresh rosemary and thyme, and put it into the oven.

She took off the bloodied dress and hid it deep in the laundry hamper. She heated water on the stove and bathed in the tin tub, then changed into a fresh housedress and apron.

Back in the kitchen, the cooking bird smelled like heaven.

Kate didn't come down to set the table. Charlotte put out the dishes. When the chicken was done, she pulled it from the oven and set it on the wooden counter. She watched out the window, pacing, then sat in the parlor for a bit, staring at nothing.

It was nearly dusk when Thomas rushed in, slamming the door behind him. The kitchen was still warm with the aroma of roast chicken, but Thomas didn't seem to notice.

He headed into the parlor. Charlotte followed. He opened the gun cabinet.

"Thomas, what's going on?"

"One of them escaped." He pulled out a shotgun and loaded bullets into the magazine. "The bad one. Where's Kate?"

"Up in her room—"

"Stay inside, both of you. Close the windows, lock the doors." He looked at her for the first time since entering the room. "Charlotte! What happened to you?" He put the rifle on the table.

She hesitated. The stain, the crime.

He took her face, alarm in his eyes, examining the bruises on her cheeks. "Char?"

"I was in the barn, putting away my gardening tools. I dropped a rake and tripped over it—"

"Oh, Char." His eyes gazed into her face lovingly. "It's not like you to be so careless." He gave her a long hug. "We have to calm ourselves in spite of everything."

Charlotte stood dumb. She had never told him such a lie. He patted her shoulder, then went upstairs, floorboards squeaking. Charlotte heard him speaking with Kate.

Don't tell! Charlotte prayed, as if Kate could hear her.

Back downstairs, Thomas opened the kitchen drawer where Charlotte kept the revolver and checked to make sure it was loaded. "Keep this near you." He grabbed his hat and went out the door.

Oh, Thomas! She wanted to cry. She wanted to tell him not to worry. The Nazi was dead, gone. But it was too late. Too late for the truth now.

Charlotte watched through the window as Thomas and one of the guards walked to the barn. *The barn!* She froze, her hand to her mouth. Would they notice the stain? Her heart thumped painfully.

After some time, the two men came back out and went to the boathouse and the shed and even the outhouse. Finally, they disappeared into the woods.

Kate came downstairs and saw the chicken cooling on the counter. "Why did you kill one of your chickens? You weren't going to serve chicken until you had a new flock."

"Best you don't ask any more questions, Kate."

Kate burst into tears. "I can't do this! Lying to Father . . ."

Kate and Thomas, so alike, so close and trusting. Would she break down and tell him?

"Kate, listen to me. We must be strong together."

"But how can we sit at the supper table with Father and watch him agonize over this . . . this lie? How can you do this to him, Mother? How can you!"

Charlotte wanted to shout at Kate to mind, to just do as she was told, but she didn't want her daughter to turn on her, turn to Thomas for support.

"Kate, I know this is hard for you," she pleaded. "It's hard for me too. It will be over soon, I'm sure. What happened, happened." She paused, searching for words that would persuade her daughter. "I wish you hadn't seen Karl in the boat. I wish you didn't have to be involved. But you did. And you are. And there's no going back."

Kate wiped her nose. "You're a liar! And now I have to be a liar too!" She ran from the kitchen. Her footsteps resounded on the stairs as she fled to her bedroom and slammed the door.

Charlotte stood for a while, watching out the window, waiting. When no one came to dinner, she covered her beautiful bird with wet cheesecloth and put it into the icebox.

IT WAS NEARLY BEDTIME when Thomas returned. Charlotte was in her nightgown and robe. She served him cold chicken and a salad of spinach and herbs. He always praised her cooking, but tonight he said nothing.

"Have they found him?" she asked, shielding her eyes. She was such a liar. Kate was right. Worse than a liar, a fraud. A fraud of a wife.

"The sheriff's men are going house to house all up and down the county, warning families to lock their doors and watch for anyone suspicious. They're checking to see if any boats are missing. That would be a smart thing for an escapee, take a boat, leave no trail." He shook his head. "People are reporting things missing—tools, animals, dry goods—everywhere from Sister Bay down to southern Door. Vehlmer couldn't possibly be the culprit in every case, but the sheriff's men have to check each lead." Thomas stood. "I'm going to bed."

After washing the dishes, Charlotte went upstairs. Thomas was lying in bed, eyes staring at the ceiling. His shotgun was on the floor within reach. She switched out the light and slid under the covers. Lying next to her, he took her hand and squeezed it. She turned her face away so he wouldn't see the tears.

Charlotte woke in a sweat. *Vehlmer's hand clutching her ankle, pulling her down, his scarred face hanging over her.* She sat up, heart pounding.

"What!" Thomas startled awake and sat beside her.

"Nothing." She whispered, shaking her head. "Just a nightmare." She rubbed her ankle.

"Oh, Charlotte." When he reached out to hug her, she fell into his arms, sobbing. She sobbed for the fear and the lies. She sobbed for Thomas, so trusting. But her sobs couldn't shake the image of the bulging eyes, the purple scar, the bloated body. All of it. Floating just below the surface.

CHAPTER TWENTY-FIVE

CHARLOTTE WOKE WITH A MOAN, HEAVING. Her bruised body ached. She slipped from under the covers and hurried down to the kitchen. *The burning eyes, sweaty hands clamping hers to the wooden floor.* She vomited into the deep porcelain sink. Stomach tight, aching. *The grip on her ankle.* She tried to will the images away, but they were there. They would always be there.

She pushed back from the sink and doused it with water, then bleach. She had to keep going. Move forward. She started a fire in the stove, heated water for a bath in the tin tub. Clean. Would she ever be clean again? Wrapped in her wool flannel robe, she returned to the bedroom and put on a fresh dress. She wanted to lie down again, but Thomas was there and she couldn't bear to be touched right now.

She could lie on the couch. Warmer downstairs. Dizzy, Charlotte held to the oak banister. *Make yourself tea.* In the kitchen, she heard herself moan and grabbed the counter for balance.

She'd go crazy if she held this in. She had to talk to Karl. He was the only one who would understand.

When Kate came into the kitchen, Charlotte struggled to control herself. She needed her daughter to see she was strong.

Kate fumed about, doing her chores, not even looking at Charlotte. She took her breakfast out to the porch, and when she was through, she stomped back upstairs to her room.

Thomas came down, ate his breakfast, scanned the morning paper. Charlotte could barely contain herself until he finally left for the orchard.

She was washing the breakfast dishes when Karl came to the window. "Mrs. Christiansen, does Kate have any lessons for me?"

A ruse, of course. *He's as eager to speak with me as I am with him.* "I'm going to the root cellar," she whispered. "Make sure no one sees you."

After Karl left the window, Charlotte went to the back of the house and pulled open one of the wooden doors that led down under the kitchen. Like a cave, the dark stone-lined room was always cool, even on the hottest summer days. She lit the wick on the kerosene lamp she kept there, and the dim yellow light revealed rows and rows of empty jars and bins.

This was where the family sheltered from the occasional tornado. Charlotte had stowed emergency provisions—a small barrel of water and tin cups, plates, and eating utensils, woolen blankets, a bottle of kerosene, matches. Except during seasonal storms, she was the only one who came down here.

Soon Karl stepped in and pulled the wooden doors closed above them. Charlotte held up the lantern to show him the way.

He moved quickly toward her. "Your cheek, it is swollen." He reached out and touched her face.

She put her hand on his and the tears came. "Karl, I'm so scared."

When she started weeping, he put his arms around her. She was shivering now. "Mrs. Christiansen, you are cold." He unbuttoned his tan PW shirt and put it around her shoulders.

"There are blankets . . ." she pointed to the tall barrel.

He moved away to take the cover off the barrel and pull out a woolen blanket. Holding it behind her, he wrapped them up together, pulling her in against his thin undershirt, his warm broad chest. He held her to him, comforting. "It's better?"

She felt his heartbeat and looked into his eyes, so close to hers. "Karl?"

"We share a secret, Mrs. Christiansen." His lips came soft on her swollen cheek.

With his muscled arms encircling her, she felt oddly safe. No longer alone. In his protective embrace, she could cry openly, and she did. She sobbed, and he held her and rocked her. Letting out so much she had held in. "Oh, Karl! You saved my life!"

"Mrs. Christiansen." He rubbed a hand on her back.

"Call me Charlotte," she murmured.

"Charlotte." He said her name carefully, as if it were a delicate blossom.

And then she recalled Ellie's words, and Kate dressing up and sitting at the picnic table, waiting for Karl. Where did they meet? What did they do? Since that morning with Ellie—the same day Vehlmer attacked her—Charlotte had been consumed with the murder, the cover-up. But now it all came back. She pulled away. "What of your secret meetings . . . you and Kate—"

"Secret meetings?" He looked stricken. "No, no. We meet only in your kitchen. For her lessons."

Could she believe him? She held his gaze for a long moment, but his eyes never wavered from hers.

The romance must be all on Kate's part, one of her fantasies. And yet, Charlotte remembered that Kate had not been the least bit concerned when she suggested that Karl might be hanged. Maybe Charlotte had been imagining things, worrying for nothing. Maybe Ellie Jensen was wrong about Kate having a boyfriend.

"How could you think it was Kate?" Karl grabbed her arms. "It is you, Charlotte. You."

She trembled. Before the murder, she would have pushed him away, reluctantly perhaps. But now, the secret they shared, dark and shameful, bound them together. He had fought for her, killed for her. *If he hadn't been there . . . !*

"Charlotte . . . ?"

Breathing in his salty scent, she pressed into the warmth of his body, felt his muscular thighs hard against her own.

They sank together to the floor, the blanket around them. His fingers threaded through her hair. One of his large square hands held her head firmly against his kiss. The other brushed across the bodice of her dress where her nipples stood erect. He touched the hem of her skirt, slow and easy, moving it up and up.

"Charlotte?"

His strength drew her, scared her. "Yes," she said, reaching beneath her dress to slip off her underpants. *What am I doing?*

He unbuttoned his tan trousers and soon he was on top of her, pulsing into her.

We shouldn't do this . . . We shouldn't . . . The words whispered around the edges of her mind as she kissed Karl's open mouth, frantic for him. Her thoughts flickered to the barn, Karl saving her. Drawn to danger, together, saving each other.

Unlike Thomas, Karl didn't recite poetry from some foreign time or place. No, Karl was physically there with her, all passion, hungry for her. Now, right now. She knew. She felt the difference.

Her skin tingled. A warm sweet river flowed through her body. She slid her hands up under his shirt and scratched at his skin, then down to his buttocks, holding him tight to her hips, her skin alive with desire, the beautiful thick slide of him inside her.

His lips murmuring her name, sweet as a song.

Her hips rising up, up, up to take him deeper into her. "Karl!"

And more and again. And now she was only her body, the heat and flow of her body coming in waves of relief. Tensing and loosening. Set free.

"Karl!"

"*Meine liebe!*" he gasped.

She fell back, panting.

Karl lay beside her, holding her until her breathing calmed.

After a while, she blinked her eyes open and turned toward him. Lamplight dusted his solid jaw. He kissed her cheek.

"So beautiful you are, Charlotte." His hand slid gently along the curve of her torso where her dress was spread open.

She didn't cover herself. She didn't mind him looking at her nakedness. She felt beautiful under his gaze.

A vision flitted through her mind—Karl coming into her kitchen, sunset, just the two of them. She reached over and smoothed his dark hair, touched his lips.

He touched her face. "I must go."

Must go. Yes, he must go.

They slipped apart and drew on their clothes. Charlotte climbed the steps and pushed up one of the wooden doors and peeked out. Her eyes took a moment to adjust to the late morning sun. She heard the tractor far off in the orchard. The prisoners were nowhere in sight. She motioned for Karl to leave.

Charlotte folded the blanket and put it back into the barrel. She stood alone at the bottom of the cellar steps for some time, attempting to compose herself. Then she took a big breath, blew out the kerosene lantern, and emerged back into the day.

CHAPTER TWENTY-SIX

BY LATE AFTERNOON, Charlotte had bathed in hot soapy water again and changed her clothes. She tried to focus on making dinner, but she could think of nothing but Karl's admiring eyes, the feel of his tight muscles under her palms. Her skin tingled from his touch. Her insides contracted with the memory. She luxuriated in the sense of it, imagining it again. And again.

A siren whined in the distance, advancing along County Trunk Q. A loudspeaker blared the sheriff's voice: "Nazi prisoner escaped. Be on alert. Inform authorities of suspicious persons."

The siren gave a short toot as the car turned down Orchard Lane and stopped where Thomas hurried to meet it. Thomas and the sheriff spoke for a few minutes before the car sped back to the highway and resumed the alarm.

Thomas came in and threw his hat on the kitchen table. "Ole Weborg's been shot."

"What? How?"

"Seems he was out looking for the escapee and Big Mike thought he was a prowler. Shot him in the shoulder. He'll live."

Charlotte crumpled into a chair and put her face in her hands. Thomas put a warm palm on her back and slowly rubbed it. He stopped at the sound of a truck approaching.

"Now what?" He went out the door.

Kate came in and washed in the sink. She didn't look at Charlotte, didn't say a word. Her body sparked with anger.

Charlotte peered out as the Army truck rumbled in. An officer got out. Thomas wasn't one to get emotional, but he was waving his arms, pointing, as he talked with the man in uniform. More talking. Then his posture slumped. He led the man toward the migrant camp.

"Mother, we have to tell him," Kate cried.

Charlotte leveled her eyes at her daughter and spoke the words slowly: "We tell no one."

Thomas came into the kitchen. "They're taking the PWs back to prison."

Charlotte's scalp bristled. "Taking them away! What about the harvest? We can't lose the harvest!" *And Karl!*

"Until they know what's happened to Vehlmer, no PWs will be allowed outside locked gates. Might be some sort of secret communications with the enemy, others may be involved. That's what they fear most." He glanced out the window. "Unless I put metal gates around the camp, they're all going."

"Then put up the gates, damn it!" Charlotte yelled.

"Mother!" Katie cried.

Thomas stared at Charlotte with a stricken look. She had never spoken to him in such a harsh way.

She hugged him. "Thomas, I'm sorry. I'm so sorry." *What's happening to me?*

He put his arms around her. "I know." He kissed the top of her head.

"It's not fair, Thomas. It was just one man. The rest aren't like that—"

"We don't know. There are prisoners assigned to farms all over the county. The Army is taking them all. The growers are angry with me for being so careless."

"It wasn't your fault!"

"Yes, it was, Char. I called Vehlmer to fix the tractor and then sent him off across the orchard alone. I trusted him to go directly to the work crew on the other side. And now families are terrified about what he might do."

"Thomas!" She clung to him.

He loosened his hold on her. "Listen to me, both of you. You are not to leave the property. Stay close to the house. Keep the doors locked."

"For how long?" Charlotte asked.

"Until he's found."

"But what if he's not found?" Kate said, her eyes flashing to Charlotte.

"Mind me. Stay close. Make do with what you have here—eggs and milk, vegetables from your garden."

After Thomas left, Kate whispered, "It's crazy to go on like this. They'll never find him."

"If they knew what that Nazi tried to do to me, it would be even worse. And what I did . . ." Charlotte's mind reeled with images— Vehlmer in the barn, Karl in the root cellar. She could barely breathe.

"I can't watch Father going out with his gun, and everyone so afraid . . . afraid of nothing!" Kate's blue eyes were wide and teary. "Mother, we have to stop this! A man has been shot!"

"Do you want me to go to jail?" Charlotte grabbed Kate's shoulders and shook them. "Do you?"

Kate pulled away. "Maybe I do!"

Charlotte reeled back in shock. "Kate . . . ," she pleaded. But she could think of nothing more to say.

Kate turned and hurried away from the kitchen.

CHAPTER TWENTY-SEVEN

CHARLOTTE HAD BATHED AND douched with vinegar, but when she got into bed beside Thomas, she still felt soiled, unworthy.

Lying on the sheets, her body remembered Karl. His face in her hair, the scent of his labor. His large hands. *Meine liebe.* What did that mean?

He would be leaving soon. She would never be with him again. Never, never.

When she sighed, Thomas put an arm around her. She turned away in shame.

She longed to go back to the way things were before. Before the prisoners came, before Ben left. Before she wanted Karl.

CHAPTER TWENTY-EIGHT

KATE COULDN'T SLEEP. Long before sunrise, she pulled on her overalls and headed out to the barn. A bat fluttered near her hair. Branches rustled all about. Vehlmer's ghost whispered through the trees.

She forced the heavy doors open and switched on the electric light, breathing hard.

It happened here. Somewhere in here. She scanned the butchering tools and imagined the huge meat hook slicing into Vehlmer's guts. There must have been a lot of blood. She shuddered and pulled her sweater close around her.

Her eyes skittered across the floor. There! A newly scrubbed patch with a faint stain. Not something anyone would notice unless searching for it. She edged away. She wanted to run and scream and run and run and fall into her father's lap and confess everything and feel his big hands smoothing her hair and hear his gentle voice telling her everything would be fine. She wiped her nose with the sleeve of her sweater.

Mia balked when Kate tried to coax her onto the stanchion and bellowed when Kate half-lifted her and tied her in place. The goat kicked toward the milk pail that Kate put beneath her. Was it because she sensed Kate's anxiety, or did Mia too feel the evil lurking in the shadows?

"Shh. Calm down, little girl." How could Kate calm the goat when she herself was so skittish? She jumped at the sound of the two cats darting in and out of the barn. The goat jumped as well. "It's okay. Just your friends, Lulu and Ginger Cat."

Mia gave only half a pail of milk, and when Kate opened the pen, the goat bounded out to the yard.

It was the same with the chickens. They hadn't laid any eggs, and they too were eager to escape.

Outside, the sun came up big and round. Blood-red.

UP IN HER BEDROOM, Kate felt her little world closing in.

Yesterday she had hurt her mother with cruel words, and now guilt washed over her. She had never spoken so sharply to anyone. No, she didn't want Mother to go to jail. How awful it must have been to have that madman attack her. Kate recalled how frightened she had been when Vehlmer came after her on her bicycle. Imagine him actually touching her . . . tearing at her clothes! Mother had always been strong, fearless even. But now, for the first time, Kate realized how vulnerable her mother really was. Poor Mother! But I would have told the truth. And Mother would be better off if *she* had told the truth, harvest or no.

Kate longed to get away. To get on her bicycle and ride until she was too exhausted to remember any of this. Ride into her future with Miss Fleming and the girls in the dorm. And Clay. Dear Clay. If only she could talk to Clay!

At the sound of a motorboat, she peered out her window. Josie's father? He was pulling up to the dock.

He tied his boat to a post and marched up the lawn toward the front door. Three hard knocks.

"Mr. Lapointe!" Mother's voice.

"I must speak with Mr. Christiansen." His tone was demanding, unfriendly.

Soon Father was on the porch with the lighthouse keeper, right below Kate's window.

"A body washed up on the island," Josie's father said. "Let's hope it's your prisoner. I'd have killed him myself if I had found him alive."

After a pause, Father said, "Let's go have a look."

CHAPTER TWENTY-NINE

CHARLOTTE WAS IN THE YARD hanging laundry when she heard the boat, Thomas returning from the island. She dried her shaking hands on her apron and hurried down to the dock to meet him. "Was it Vehlmer?"

Thomas nodded. "We don't have to worry about him anymore."

Charlotte's heart beat fast. This was a good thing, wasn't it? The hunt would be over. But would they know he'd been murdered? Were there clues to lead them here, to the barn, the knife? She crossed her arms to hold in the trembling.

Thomas maneuvered the boat onto the track and hooked it on the ring. Charlotte followed him into the boathouse, where he turned the winch.

"The prisoners can come back then?" Her dry mouth gave her words a sticky sound.

Thomas's jaw clenched. "I don't know, Char. Listening to that lightkeeper, he's going to do all he can to rile up everyone against their return." After a pause, he added, "The sheriff was there. He's on his way now."

"He's coming here?" Just then she heard a car door closing.

The sheriff walked down the lawn to the dock, his badge prominent on his round, rimmed hat. It was that heavyset German, Sheriff Bauer. At the county meeting he had said the prisoners were no different from "our boys," just on the wrong side. He had voted for their release to work. He was on their side.

"Morning, Mrs. Christiansen." He took off his hat. "Sorry to bother you, but I need to ask Mr. Christiansen a few questions."

"Please come in, sheriff." Charlotte led him up to the house, through the front door, into the living room. She offered him a deep, upholstered chair, the most comfortable one in the room. She sat on the couch and smoothed her dress to keep her hands still. Thomas sat beside her.

The sheriff put his hat on the end table, and when he turned to face them, he raised an eyebrow. "Mrs. Christiansen, looks like you had a bit of an accident there."

She flinched. The swelling had subsided, but yellow-green bruises lingered, especially on the right side. "I tripped over a rake in the barn," she said, maybe too quickly.

"Must have been some fall. Bruises on both sides."

"It looks worse than it is." She saw that he was staring, waiting for more. "Fell onto . . . onto sacks of feed." She tried to keep her voice steady. She hadn't thought this through. She laughed. "I should have put ice on it right away."

"And your neck?" His eyes fixed on a bruise that started on her throat and ran down under her dress.

Charlotte tugged on her collar. "From the rake." She shrugged her shoulders.

"I see." He squinted at Thomas as if waiting for confirmation.

Thomas gave Charlotte a questioning look, scratched his head. "Been meaning to move those feed sacks. They're sitting on a metal grate near the garden tools."

The sheriff eyed Thomas's hands. "You a lefty?"

Thomas flexed his left hand, weathered with work. "Yeah. Not very convenient. Every tool . . . everything designed for right-handers. Why do you ask?"

The sheriff picked up his hat and twirled it. After a pause, he said, "A man would hardly blame a husband for rescuing his wife."

"What?" Thomas leaned forward, eyebrows up.

"Were you with Mrs. Christiansen?" he asked, his fingers circling the rim of the hat, "when she tripped in the barn?"

Thomas shook his head. "I was in the orchard all afternoon, taking Brix measurements."

"Brix?"

Thomas sat up to his full height. "We use a hydrometer to test the specific gravity of the fruit and enter that into a Brix table. That measures the sugar content and . . ." He stopped and looked at the sheriff. "It's how we know when to harvest."

"Ah." Bauer opened a notebook and wrote something down. After a pause, he said to Charlotte, "Mrs. Christiansen, have you ever had any contact with this man, Fritz Vehlmer?"

"Contact?" Feeling the spotlight, her face went hot.

"Maybe a word between you, eye contact, anything like that?"

"The PWs work off in the orchard, away from the house," she said. She had to leave, get away before he noticed her color, her shaking hands, her thin voice. She pretended a sneeze. "Excuse me." She rose and hastened out of the room.

She stood in the kitchen, bracing herself against the counter, trying to calm her breathing. If she didn't go out there, they would know something was wrong. The sheriff would know, Thomas would know. She pretended another sneeze, then blew her nose.

Kate came in through the back door. "Why is the sheriff here?" she whispered. "Did they find out what happened?"

Charlotte chilled at the thought. She had no idea what the sheriff knew, what the Army had told him, whether Karl had confessed. She whispered as well. "He's asking what we know. And we don't know anything." She gave Kate a steady look. "And then he'll go, and it will be fine."

"Fine? How can anything ever be fine again?" Kate spun around and left the room.

Charlotte heard Kate's footsteps hurry toward the staircase and up to her bedroom. Charlotte returned to the living room and sat next to Thomas on the couch. He patted her hand. Her guilt surged. *Thomas thinks I'm as innocent as he is.*

"Defensive knife wounds," the sheriff was saying. "Must have been a hell of a struggle. The victim looks to have been pretty strong."

"That he was," Thomas said. "I wouldn't have wanted to be on the other side of that fight."

After a pause, the sheriff's voice fell to nearly a whisper. "Vehlmer had his trousers down around his ankles." He paused. "Pretty strange, don't you think?"

Thomas nodded. "Thought the same myself."

"We'll check the prisoners' privy for blood . . ."

Thomas put up a hand. "Sheriff, please. Not in front of my wife."

Charlotte was avoiding Bauer's eyes when he pointed a question at her. "I know this is a delicate subject, Mrs. Christiansen, but were you aware of the details of the—"

"I had no idea." She put a hand to her mouth. "It's horribly vulgar. I do not wish to imagine it."

"Of course," the sheriff said. After some silence, he squinted toward Thomas. "That island with the lighthouse, it's about half a mile north of here?"

"About," Thomas said.

"And the current flows north?"

"Depends. It could go either way."

Bauer sat forward. "So it *could* have been going north." He twirled the hat in his hands.

Charlotte stiffened. *North from here, he's thinking.*

"Well, Ole'd know," Bauer said.

"Ole Weborg." Thomas nodded. "Knows the flow of this lake like the time of day."

"Course, he's still in the hospital, recovering from that gunshot wound . . ." The sheriff set his hat back on the table and turned to Charlotte. "Feed sacks, you say."

Charlotte felt blood rush to her face. Thomas was staring at her as well. She tugged at her collar, tried to keep her hands steady.

"Be hard to tell what actually happened," the sheriff said. "But our hounds could lead to the murder scene."

Hounds! Dogs would sniff out the blood in the barn, the hints in the boat. The cover-up would unravel like a badly knit sweater. Charlotte attempted a smile, as if hounds would be a good thing, but behind the smile she trembled.

"That's what we need." Thomas slapped a thigh. "Let's get this business behind us."

The sheriff nodded. "Thing is, the Army sent our best hounds off to war. The ones left are skittish, can't be trusted."

Thank you, Jesus! But why had he brought them up? He was watching her.

The sheriff drummed on his notebook. "Tell me again, Mr. Christiansen. When did you first notice the victim missing?"

Thomas explained that he had called on Vehlmer to get the tractor started, and Vehlmer repaired it; then Thomas sent him off across the orchard to join the other PWs. "Until we finished for the day, I didn't know he hadn't gone to the other site. And the guards didn't know I'd dismissed him."

"That's what the guards told me." The sheriff paused. "I couldn't believe it, wanted to hear it from you."

Thomas stiffened.

"Thank you for being truthful, Mr. Christiansen."

Charlotte winced. Thomas was so trusting. His negligence might be held against him in bringing the PWs back. It was his fault, really it was, for having let Vehlmer go alone. None of this would have happened. But it had happened, and that was that. She stood and tossed her hair. "Sheriff Bauer, would you like a glass of chilled goat's milk?"

"Ah, Mrs. Christiansen. That would be most delightful."

"None for me, Char." Thomas raised a hand.

They were quiet until she returned with the glass and handed it to the sheriff.

He took a sip, smacked his lips. "Splendid."

She turned to escape back into the kitchen.

"I have a few questions for you, Mrs. Christiansen." He picked up his notebook. "And for your daughter. Kate, isn't it?"

Kate? Oh dear Jesus, not Kate.

"Just routine."

Charlotte rose and went upstairs, her shaking knees threatening to give out with each step. She found Kate standing in the doorway of her bedroom, listening.

"I'm not going down there," she hissed.

"You must."

"I'm not going to lie."

"If you don't come down, the sheriff will suspect something. Suspect you. Or your father." *Oh, what a bad mother I am!*

Kate glared at her for a minute, then set her jaw and followed Charlotte down the stairs.

The sheriff stood. "Hello, Miss Kate. Thank you for joining us."

Keeping her eyes down, Kate said hello, then slid into a chair in a corner and flashed Charlotte an irritated look.

Charlotte sat next to Thomas on the couch and returned Kate's look with a smile. *Be calm.*

The sheriff picked up his pad. "Mrs. Christiansen, would you recognize the man who escaped?"

She hesitated. What would her answer mean? How would she have recognized him?

"I could," Kate blurted. "He tried to knock me off my bicycle."

"Kate!" Charlotte jerked toward the edge of the couch.

The sheriff's eyes were fixed on Charlotte.

"I saw it too," Charlotte said quickly. Anything to take the focus off her daughter.

Bauer's eyebrows went up. When did this incident happen? he wanted to know. Why wasn't Vehlmer returned to prison? Thomas explained that the guards had said Vehlmer was a mechanic; he wasn't after Kate, only concerned that her bicycle chain was rattling. And if he had been sent back, he wouldn't be replaced.

The sheriff wrote something in his pad, then looked to Charlotte. "Mrs. Christiansen, were you at home the afternoon of the disappearance of this man?"

"I went to town that morning. Bought stationery at Ellie Jensen's dry goods store. I have a receipt," she added, rising, eager to be out of the room.

"That won't be necessary just yet. Please continue."

She tried to relax into the couch. "I arrived home sometime late in the afternoon." Her heart was beating too fast.

"And did you spot this man anywhere on your property?"

Charlotte hesitated, her mouth dry.

"We're talking about Saturday now. July eighth. Late afternoon."

She willed her heart to slow, willed her mind to calm. "I parked my bicycle in the barn and did some work in the garden. I was putting my tools away when I tripped over the rake . . ." Her throat was closing. She could barely squeeze out the words.

"Ah, the feed sacks." The sheriff shook his head.

She tugged at her collar. Thomas was watching her.

"And Miss Kate?"

"I wasn't home," Kate said, in no more than a whisper. "I was visiting a friend."

The sheriff circled back to Charlotte. "Have you checked to see if you're missing anything?"

She glanced about the room. "I haven't noticed anything missing."

"Not as far as I know," Thomas said. "But I haven't had time to do a thorough check."

Charlotte caught her breath. If he did do a thorough check, would he notice the bloodstain in the barn? Was there blood on the dock? In the boat? He had taken the boat to the island, but his mind would have been focused on identifying the body. She'd go to the boathouse later and make sure nothing gave away the crime.

The sheriff bounced a pencil on his pad a few times. What was he thinking? The room was heavy with silence. Charlotte wanted to jump up and yell, *Who gives a goddamn about that crazy Nazi? Bring back the prisoners so we can have our harvest . . . and Karl . . .*

"Do you have any idea who might have wanted to murder this man?"

Murder. The word hung in the air.

Thomas sat forward. "Just about anybody who met him, I reckon. Nasty brute. Only kept him on because the Army wouldn't replace him. But I couldn't imagine any of the prisoners doing it, knowing they could face hanging."

"Hanging!" Charlotte cried.

The sheriff cleared his throat before responding. "Yes, Mrs. Christiansen. Does that surprise you?"

Maybe he knew everything. Maybe they had tortured Karl. And if he confessed about the murder and hiding the body . . . or what if he confessed about the root cellar? No, he would never . . .

"This is murder," the sheriff continued. "Grisly business."

She couldn't breathe. Her cheeks were hot. "I don't like to think that anyone would be put to death. Especially for this . . . this . . ." The room had grown small. Charlotte's palms were clammy. She felt faint. She rose and opened a window and the morning breeze came soft off the lake.

After some time, the sheriff said carefully, "Especially for this what?"

Charlotte's mind reeled. "Well, we don't know, do we? We don't know what happened. He was a bad one. The enemy. Do you really care what happened to him?"

The sheriff picked up his hat, twirled it. He was watching Charlotte watch the hat. He put the hat on the table. "So you believe individuals should take the law into their own hands, commit murder if they think someone is 'a bad one'?"

"No, no . . ." She sucked in her breath. "I'm sorry. I haven't been sleeping. I have feared that man since he went after Kate on the bicycle. Now he's gone, and I'm not unhappy about that. But the others, they have to come back to finish the harvest."

"Thank you for your honesty, Mrs. Christiansen." He wrote in his notebook.

Charlotte sensed Kate's eyes on her and didn't dare return the look.

"I'm not concerned about the prisoners," the sheriff said. "The Army is doing its own investigation. I only want to make sure we clear up any concerns about our citizenry." He shifted his attention to Thomas. "Notice anyone on your land that day, the day of the disappearance? Anyone who didn't belong?"

"Don't recall seeing anyone." Thomas scratched his head. "We don't get many visitors here, at least not until harvest time."

"What about Mr. Lapointe, the lighthouse keeper? Did he make any threats?"

My God! He's looking for suspects. Charlotte hadn't expected that innocent people would be pulled into this. As much as she disliked the lighthouse keeper, if he were accused . . . then what?

Thomas put his hand to his chin. "Haven't had much contact with him, not until he came here this morning." He pushed a hand through his hair. "Didn't threaten me personally. Said he didn't want the prisoners coming back, but I couldn't imagine he'd kill a man . . ."

The sheriff made a few notes, then looked up. "Told me he had predicted something like this would happen. And then this dead man turns up on his island with defensive wounds—"

"No!" Kate sat forward, eyes wide.

"Kate!" Charlotte yelped. Would Kate tell the truth to protect the lighthouse keeper? She frowned at her daughter and shook her head. *Stay out of this, don't do this. . .*

She felt the sheriff's stare.

"I was on the island all that afternoon." Kate's words came out dry and jerky, as if her tongue was sticking to the roof of her mouth.

Charlotte held her breath. *She's going to tell!*

"And was Mr. Lapointe with you there?"

"He was working in the yard. I was with Josie, my friend, up in the lighthouse. His boat was tied to the dock the whole time. No one came, and no one left but me."

Charlotte breathed in relief.

The sheriff nodded. "Thank you, Miss Kate. You have been most helpful."

The room was quiet except for the sheriff's pencil scratching.

"Thank you, Mr. Christiansen." He stood and shook Thomas's hand. "Mrs. Christiansen." He gave a slight bow.

Charlotte jumped up. "But what about the workers? We need them!"

"Yes, I'm well aware." The sheriff picked up his hat. "Other growers say the same. But the townsfolk." He squinted. "They're afraid. Or angry, like that lighthouse keeper. And this thing about Ole." He started toward the door, then turned. "I expect the Army investigators will be paying you a visit."

LATE THE NEXT DAY, Charlotte heard the Army jeep approaching down the lane. Soon Thomas was leading two officers around to the front door and into the living room. The older one was short and stocky, the younger one tall and thin. Charlotte stood at the kitchen door, listening. They were talking about the prisoners, names she didn't know. Not until she heard "Karl Becker." That was when she went in to join them.

Thomas introduced her. She sat on the couch, but the men remained standing, making her uncomfortable.

The younger one spoke first. "Seems Becker had special privileges. Could move about without supervision." He rocked on his boots, squeaking back and forth.

"Even welcome in your home," said the older man in a gravelly voice. "Is this true?"

Karl! What do they know?

"When he's in my home, I supervise him," Thomas said.

"So it's true?"

Thomas nodded, as if he didn't understand the implications. "He tutors my daughter in math, helps my wife with heavy chores. He's educated, speaks English, translates for the others. Good worker too."

"He had the run of the place, then?" Squeaky Boots said.

"He did as I directed."

"But not under the supervision of the guards," Squeaky Boots continued. "You do know that the prisoners were to remain—"

The older fellow cut in. "Where was Becker at the time of the disappearance of the victim?"

Charlotte put her hand to her mouth. Her heart jumped, then beat rapidly. Did anyone notice? She put her hands in her lap, trembling, trying to calm her expression. She didn't dare look up.

"I can't say. I was focused on my work." Thomas's words were rushed, as if to match the pace of his interrogators. Yes, that was what they were doing, interrogating. "Karl makes himself useful. Fetches supplies from the barn—"

The stocky man's eyebrows went up. The two Army men exchanged glances.

"You call him Karl," the older man said. "Pretty familiar."

Thomas went pale.

"Did you call all the prisoners by their first names?"

"It was different with Karl—"

"Did the other men resent that?" the young one challenged. "Did Vehlmer resent the freedom that Becker had on your property?"

"I don't know. Maybe . . ."

Dear Thomas! They shouldn't be treating him like this, like a criminal. Charlotte wanted to shout, Enough! Get out! Instead, she simply looked down to avoid giving herself away.

"They say Becker was absent a good part of the time that afternoon. Are you aware of that?"

"No, I—"

"Is there any reason the other prisoners would want to single Becker out?" Squeaky Boots rocked back on his heels. "Jealousy? Or perhaps a situation between Becker and Vehlmer?"

Thomas held up a hand. "Look. You've spoken with Karl, I expect. He's not antagonistic. He's not a killer."

After a moment, Gravelly Voice said, "He was captured fighting for Rommel. You don't think those Nazis are killers?"

Charlotte jumped from the couch. "Karl was with me."

The officers stared at her.

"With you?" Thomas said.

Charlotte put her hand to her chest, swallowed, and spoke as calmly as she could. "He came to the barn to get some tools. I had just butchered a chicken and it got away, running around without its head. That's what chickens do." Her eyes swept the ceiling, looking for the words. "Karl helped me catch her."

"He himself said as much," Boots squeaked. "But that doesn't explain the length of time he was away from his duties."

Charlotte knew she couldn't make anything up because she didn't know what else Karl had told them or what the others had told them. "He always helps me," she said. "I don't recall exactly what he did that day, but he's helped me chopping wood and mending my garden fence and lots of things." Her voice was shaky. She clutched at the skirt of her dress.

"He's handy with tools and such," Thomas said. "A big help to my wife since our Ben went off to war."

"May I be excused?" Charlotte stood.

Gravelly Voice cleared his throat. "Yes, thank you, Mrs. Christiansen."

Charlotte went up to her room and lay on the bed facing the ceiling, her breath as rapid as her heartbeat.

They've questioned Karl, and he stuck with the story. But what if they accuse him, condemn him?

She rolled over and put her face into the pillow, stifling sobs. Would they really hang him?

She couldn't expect him to face such a fate without telling the truth. Of course he'd tell the truth. Charlotte sat up, moaning. She stood and paced, then lay down again. *What's going to happen?* She hadn't slept since the assault in the barn, since the bad one . . . only two days ago and it seemed like another life.

"Charlotte?" Thomas's voice came from the stairway.

Charlotte jumped up and straightened the bed covers and wiped tears from her face.

"You didn't tell me about the chicken." He stood at the door.

"The chicken? I thought that . . ."

He was staring at her eyes. Was he angry?

"Thomas, you were agitated that night, grabbing your gun on the way out the door. The chicken was not important. Thomas, I was embarrassed about my sloppiness in the slaughter of it. It was insignificant in the face of . . ." She heard her voice, frantic. She stopped.

Thomas waited, and when she was silent, he said, "I see." After a pause, he asked, "Why did you kill one of your chickens? You've been saving them for eggs—"

"Yes . . . yes . . ." Her thoughts reeled. "But we're so close to the harvest and . . . I can start a new flock. I'll go to the fair and buy young chicks." She swallowed. "We had chicken for supper that night, don't you remember?" She put a hand on the dresser to steady herself.

Thomas studied her.

She could tell him. She could tell him the truth right now. After all, he was the one who had let Vehlmer loose. But then he'd want to know why she hadn't told him the truth from the start. Why she agreed to dump the body in the lake. *Are you protecting Karl?* That was what he'd think. No, it wasn't about Karl. It was about the harvest. About providing for her family. No, it wasn't to save Karl. She was dizzy.

"Thomas, I want to put all this behind us and get the harvest over and have Ben home and everything the way it was." She went to him and hugged him and sobbed. "Everything has gone spinning out of control . . . I can't . . . I need to get hold of it again."

"Spinning out of control." He put his arms loosely around her, but his words were detached. "Turning and turning in the widening gyre / The falcon cannot hear the falconer."

"What . . . ?" She shuddered. *Falconer?* "What are you saying?"

The back door slammed. "Father?" It was Kate. "Father? Mother? Where are you?"

Thomas let go of Charlotte and went to the landing. "Up here, Kate."

"A letter from Ben." Kate ran up the stairs, nearly breathless. "It's for you, Father." She gave him the letter.

"For you?" Charlotte said.

Thomas stared at the envelope a moment, then opened it and read it to himself.

Charlotte squeezed out the words: "What does he say?"

"He wants me to send the prisoners away."

"Oh." She sighed. That was all. She tried to laugh. "He wants us to send them away, and they're not even here. We need them back!"

Thomas handed the letter to Charlotte. It had been written with such force that the lead of the pencil had torn the paper in places and then dulled before Ben got to his signature.

June 3, 1944

Father,

I expect you heard of our successes, chasing the Germans home, but BLACKED OUT. I can't get the picture out of my mind. I'm the last of the original squad. Alone. And you are harboring the very men who did this?

Send those Nazis away! You have no idea what they're capable of! You MUST send them away!

Charlotte clutched at her dress. *Ben! Oh what he must be going through!* Tears rolled down her cheeks. "He doesn't understand! He sees only the men who are shooting at him. Of course he must think they're all killers. Ben was not born for this—living in fear, having to kill men, learning to hate!" She wiped her nose with the back of her hand. "Thomas, we're so close. We can't change what's happening over there, but we need to have a home for Ben to come back to."

Thomas put a hand to his forehead and rubbed his temples. "Ben shouldn't be worrying about us when he has a dangerous job to do over there."

"The orchard is his future. We can't lose it! There was one bad one and he's gone. But the others . . . Karl—"

Thomas raised an eyebrow. "What about Karl?"

Charlotte blinked. Her cheeks grew hot. Did he notice the blush? "Not just Karl. He's especially useful . . . for Kate . . . We need them all." She took his arm. "Write to Ben, Thomas. Tell him things are under control."

"Under control?" Thomas snorted.

"You must tell him. You must!" Charlotte pleaded. "If he's

worried about Nazis on our property . . . oh, Thomas, he won't be focused on what he needs to do to keep himself from harm."

"I'll write and tell him they're gone." Thomas sighed. "At least that's the truth at the moment."

IN BED THAT NIGHT Charlotte tossed this way and that, trying to get comfortable. Though her body was exhausted, her mind whirred. Ben was the last of the squad. What had he seen? What had he lived through? And in spite of all that, he worried about his family back home. *Damn that Josie for telling tales!*

Charlotte must have fallen asleep because when she woke she had been dreaming she was with Karl, her body excited by his touch, his arms slipping around her, lying close in a green meadow, a gurgling creek, the call of redwing blackbirds.

Thomas turned toward her in his sleep.

She slipped out of his reach, out of bed, and put on her robe. She tiptoed downstairs, out to the front porch, where she sat on the wooden bench swing. The warm July night was alive with crickets. The beam from the lighthouse swung through the sky, then disappeared and swung back, methodical. Charlotte pushed a foot against the porch rail and set the swing rocking. She breathed in the cool lake air, tried to bring back better nights. But they were gone. All gone.

Ben's letter was dated June third, more than a month ago, the day before his unit reached Rome. Maybe his attitude would change now that they had won another major battle.

The door opened behind her. "Kate!" Charlotte whispered.

"Oh, it's you." Kate said flatly. She must have thought it was Thomas out here. Of course she would rather be with Thomas.

Charlotte patted the swing, inviting Kate to sit beside her. Instead, Kate remained standing, facing the lake, hugging herself. "What's your plan, Mother?" She turned to Charlotte and leaned against the porch railing. "What now?" she whispered.

"Keep going, the way we've always kept going. We are strong women. This is what we do."

"Maybe this is what *you* do, but not me." She wiped her face on the sleeve of her cotton robe.

"Kate." Charlotte stood and took hold of her daughter's shoulders. "I never wanted you to be part of this . . ."

Kate shook away. "*I* don't want to be part of it either. So let's just end it. Let's tell the truth and it will be over."

"Kate . . . no—"

"Don't you see how you're hurting everyone? Father, you, me . . . even Karl. Whose idea was this anyway?"

Charlotte stood dumb.

"You and Father taught us to be honest in all things. Our work, our lives."

"This isn't about—"

"You want me to lie . . . and lie—"

"Kate—" Charlotte reached out.

"And the worst part . . ." Kate opened the front door. "The worst part is . . . I don't even know why!"

The door closed, leaving Charlotte alone.

CHAPTER THIRTY

IT WAS ONE OF THOSE hot sticky July days, flies buzzing.

Kate propped open the outhouse door with the big mossy stone and set a pail of pungent ammonia water on the floor. She wore khaki shorts and a sleeveless blouse and had braided her hair to keep it off her face. But she was already perspiring.

She dunked a rag into the water and wiped down the wooden seat and bench.

If only she could talk to someone. Josie was the one she always ran to, but Josie was such a blabbermouth. Josie would tell her mother and father . . . and Ben! Kate's mind reeled with the consequences. Kate hadn't been to the lighthouse since she'd witnessed Karl dumping the body—the boat listing to one side, the heavy thing rolling out of the blanket, Karl's face as he turned—it kept her awake at night, and when she did sleep, dark images haunted her dreams.

She twisted the rag and dunked it again.

Clay. He was the only one. He had trusted her with his own secret, told her he was enlisting before he told his family. Kate tried to hold to the sweet memories—the way his eyes smiled at her, the vanilla warmth of his skin, his sure touch on her back as he danced her around the floor. He was writing to her regularly now. *Dear sweet Kate . . .*

In her letters to him, she had been holding back, trying to stay light and fun. How could she possibly tell him about this in a letter? *My mother and one of the prisoners murdered a PW and dumped the body into the lake.* She couldn't write that. There was too much to explain.

Kate scrubbed at the floor. *And I lied about it . . . to Father . . . and the sheriff.* She wanted Clay's advice, his understanding, but would he understand? What would he think of her sordid family? Could she trust him to keep this awful secret?

She'd have to wait to tell him in person. With his arms around her, she'd know how much to say.

She dumped the dirty water down the hole.

But when? His schedule was controlled by the Navy now. He could only guess at a date, weeks away.

Walking to the house, Kate noted that Mother was out in the garden. *Good, stay there.* Mother wanted Kate on her side, but until Mother told the truth, Kate would have no part of it. Whenever Mother approached, Kate moved away. When questioned, Kate answered simply "yes" or "no" or "I don't know" or, more often now, "I don't care."

Alone in the kitchen, Kate washed the pail and heated water on the stove. As she added fresh ammonia, she turned her face away from the burning fumes.

Though she had opened the windows and back door, there wasn't even a hint of a breeze. Her whole body glistened with sweat. She placed the rubber pad on the wooden floor and knelt down. When she plunged the sponge into the hot water, her hands stung raw.

She swatted away a horsefly and slowly, methodically, worked her way across the room. Halfway to the door, she sat back on her heels. *I have to tell Father.*

Yes, she would go out into the orchard. He would smile at her approach. "It's about that Nazi, Vehlmer," she would say.

"Oh?" His eyebrows would go up.

"I know who killed him." Yes, that was all she would need to start the conversation. Father would ask questions, and Kate would tell him everything, and then she'd be free of it. Free of the secret, the guilt.

And then what?

Father would confront Mother and she would confess. He would go to the sheriff, and it would be over. It was self-defense, simple as that. Karl came into the barn just in time to save Mother. No one was at fault except Vehlmer, and he was gone.

She resumed her scrubbing, faster now.

Josie had told Kate about the confessional. You tell the priest your sins, and he gives you some prayers to say in penance and your soul is washed clean. Yes, this must be how Catholics feel on their way to confession. If you don't confess, Josie said, you go to Hell.

If ever there was a Hell, this was it.

She wrung out the sponge. A light breeze came from the door. When she reached that door, she would go out where Father waited. And everything would be fine again.

Except that Mother and Karl had dumped the body. That was worse than a lie. It was a big fat crime. As much as Kate blamed Mother for all this, she didn't want her to go to jail. And Karl—Father and the sheriff had talked about the murderer being hanged.

Maybe Father wouldn't go to the sheriff after all. He'd want to protect Mother. And Karl too, because Karl had saved her.

Kate sat back and wiped her forearm across her sweaty face.

Father would blame himself for what Mother had endured. After all, he was the one who let Vehlmer free in the orchard. His fault. Kate didn't want him to suffer for that. And why did Mother not tell him about the assault in the barn? Why did Karl dump the body? Why didn't Mother and Karl tell the truth?

What is the truth? If Mother can lie to Father, she can lie to me.

Was it really about the harvest? Surely Father would have been able to make it right with the Army, protect Karl and return the PWs to the orchard. If only they hadn't dumped the body.

When Kate reached the door, she tossed the ammonia water onto the back porch.

Mother wasn't one to take risks. She wouldn't have done this unless there was something else. Something she doesn't want Father to know, doesn't want me to know.

And Karl's in on it.

CHAPTER THIRTY-ONE

LATE IN THE DAY Charlotte was in the garden when she heard it. The Army truck.

It had been nearly two weeks since they'd left, and now she held her breath as they piled out from under the canvas, one by one, until—yes! Karl, thank God! Even from this distance, she knew his stance, his bearing, so comfortable in his body. He had remained true to his word. They were safe. He looked her way. Though she couldn't see his eyes, they drew her. She didn't move.

She wanted to run to him, hug him to her, thank him for keeping their secret. She wanted to hear about the interrogation at the prison, tell him she had feared for his life. She wanted to feel his arms around her. But she didn't move.

Now he was coming. Thomas was leading Karl toward the barn, toward her. Heart pounding, she hurried to the house. Inside, she steadied herself at the kitchen counter. Quick breaths. After some time, she went out the front door and sat on the porch swing, focusing on the lake sparkling in the sun, placid in its ignorance.

"Char?" Thomas called from inside.

Suppertime already?

She hurried to the kitchen. Thomas bowed at her approach and said:

> *Now therefore, while the youthful hue*
> *Sits on thy skin like morning dew,*
> *And while thy willing soul transpires*
> *At every pore with instant fires,*
> *Now let us sport us while we may.*

He hadn't spoken in poetry to her since before Vehlmer disappeared. *He's forgiving me. My dear Thomas is forgiving me. He doesn't know what he's forgiving, but he wants us to go on as before.* "You're ready for supper, then?" Charlotte said, trying to smile.

"It's the cherries that are ready. Tomorrow we start picking the fruit."

Finally! They would have their harvest. Then Karl would leave. Yes. And she would stop thinking about him. She needed to stop thinking about him.

CHARLOTTE WAS CLEARING PLATES from the supper table that evening when the knock came at the door.

"*Hallo.*" Karl's voice. "*Guten Abend.*"

Blood surged through her veins, heat rose to her face.

When he entered the kitchen, Karl's eyes locked on hers, and she read in them a hunger that mirrored her own, a tightrope between, an abyss below.

She looked away, and there were Kate's eyes, watching her, watching Karl, squinting in question.

Charlotte untied her apron and hung it on the knob. Leaving dishes in the sink, she went to the parlor and sat on the couch. But she couldn't shut out the voices, Karl's deep, evocative voice. She switched on the radio. Bing Crosby. "You'll never know dear, how much I love you. Please don't take my sunshine away . . ."

When she reached for her mending basket, her hand shook. On top was the dress she had worn that fateful day in the barn. She had washed it and purchased blue buttons from Ellie. Now she threaded a needle and stabbed into the fabric.

Karl would have liked to stay on his family's farm, he'd said, but his brother inherited it. What would it be like to live on a farm with Karl? A dairy farm, perhaps. She put her work in her lap and closed her eyes, imagined a cozy kitchen at dusk. Karl would come in from the barn, strong and happy, smelling of animals, eager for the meal she'd prepared, hugging her with pleasure. Content. Both of them content with the rhythm of the seasons. She'd like to have cows again. Big, warm, dependable gals who'd give a calf every spring and milk for cheese and butter and ice cream. How could anyone not love cows?

She picked up the needle. A few prize calves to start, that was all they'd need. Fruit trees would be nice—cherries, apples, peaches— not too many, just enough for canning. And pies. Karl would love her pies.

The radio announcer intruded on her daydream with the eight o'clock news. "US Marines . . . amphibious landing . . . Japanese-held island of Guam . . . in the Marianas." Charlotte didn't know where Guam was. She had never heard of the Marianas. She only knew that it was part of the Pacific war, not the war Ben was in. She picked up the dress and pushed the needle in and out.

Ben! How could she ever leave Ben?

Karl's laugh came from the kitchen, hearty, resonant. She put her hands to her ears. She would write to Ben, tell him the harvest was starting. She wouldn't mention the PWs. By the time he received her letter, they'd be gone.

Gone! She closed her eyes and swirled back there again, back to the root cellar, Karl's arms pulling her to him, his hard body against her own, his fingers on her breasts, his strength pushing into her . . .

"*Owww!*" The needle pricked her right index finger. She sucked on the blood. His lips on her mouth, his breath quickening in her ear . . . *Did I ever feel this way about Thomas?*

Charlotte tore a scrap of fabric from out of her basket and wrapped her finger. It wasn't a deep puncture, but it didn't want to stop.

Stop. Yes, she had to stop thinking about him. It was folly . . . a silly fantasy. She would lose everything—Thomas, Ben, Kate, the farm, respect—everything!

Kitchen chairs scraped the floor. Voices, good-byes, the door opened, closed. Thomas came into the parlor and sat in his wingback chair. Soon he was tapping his pipe on the ashtray. He refilled it with tobacco and struck a match. Charlotte knew what would come next. *Puff . . . puff . . . puff.* Annoying little puffs.

"That Karl," Thomas shook his head. "He sure does know how to keep a girl interested."

"What?" Charlotte stammered, nearly choking.

"Kate's actually excited about calculus." He picked up his book. "She's going to do just fine at the U."

Charlotte slouched back, stomach churning, the Mills Brothers singing brightly, "You always hurt the one you love." She fingered one of the blue buttons. "When are they leaving?" she blurted.

"Who?" He peered over the edge of the book.

"The prisoners. When will we be alone again?" She ached to be rid of her guilt, her shame.

"In a few weeks, weather holds." He turned a page. "But they'll stay in the camp through the apple harvest in September."

"They'll be gone during the day," she said. "Working at other orchards. So we won't have to see them?"

"You need not look at them again, Char. They'll sleep in the camp, out of sight."

She folded the dress and smoothed it with her hand. Done. It's done.

From behind his book, Thomas said, "Only Karl. He'll be coming to help Kate with her lessons."

Charlotte froze.

CHAPTER THIRTY-TWO

EVERY YEAR THE CHERRY FESTIVAL started in southern Door and moved north with the ripening fruit, week by week, orchard by orchard, up the peninsula. Locals celebrated. Tourists came from as far away as Chicago.

It was a carnival atmosphere. Parents hoisted children up ladders to fill buckets and baskets. Teenage girls and boys flirted from branch to branch. The butcher brought bratwurst to cook on a wide grill. Kate sold lemonade, cherries, and pies.

But not this year. The butcher had died, men were at war, and the locals and tourists alike were afraid of the prisoners. No one would come.

In the eerie gray predawn light, Charlotte watched the PWs load three-legged ladders and black buckets onto the flatbed behind the tractor. The men wore rope belts with hooks for buckets. Each would work a tree alone until it was stripped of ripe fruit, then go to the next open tree down the line. They'd empty their loads into lugs that held eight to ten buckets of fruit.

Wearing his broad straw hat, Thomas rode the tractor up and

down the rows, stopping to pick up filled lugs and set empty ones on the ground.

Kate was out there in shorts and a sleeveless blouse, working a tree. When Charlotte finished the breakfast dishes, she changed into summer work slacks and a blouse, put on a straw hat, and went out to join the others. She took her place in the tree next to Kate's. "What a beautiful day!" she said.

Kate didn't respond.

There was nothing Charlotte could do about Kate's attitude. Things would change after the harvest. But now, right now, the rising sun was spreading golden light out across the orchard. Charlotte breathed in the fresh morning air.

Soon Karl came down the row seeking the next open tree. "Hallo, Kate," he called as he approached.

"Hi." Kate's voice was flat, sullen. Her attitude toward Karl had changed since his return.

She blames him too, Charlotte thought.

"Hello, Karl," Charlotte said brightly, for Kate's sake as much as for Karl's.

Karl planted his three-legged ladder near where Charlotte was working. The wooden rungs squeaked as he climbed to the top.

Charlotte tried to focus on her work. Cherry juice ran down her arms, itching, attracting bugs. When she raised an arm to shoo away a swarm of gnats, she knocked her hat from her head.

Karl grabbed for it, and his ladder wobbled sideways.

"Karl!" Charlotte reached out, as if she could stop his fall, and nearly fell herself.

He jumped from the unsteady ladder, laughing. He picked the hat off the ground, climbed back up, and handed it to her. "*Hier ist es!*"

She held it to her chest, her heart beating fast. "I was so frightened!" She touched his hand. "I thought you might . . ."

"Don't worry." A tender look.

When she turned back to her work, she met Kate's eyes.

"I was just worried that . . ." Charlotte murmured.

Kate stared at her, unblinking.

Charlotte's cheeks burned. When she was done with her tree, she climbed down the ladder and went to the barn. Thomas helped her load the pickup for the trip to town. He would send the bulk of the cherries to the cannery, but they got a higher return from the retailers, and it was Charlotte's job to sell as much as she could to local markets.

After Charlotte washed up and changed into a dress, she drove down Orchard Lane and stopped the truck at the end of the row where Kate was picking. She gave a toot on the horn.

From the time she could walk, Kate had enjoyed helping Charlotte with the deliveries. The merchants delighted in seeing the curious little girl. Charlotte made a special day of it, including lunch at the Dew Drop Inn. An annual ritual. The café had closed, but they could get a burger at the soda fountain.

When Kate didn't respond, Charlotte got out of the truck and walked along the row and stood under the tree Kate was working. "About ready to go?" she called up.

"I'm not going." Kate didn't look down.

Charlotte felt the chill. She stood a moment in the shade, then returned to the truck. No, she wouldn't try to coax her daughter. Kate had obviously made up her mind.

CHAPTER THIRTY-THREE

ALL THROUGH THE WINTER, the wooden fruit stand at the end of Orchard Lane waited patiently for the cherries to ripen. A simple clapboard shack with a tin roof, it proudly displayed a weathered red-and-green sign: CHRISTIANSEN ORCHARD—BLUE RIBBON CHERRIES & PIES. But everyone called it the cherry shack.

Long ago someone had painted the outside of the place green, and then a few years back, when Kate found a bucket of paint the color of the barn, she added clusters of red cherries.

Approaching it now, Kate recalled the old days when she and Ben used it as a playhouse, trading acorns and pinecones for mud pies. She parked her bicycle in the gravel lot and opened the door to let out the musty air. Swatting away cobwebs, she hooked up the heavy awning that projected out over the wooden counter, protecting displayed produce from the weather, and unlatched shutters on either side of the place, letting in air and sunlight. After all these years, it still felt like playing house. She hummed as she dusted and swept and wiped the counter and washed out the big icebox that held metal racks for Mother's pies.

Kate had grown up helping Mother sell cherries and pies, and now it was her job, her favorite job, to sit out here on her own, greeting people and reading or writing or just daydreaming during quiet spells.

Out in the leafy maple grove, Kate wiped down the picnic tables and benches. This was where customers would normally sit. But not this year. With the war, and the prisoners in the orchard, she didn't expect anyone to linger.

Soon Father arrived on the tractor with a lug of cherries. Once he'd left, Kate filled pint-sized straw baskets and set them on the counter. She took a quick trip to the woods and picked a handful of yellow lady slippers to embellish the display, then put out the sign: OPEN.

She'd washed the sticky cherry juice from her arms and changed into a baby-blue summer dress, and now, as she walked to a picnic table, she relished the light summer breeze that floated through her hair and lifted the hem of her skirt.

Miss Fleming had sent a new book, *Pale Horse, Pale Rider* by Katherine Anne Porter. Kate loved immersing herself in a new story, another life. She sat at the table and began reading about Miranda. In the midst of the 1918 influenza pandemic, Miranda, a newspaper reporter, has a vivid nightmare. She sees herself on horseback desperately racing from Death, the pale rider, who has already taken her grandfather, an aunt, a cousin, her "decrepit hound, and silver kitten," and when Death reaches her—

A car horn tooted. The red convertible! Kate dropped the book and jumped up from the bench. Her heart leapt forward. "Clay!"

He emerged from the automobile, neat and trim in a sharp white uniform, and grabbed Kate up and swung her around. And when he put her down, his mouth was on hers. Her insides rushed toward that kiss, her hands on his neck, fingers pushing up through his hair.

"Your hair!" She grabbed his Navy cap. His thick dark curls were gone. His head was a bristle.

"It'll grow back," he reassured her with a grin.

She returned the cap to his head and stood back, admiring him. "You look so official."

"Wait till I get my pilot's wings." He flew a hand up into the air and down and caught her around the waist. "One day, you and me, Kate, we'll go flying together."

Flying! "Promise?"

"Promise." He kissed her lips. "Wherever you want to go."

"Everywhere!" *I want to go everywhere with you!* "But why didn't you tell me you were coming?"

"I found out only yesterday. My dad pulled some strings and got me an emergency furlough for a few days. My mom's having a fortieth birthday bash, up at the beach house."

"Only a few days?"

"Yes, but I have all the time in the world for you right now."

"Well, then." Kate put her arm in his and led him to a picnic table. "You must try our blue ribbon cherries." She went to the stand and chose a basket. "I picked some of these myself."

Clay put one into his mouth and sighed with pleasure. "Mmm. Yes. I can taste your touch on this one . . . and this one."

She couldn't stop smiling, even when he kissed her. "Let's play the spitting game," she said.

"The what?"

Kate blanched, realizing her mistake. Spitting wasn't something polite people did. "Never mind. I was just—"

"Tell me."

She took a big breath. "All right. Well . . ." She hesitated. "It's about who can spit a cherry pit the farthest. Stand up." She picked up a small tree branch and laid it on the ground. "Toes at the line."

"Yes, ma'am!" Clay stood and popped a cherry into his mouth and spit a pit into the field nearly a yard.

Relieved at his willingness to play, Kate marched to where the pit had landed and planted a stick. "Good start." She returned to Clay's side and spit a pit just beyond his.

He mussed her hair. "I forgot what a competitive little minx you are." He plopped a cherry into his mouth and leaned his head back and let go. The pit went inches farther than Kate's.

Next, Kate stood and curled her tongue and threw her head with her special trick and sent her pit at least a foot beyond his.

"What was that thing you did?"

"I'll never tell."

He put an arm around her waist. "Come to dinner with me tonight."

Oh, to be with Clay alone for the evening! How wonderful, how simply wonderful!

"There's a little roadhouse out by Kangaroo Lake," he said. "Do you know the place?"

It was rare that Kate ate at a restaurant. "I've ridden by, but I've never eaten there."

"I'll pick you up at seven?" His eyes smiled.

"Not at the house. Not yet." Kate would need to make a plan. She'd have to enlist Josie's help, set everything up ahead of time. "Tomorrow. We'll go tomorrow . . ."

A car pulled onto the gravel lot and a couple got out and approached the stand. Kate excused herself to attend to the customers. When she returned and sat next to Clay on the picnic bench, he asked her what she'd been doing since he'd last seen her.

In her excitement over Clay's arrival, Kate had nearly forgotten about the ugly secret. But now dark thoughts returned. She looked away. She had longed for this moment, to tell someone, tell Clay, and now here he was. She wanted to trust him . . . wanted his advice . . . but what would he think of her?

"Kate?" He sat forward. "What is it?"

"It's all twisted and . . . my mother . . ." Kate turned away and started crying.

"Is she ill?"

"No . . . no." Kate shook her head. "It's . . . my mother and Karl . . . he's a PW . . . they killed one of the Nazis and—"

"They what!" His eyes filled with alarm. "Killed! Why? How?"

"He attacked her—"

"Oh no! Was she hurt?"

"Yes, but . . ." Kate wiped her nose with the back of her hand. "They stopped him before . . ."

Clay offered her a freshly pressed handkerchief. She blew her nose. "You can tell me."

And she did. She told him about Father releasing Vehlmer, about the attack in the barn, about seeing Karl dumping the body. "Mother told me to lie to the sheriff. I lied to my father!" Tears came.

He squeezed her shoulders.

"There's more." She paused. Could she trust him? "I think they're . . . What if there's something going on between them . . . Mother and Karl?" Kate stood and walked away and back and finally sat across the table from Clay.

"The way they look at each other," she whispered. *The way Mother reached for him on the ladder. The way their eyes lingered, their touch when he handed her the hat, the way she held it to her. They had a secret. The murder, yes, but something more, something intimate.*

"Why was he with her in the barn?" Kate put the handkerchief to her face and cried.

Clay moved to her side of the table. "C'mere." He softly enfolded her in his embrace. "My darling girl. Holding this in, all by yourself."

"You must think we're some sort of —"

"I think you're strong and smart and sensitive."

She pulled back and looked into his face. "I should tell Father. I'm sure he suspects . . . suspects something."

"What would you tell him? About the attack on your mother, the killing? Or about your suspicion that Karl and your mother are—"

Kate put her hands to her ears. "I don't want to hear it."

Clay was silent for a moment, then said, "Killing the rapist, that's done and over, so what would you gain, what would your father gain, in knowing about that?"

"I worry that Father would suffer for what happened because he let Vehlmer go, but . . . don't you believe people should tell the truth?"

"Well, then, let's consider what you know for sure. Your father has his harvest. And the PWs will be leaving, right?"

"Yes."

"And then it will be over. All of this will be over."

"But—"

"Kate." Clay put a hand under her chin and held her face toward his. "Your mother may have done something that disturbs you, but this man, Karl, will soon be gone. End of story."

"Father may never know—" Kate blurted.

"And maybe that would be best."

Kate stared at him.

"It's not up to you to work this out. Think what it would do to your family. As long as you and your mother put it behind you, it doesn't exist."

Like a story. Just change the ending.

Clay touched her hand. "You said you think your father suspects something?"

Kate nodded.

"If he wants to know the truth, don't you think he'd ask your mother?"

CHAPTER THIRTY-FOUR

DRIVING THE PICKUP NORTH on County Trunk Q, Charlotte listened to the radio—clear weather, rising grain futures. Good times. First day of harvest, her favorite day of the year.

At Zwicky's Market, Charlotte traded baskets of cherries for three bins of flour, two canisters of Crisco, and a ten-pound sack of sugar. At the greengrocer's, she sold cherries for cash, then purchased five pounds of butter at the creamery. Ingredients for her pies. With the remaining cash, she could splurge on their harvest supper, their true Thanksgiving.

In the butcher shop, Charlotte paid for a fresh leg of lamb and told Olga she'd be able to pay her IOU within weeks.

"I have a bag of wild rice I've saved from last year," Olga offered. "It'd go well with the lamb."

Charlotte didn't hesitate. With the roast and wild rice in her satchel, she held her head high as she pushed out the door, setting the happy bell jangling.

At the barbershop, Charlotte offered Old Man Berger a large basket of cherries—their annual ritual, her cherries for the use of his phone. The elderly men, gathered about in cracked leather chairs, looked up from their pipes and newspapers and nodded her way. Charlotte pulled out her address book and called every market in Door County. Having missed Christiansen cherries and pies the previous year, grocers put in generous orders.

Back home, shifting onto Orchard Lane, Charlotte noted that Kate had opened the fruit stand. Even Kate wouldn't be able to stay mad for long, not today. And customers already. A sleek red convertible, the likes of which Charlotte had never seen, was parked at the edge of the orchard. A man in a military uniform sat on a picnic bench with Kate. *Must have been wounded.* Kate would be good to him, she'd be thinking of Ben.

Charlotte found Thomas in the barn and hurried toward him to tell him of the orders. He hugged her and kissed her cheek. Yes, Thanksgiving.

From there, she went out to the summer kitchen, a separate building that housed the big ovens. Thomas had left a lug of cherries on the wooden counter. Charlotte donned an apron and fed the fruit through the trough of the cast-iron cherry stoner clamped to the edge of the counter. She plopped a few pitted cherries into her mouth and savored the taste. Though Thomas grew a variety of cherries, it was his tart Montmorency that made the best pies.

Charlotte might make fifty or sixty or even one hundred pies, but she made them one at a time. When people asked for her recipe, she gladly gave it. It wasn't about the ingredients, however; it was in the handling of the dough. The secret was to handle it as little as possible, fingering it just enough to break up the fat, adding the smallest amount of ice water, a drop at a time, then quickly rounding the dough into a ball the size of a large orange to chill in the icebox. The perfect dough for rolling the perfect crust, thin and flaky. It was the touch that made it special. And Thomas's prize-winning cherries, of course.

She smiled as she pushed the first six pies into the ovens, then went to the garden to choose vegetables for supper.

"AH, HEAVEN!" Thomas came into the kitchen and sucked in the bouquet of lamb roasting in garlic, rosemary, and thyme. Charlotte laughed as he came up behind her and slipped his arms around her waist and breathed into her ear. "A good year. Thanks to you, Char, we will have a good year."

Charlotte patted his hand. She was pleased with Kate's excitement as well. Kate had added a centerpiece of wildflowers. *She's happy again.* Could anyone not be happy today?

Once supper was served and conversation turned to the food, Charlotte closed her eyes and savored the lamb. How could she ever think of leaving this place, this family? Home. She was eager to show Thomas how she loved him for forgiving her, how she wanted him, needed him. She watched his face until he looked up, excited eyes smiling her way.

After Kate cleared the dishes, Charlotte put a warm pie on the table, the first pie of the year. She picked up the knife.

"*Hallo!*"

Charlotte froze.

"Come in, come in!" Thomas greeted Karl warmly.

"Oh! You are eating." Karl bowed. "I will return."

"No, no. You're just in time." Thomas waved Karl forward. "You must taste Charlotte's pie. She makes the best cherry pie in all Christendom."

Karl took a seat. "*Danke.* I would truly thank you for offering your pie."

Charlotte felt him watching her, and though she looked away, her emotions raced toward him, embraced him. In this, her own kitchen, with her family, the family she loved and needed. She blushed with shame, with desire. Her eyes stayed on the pie, on the knife slicing through the pie. Flashing like the knife in the barn. Kate watching.

She was cutting the last piece, her own piece, voices chattering like a distant radio, when a knock came at the front porch.

"Who could that be?" Thomas rose to answer it.

Charlotte stood in the kitchen doorway, listening. What did that boy say? *Telegram?* She held fast to the door frame. She didn't want to know. Yet her legs pulled her into the living room.

Thomas stood with the yellow page in his hand, looking pale.

"No!" Charlotte slogged forward as if through quicksand. She groped for a chair, fell onto the couch. She covered her face with her hands. "My precious baby!"

"Char." Thomas grabbed her shoulders. "Ben's coming home."

"What?" She sat up.

He handed her the telegram: ARRIVING RR DEPOT WASH ST GREEN BAY 7/24 15:20 HOURS STOP WOUNDED BUT OK STOP BEN STOP.

"Thomas?" Charlotte touched his arm. "What does this mean?"

"I don't know, Char."

Kate appeared, alarm in her eyes. "Is Ben all right?"

Charlotte held to the armrest. She tried to say it, "Of course he is." But the words came out soft, tentative. She took a breath and spoke louder. "He said he was okay."

Karl's face across the room. His eyes met hers, solemn. She looked away. Then he was gone.

Charlotte pushed herself up from the couch. "I have to . . . I have to get his bedroom ready." She went to the stairs and grasped the banister. One step, then another.

Wounded?

She had entered this room many times since Ben's departure, to touch his things, feel his presence. The menagerie of figurines he had carved looked up happily from his dresser. They needed dusting, the room needed airing and sweeping. She would put on fresh sheets, shake out the rugs and curtains.

Her mind saw Ben's bright eyes, his sturdy body. Other boys had come back blind, deaf, paralyzed, crazy. *Not my Ben. Please, God, not my baby!*

A broken arm, that wouldn't be so bad. Something that would heal. Or a finger, he could work with a missing finger, she bargained.

Why would God listen to me? Was this punishment for her sin? *No, no, no!* Ben's alive. That's what matters. *For us, the war is over.*

She would get cotton yarn from Ellie and knit him a pair of summer socks. She sat on the blue-and-brown afghan she had crocheted for her boy so many years ago and began a mental list of all she must do.

"Char." Thomas stood in the doorway. "Come to bed."

"But I need to—"

"It can wait until morning."

"I'll be along."

After Thomas left, Charlotte picked up Ben's pillow and hugged it to her breast.

CHAPTER THIRTY-FIVE

KATE RAN TO THE BARN and grabbed her bicycle and raced down the path. *Ben tells Josie everything. She knows what's happened. She must know!*

The evening sky had clouded over. Was that thunder?

When Kate arrived at the lightkeeper's house, Josie was helping her mother with the dishes.

"Kate! Where have you been?" Josie led Kate upstairs to her bedroom. "I was so worried . . . that dead Nazi, and then I didn't see you for so long! And my parents wouldn't let me go to your place. What's going on?"

Movie posters adorned Josie's walls—Judy Garland skipping down the Yellow Brick Road with the Tin Man, the Lion, and the Scarecrow; Scarlett O'Hara in Rhett Butler's arms against a fiery backdrop; Laurence Olivier and Joan Fontaine. Josie closed the door.

"What have you heard from Ben?" Kate said.

"I haven't received a letter since . . ." Josie stopped and stared at Kate. "What happened? Something's happened!"

Kate hesitated. Why hadn't Ben notified Josie?

"What!" Josie demanded.

"He's coming home."

"Home!" Josie shrieked and gave Kate a quick hug. "Really? He's really coming home?"

Kate nodded. "Day after tomorrow. He sent a telegram."

"Day after tomorrow!" She laughed. "But . . . but why didn't he write to *me*?" Her eyes darkened. "Did he meet another girl? He wouldn't—"

"No . . . Josie, he's wounded."

"Wounded! Wounded how?"

"He didn't say."

"Oh, my poor Ben!" Tears rolled down Josie's cheeks. "I'll take care of him. I'll nurse him until he's well again. No matter what it is. He did his duty, and I'll do mine."

For once Kate was grateful for Josie's romantic notions. "Yes, he'll need someone to take care of him," Kate said. "He's coming home to *you*, Josie, the girl he loves. You need each other now."

Josie grabbed Kate's arms. "What time is he arriving?"

"Three o'clock train. Green Bay."

"I'll go with you."

"There's only room for three in the truck—Mother, Father, and Ben. I can't even go."

"Ben and I can ride in the back on the way home." Her nails dug into Kate's arms.

"In the bed of the truck?" Kate pulled away. "It's a two-hour drive each way. And if Ben's wounded—"

"But he'll want me there!"

What *did* Ben want? Kate considered the options. Mother, Father, and Ben would be home from Green Bay in time for supper. Kate would prepare the meal. She could invite Josie to help, invite her to dinner. But no, Mother wouldn't like that. "Come over in the evening, after Ben's settled." Mother wouldn't like that either. Mother didn't like anything about Josie.

"Day after tomorrow!" Josie twirled around, then went to her closet. "I'll go to the cottage and fill it with flowers. And bring fresh sheets for the bed—"

"The bed?"

"What should I wear?"

Thunder rolled in the distance.

Kate opened the door. "I have to go."

CHAPTER THIRTY-SIX

THE SKY THUNDERED THROUGH THE NIGHT. Waves pounded the shore, wild and violent. Lightning flashed and crackled. And in the dark of morning, rain poured down around the farm.

Trudging through the mud on her way to the barn, Kate recalled mornings before Ben left. He'd be standing in the boat out beyond the dock, casting his fishing line. Or she'd find him in the barn fixing some piece of equipment, Scout lying at his feet. That mutt would follow Ben everywhere.

She pushed aside the heavy wooden door, threw off her slicker, and tied her hair back into a knot.

Wounded! Images flooded her mind. Pictures she'd seen in magazines, boys on stretchers, heads wrapped, limbs missing. He'd be home tonight. Whatever it was, she'd know tonight.

Kate cleaned Mia's udder and teats and set the empty pail on the stanchion.

At least he was coming home alive. She had known other boys who didn't.

After breakfast, Kate rode her bicycle down Orchard Lane,

splattering through puddles. Off through the trees she saw Father with the PWs. Lightning or tornadoes might keep pickers from the treetops, but not a simple rainstorm.

Kate hurried into the cherry shack and hung up her slicker. Driving rain drummed on the tin roof above. She pushed open the front shutter that served as an awning and put out baskets of cherries. She glanced up at each car that came splashing down County Trunk Q. Most drove past, but now and then a driver pulled up to the stand, dashed out with a handful of coins for a basket of cherries or a pie, then disappeared off into the rain.

Clay. She wouldn't be able to go with him tonight after all.

Kate picked up *Pale Horse, Pale Rider.* Miranda was in the midst of a whirlwind romance with a young Army officer. Kate smiled—a writer in love with an officer. But on the next page, Miranda collapsed from the influenza. Her officer came home and nursed her through her delirium, but when she awoke, she learned that he had caught it from her and died.

Kate wiped her eyes as she read the last sentence: "Now there would be time for everything." *What was that supposed to mean?* Kate longed to discuss the book with Miss Fleming. She'd be at the university in just five weeks! Maybe the war would be over by then. Maybe Clay wouldn't have to go. And she could visit him and he could visit her.

The rain let up, and the drumming on the roof quieted to occasional *plips* and *plops* from overhanging trees. Wet leaves sparkled in a patch of sunlight. Kate inhaled the earthy scents, the freshly washed air.

A pickup truck pulled to a stop in front of the stand, and a burly man in overalls got out and approached the counter. "Came to get the order for Robert's Market, Green Bay. Two lugs of cherries, seven pies."

Kate ushered him into the shack, where Father had set aside the order. He loaded up, paid the bill, and crunched back out of the gravelly lot.

Clouds moved across the sun and Kate shivered. The rain came once more, hard and cold, closing her off from all sights and sounds, a gray curtain around her.

Kate thought of the soldier who saved Miranda. Clay would do that for her. He would come home and take care of her. But he wouldn't die.

The sky thundered close. Then lightning. Father would call off the harvest. It was just past noon when the truck pulled up at the stand, and Mother rolled down the passenger window. "We'll be back around five-thirty. The rib roast is in the icebox. It should cook about three hours."

"I'll have dinner ready by six," Kate said.

Mother nodded and rolled up the window, and the truck veered south onto County Trunk Q. Ben would be with them when they returned. Dearest Ben!

A few hours later, Kate was about to close up for the day when she saw it, a vision emerging from the foggy rain. The red Duesenberg. Clay dashed inside and threw off his hat and gloves and coat and pulled Kate into a hug, his arms warm and solid around her. He was kissing her and she was kissing him, hungry together, not worrying about anything because they were alone and loved each other.

"I came to see you last night, but your house was dark except for one lighted room upstairs." His voice was low, sensual. "If I had known what room you were in . . ."

"Oh, Clay!" She pulled back. "Ben's coming home."

Clay's eyebrows drew together in concern. "Is he . . . ?"

"He's wounded."

"He's alive, then. Thank God."

"Yes, but . . ." Tears flowed down her cheeks. She had held them in, but now they came. "He didn't tell us what. I don't know what it is. I fear . . . I just don't know!"

"My sweet girl." He rocked her. "He's coming home alive." He kissed her tears.

She looked into his eyes. "If it could happen to Ben, it could happen to you—"

"Don't worry about me. I'll be up in the sky, watching it all from above."

"I've seen newsreels of planes going down in smoke and flames . . . I do worry." Rain beat on the tin roof. "I worry about you!"

Thunder rattled the shack. Lightning flashed white.

He hugged her to him, his body against hers, rain all around. His fingers undid the top buttons of her pink summer dress, touching her breasts, sliding into her bra, kissing her breasts. She sighed, moving against him, her own hands beneath his starched military shirt, then beneath his undershirt, his skin slick and humid. Headlights drifting just beyond the curtain of rain, swishing off into the mist, his hands leading hers to his trousers.

She pushed away.

He backed off. "I didn't mean to—"

Nor did she. Confused, embarrassed. The spell was broken. Looking down, she covered her breasts, buttoned up.

He moved forward. "We don't want to do anything that would—"

"No, it's not right—" Though she did want to. She wanted to do everything.

He cupped her face in his hands. "We'll have fun tonight at dinner."

"Oh! I can't. Ben's coming home *today.*"

Clay's smile dropped.

"Mother and Father are on their way to Green Bay right now to pick him up. I need to go make dinner soon."

"But I'm leaving—"

"Tomorrow," she said. "I'll go with you tomorrow night. Meet me here." She had no idea what she'd tell her parents. With Ben home, Josie, wanting to be with him, would no longer be available for an alibi.

Clay took hold of her shoulders and kissed her strong and hard, his body firm against hers. "Tomorrow, then. I'll find a way to stay another day."

When Clay left, Kate felt a chill, as if a fire had died. She pulled her cardigan sweater tight around her and thought of tomorrow evening. She would bathe and wash her hair. If only she had a bar of perfumed soap. What should she wear? Her mind coursed through her closet, her underwear drawer . . .

"What am I doing?" She said it aloud. She thought of the girls who had gotten pregnant before finishing high school, closing off future options. *This is how it happens.* She had always thought of those girls as sleazy, desperate even, but now she saw how it was, how easy it was, how sweet it was to love a special boy who loved you too.

She picked up Porter's book. Miranda, losing her love. "Now there would be time for everything." Was that the choice—love or everything else?

She brought the baskets in from the counter and pulled down the shutter. She put on her slicker and walked her bicycle to the house.

Did Miss Fleming ever have a lover? Would she understand what it meant to want a boy and want everything else too?

CHAPTER THIRTY-SEVEN

"I'M FRIGHTENED," CHARLOTTE WHISPERED, moving closer to Thomas, tugging her cloche hat down tight. They sat on a wooden bench in front of the yellow stone depot. The air was chilly with rain.

They had been silent most of the sixty-eight miles to Green Bay, afraid to voice what possible wounds Ben might have. At least that was why Charlotte had been quiet. Along the way she had nearly finished knitting two pairs of socks for him.

When Thomas turned toward her, rain dripped from his fedora. "We'll know soon enough, Char." He patted her leg.

That was when Charlotte heard it, the faraway wail of the locomotive. Then louder. And louder still. The ground shook and steam filled the air, and the engine came to a squealing stop. Not a stop, really. It shivered and shuddered, anxious to be on its way again.

Charlotte grasped Thomas's arm and scanned the windows.

"There!" She pointed. "Ben!" She waved frantically.

Ben peered out the window, but he didn't look her way. He wasn't smiling. His cheeks were hollow, his baby face gone. In a flash she saw sharp cheekbones, a steely jaw. But no bandages, no patches. She watched as he stood and reached for things. She saw his shoulders, his arms. "See! He's fine. He's just fine! He needs wholesome food and sun . . ." And motherly love. Yes, that was what he needed.

She ran to the platform of the railroad car and waited, impatient as other passengers came forward down the steps. What was taking him so long? She was about to climb up after him when there he was, standing tall on the platform, shoulders square in an olive green Army jacket. "Ben!" she cried out, laughing.

He grinned down at her. But then he was struggling on the metal steps. He had crutches. A broken leg?

That was when she saw it. Saw it wasn't there. "Oh!" She put her hands to her mouth. His left trouser leg was bunched up at the thigh with a big safety pin. *Dear God!* Nauseous, dizzy, she grabbed Thomas's arm to hold herself up.

Thomas reached out his other arm to help Ben down the last step. "Welcome home, son,"

"Hello, Father." Ben rested his right arm on a crutch and held out his hand for Thomas to shake.

Charlotte threw herself around him. Her tears fell on the front of his jacket. "Ben! Oh, Ben. We missed you so."

He tucked a crutch under one arm and put the other arm around her.

Another man in uniform, a patch over an eye, followed Ben with a duffel bag and set it on the ground. "Good luck, buddy," he said, then climbed back up the steps.

Thomas picked up the duffel and led the way to the truck. Charlotte walked alongside in stunned silence.

Ben spoke first. "Let's get one thing out of the way." He gave that old grin. "Just don't be calling me Peg Leg."

Charlotte laughed, but there were tears forming at the corners of her eyes.

In the truck she slid to the center of the seat and put her knitting basket on her lap. The socks.

When Ben climbed in, she held tight to his arm. "Thank God you're home. Safe," she quickly added.

"Sure feels good to be home." Ben rolled down the window and sucked in the cool, misty air.

The missing leg, the left leg, was next to Charlotte, half a thigh. Ben reached down as if to scratch the part that wasn't there. Then his hand moved up and he scratched the edge of the stump. The knee she had bandaged when he fell off his bicycle. Gone!

Charlotte focused on the wipers slapping back and forth as if they could slap it all away. But the rain kept coming.

Thomas glanced toward Ben. "See by your stripes you made sergeant."

"Yup."

"We didn't know," Charlotte said brightly. "That's pretty impressive." She was about to pat his leg but then remembered and clenched her fist.

Ben stared out the passenger window.

"What's that medal you got there?" Thomas said.

"Purple Heart." After a pause, Ben added, "Wounded in action."

"Ah," Thomas said.

Charlotte tilted her head back to hold the tears from falling. All was quiet for a while, save for her few quick sniffs. She took out her handkerchief and blew her nose.

Thomas cleared his throat. "How did it happen, son?"

"Machine gun tore it apart."

Charlotte cringed at the image, Ben blown off his feet, writhing in the mud, screaming with unspeakable pain, chaos blasting around him.

"Can't recall feeling anything." He paused. "Not until I woke up in a field hospital. Didn't even know it was gone until I tried to sit up." He looked off. "Nurses were nice . . ."

Charlotte stared at the bunched-up pant leg, the safety pin. "You didn't write—"

"I didn't want you to worry." He cut in. "Not until I knew how it would be. Not until I got to Walter Reed."

How will it be? Charlotte didn't want to ask. Ben rolled up the window and bent forward and unzipped his duffel. He pulled out something blue.

"The vest!" Charlotte said. The one she had knit for him, the one she had traded with the lighthouse keeper's wife for fish. The blue of his eyes.

Ben beamed. "Josie made it for me."

Charlotte's cheeks burned, anger rising. She breathed fast, holding it in. Barely holding it in. That little liar! But no, this wasn't about who made the vest. It was meant for Ben from the start, and she was glad he had it. She touched the cabling she had knit so lovingly late into the night.

Josie. Charlotte had never liked the girl, but now she realized she needed her. Ben needed her. They all needed her. "We'll invite her to supper tomorrow," Charlotte said.

Ben didn't smile. He put the vest against the window, laid a cheek on it, and closed his eyes.

All the way home Charlotte's mind spun with plans. Kate would be leaving for school soon. Josie would take her place. She'll have to learn how to do Kate's chores. Yes, we need her now. Ben will marry her right away, before Kate leaves. That would be best.

It will be nice to have grandchildren on the farm, she reasoned, even if they do have to be Catholic. With Josie's limited domestic skills and Ben missing a leg, the children will have to learn their chores early. Charlotte would see to that.

BY THE TIME THOMAS TURNED onto Orchard Lane, the rain had let up.

Kate ran out from the house. "Ben! Ben!"

"Hey, Kitty Kat!" Ben called from the open window.

Charlotte watched Kate's expression as Ben opened the passenger door, as he held to Thomas in getting down. Kate put a hand to her mouth, her eyes wide. But then she grinned and said, "Guess what I made you for supper."

"You? Cooking?" he teased.

"Your bestest favorite." She took his arm as if there were no crutches between them.

"Not rib roast." He looked at her sideways.

"Yes, rib roast. And potatoes. And kale and eggplant from the garden. And I picked wild leeks from our hiding place in the woods, remember? And that's not all—Mother's cherry pie!"

Ben gave a happy groan. "That's what I've been dreaming about all this time. Rib roast and cherry pie."

Tears came to Charlotte's eyes as she remembered how beautiful life had been, but would never be again. She put her head back and sniffed. *No more feeling sorry! From now on, we move forward, focus on what we have, focus on the good.*

"Where's Scout?" Ben gave a whistle.

Charlotte's eyes watered.

Thomas cleared his throat. "Scout, he didn't make it. Soon after you left."

"Scout?" Ben stopped and stood for a bit and wiped a sleeve across his face.

"He was getting old, Ben," Charlotte said.

Ben nodded and swung slowly forward on his crutches.

Entering the kitchen, Ben breathed in deeply. "Can't believe Kate's cooking would smell so good."

Kate gave his shoulder a friendly punch, like in the old days. He pretended to duck.

Kate took the roast from the oven and put a bowl of vegetables on the table. "Go ahead. Sit," she said.

"Yes, ma'am." As Ben moved toward his place, one of his crutches caught on the chair leg and he crashed to the floor. "God damn!" He struggled to rise.

"Ben!" Charlotte jumped up.

Thomas reached to help him, but Ben pulled himself up and stood against the wall, breathing heavily. A leg of the chair was broken.

Charlotte held in her fright at his outburst and touched his arm. "Are you all right, Ben?"

He stood, unmoving, eyes closed.

Thomas brought in a chair from the dining room.

Ben opened his eyes and stared at the broken chair. "Looks like I got myself a project here."

Charlotte took a breath, relieved.

Kate put the platter of sliced beef on the table. "Supper's getting cold."

AFTER SUPPER, THEY SAT IN THE PARLOR. Thomas must have told Karl not to come to the house because he didn't, and Charlotte was grateful for that.

Ben took a pack of Camels from his pocket. "Could you toss me the matches, Pa?" He caught the matchbox in midair.

"When did you start smoking?" Charlotte said.

"Boot camp, I guess." He struck a wooden match against the flinty side of the box. "No, I started on the train to boot camp. Sat with a fellow who offered me a smoke." Ben paused. "Eddie was his name. Never saw him again. Wonder where he is now."

A chilly breeze came from the direction of the living room. Ben laid the cigarette on an ashtray, got up on his crutches, and reached toward his duffel bag. Charlotte had to stop herself from getting it for him. He had taken off his Army jacket and now put on the blue vest. It looked so good on him. Once he was settled back on the couch, Charlotte placed an afghan across his lap, for her sake as much as for his.

He bristled, frowned.

"There must be a window open." She rose to check.

"What's it like to serve under Clark?" Thomas was saying as Charlotte left the room.

Sure enough, one of the living room windows was wide open. The rain came soft and sweet beyond the porch. Through the window she heard the drone of a motorboat. She watched it approach the dock. Josie! Oh please, God, if you exist, give this girl strength.

Charlotte waited on the porch while Josie tethered the boat, then walked up the lawn. Spoiled girl. Probably never milked a cow or hoed a garden in her life. Charlotte would teach her. For Ben's sake, Charlotte would teach Josie about being a farmwife.

When the girl saw Charlotte on the porch, she stopped, then moved slowly forward.

"Hello, Josie," Charlotte called, forcing a friendly expression.

"Hello, Mrs. Christiansen . . ." Once she was under the cover of the porch, Josie pushed back the hood of her yellow slicker to reveal lush dark curls, a yellow ribbon holding them neatly off her face.

"I'm glad you came," Charlotte said.

Josie beamed at that. "Kate told me Ben was coming home."

"Yes, he's here." Charlotte studied the girl's face.

"She said he was . . . wounded . . ." Josie bit her lip.

"You'll need to prepare yourself."

"What is it?"

"I'll let him tell you." After a pause, Charlotte said, "By the way, he's wearing the blue vest . . . the one you knit for him."

Josie's cheeks went scarlet.

"The cabling down the front is particularly lovely," Charlotte added.

"I'm sorry . . . I'll tell him—"

"No need. I'm glad he has it. And if you don't know how to knit, I'd be happy to teach you."

Josie gazed up at Charlotte reverently. "Thank you, Mrs. Christiansen."

"Let's go in, then." Charlotte opened the door and took Josie's slicker to hang.

In the parlor, Josie stood on the edge of the room and smiled at Ben. A tentative smile, unsure.

Charlotte noted her look. *She's wondering why Ben doesn't jump up to greet her.*

"Hello, Josie." Ben's smile was also tentative. "You look swell."

Yes, Charlotte had to admit, Josie was an attractive girl. Tonight she wore a ruffled yellow summer dress that showed off her curvy figure and shapely legs. They would have handsome children.

Josie entered the room and sat next to Ben on the couch. "You look swell too." She glanced down, then back to his face. "How are you?"

What did she see? His face was hardened, but his eyes remained warm. His shoulders appeared broader than Charlotte remembered, and he sat up tall. A most handsome boy. A handsome man. A perfect model for a Greek god.

After a short silence, he lifted a leg under the blanket, his good leg. "I lost the other one." He was watching Josie's face.

She gasped. Her eyes wide, mouth open. She turned away.

"It's okay," he said matter-of-factly. "They're making me a new one. At Walter Reed."

"Oh . . . that's . . . that's good."

"I can get around."

Josie nodded.

All was quiet.

"Why don't you two go out on the porch?" Charlotte finally said. "I'm sure you have a lot of catching up to do."

Josie stood and watched as Ben pushed aside the afghan and pulled his crutches from behind the couch. He led her slowly to the front door.

When the door closed behind them, Kate whispered, "It's not

fair. It's not fair what happened to Ben! I want to help him, but I don't know what to do."

Thomas emptied his pipe. "He needs you to be a good sister, as you always have been."

"He needs you to be strong, Kate," Charlotte added. "He needs all of us to be strong. We must go on, as always."

CHAPTER THIRTY-EIGHT

KATE WAS CARRYING MILK PAILS to the house the next morning when she saw one of Ben's old high school chums riding his bicycle down the lane. She hurried into the kitchen and put the pails on the counter and went out to the back porch to greet him. "Craig!" she waved. As he came closer, she saw he had a patch across an eye. His face was caved in on one side.

He stopped at the porch and put down his bicycle. "Hey, hi ya, Kate."

"Craig! Great to see you!" She moved forward and gave him a hug. "How are you?"

"I'm okay," he answered from the good side of his face. "Heard Ben's home."

"Yes! He's in the barn." This was wonderful, just what Ben needed, a friend who would understand what he went through, someone to share it all with.

Kate watched Craig walk his bicycle to the barn, heard Ben call out in welcome. She wondered about bringing them iced tea but decided to leave them alone.

After some time, Kate spied the two of them walking side by side, Ben on his crutches, Craig pushing his bicycle. Laughing. Craig slapped Ben on the back. They shook hands. "See ya, buddy." Then Craig rode off down the lane.

When Ben came into the house, he shook his head. "Poor guy. Lost his face. Can you imagine?" After a pause, he smiled. "He's going to round up some of the other guys who've seen action, get us a poker game going."

"Great. That's just great, Ben."

"Okay," Ben said. "I'm going out to see if Father wants any help."

"No . . ." Kate hesitated. He might run into the PWs in the orchard. "I'd love your advice. I'm . . ." *I'm what?* "I'm putting in a new flowerbed out front."

"Yeah, sure." Ben grinned. "Let's do it."

JOSIE ARRIVED LATE IN THE MORNING, and when she sniffed and pulled out her hankie, she said she had a cold. Kate noted her friend's blotchy skin and swollen eyes and judged that it wasn't a cold at all. Still, Josie wore a fresh pink dress and her hair was neatly waved. A good sign.

In the barn, Ben was whittling away, whistling.

"Look who's here to see you," Kate said.

He grinned, smoothed his hair. "Hi ya, Josie."

"Hi."

Ben picked up his crutches and moved forward. "How 'bout we go to the cottage?"

"Come with us," Josie whispered, tugging Kate's sleeve. So Kate followed the two of them down the path through the cedar trees. Josie held awkwardly to Ben's right arm, a crutch between them.

It was a balmy day, the sun bright on the lake. The well-trampled pine needles were soft under Kate's bare feet, each step emitting a spicy fragrance.

"Wait until you see what Josie's done," Kate said. "Everything's so pretty."

Approaching the cottage, Ben stopped and looked about. "Flowerbeds. Those are new."

"I love flowers!" Josie said, perking up.

Josie and Kate had transplanted wildflowers from the woods and meadows. Those that hadn't died came up again in the spring, and now the yard held beds overgrown with buttercup, marigold, pansies, and mounds of downy purple phlox.

"Come see." Josie led Ben to a patch of wild strawberry she was encouraging along the edge of the woods.

Ben beamed. "My little gardening genius. I had no idea."

"I like making things pretty," Josie said. She didn't acknowledge Kate's part in it, but Kate tried not to mind. She just wanted them to be happy together.

Inside, Josie showed off the newly painted kitchen—yellow and white. She opened freshly scrubbed cupboards ready to be filled with dishes and dry goods. "Do you like it?"

"I'll build a pantry for you," Ben said, motioning toward an empty space between the cupboard and the icebox.

Josie looked up at him, a loving look. "I'm glad you're home." She opened windows, and the soft lake breeze filtered in along with the sweet music of songbirds. "We'll need curtains. Kate will help make them. Right, Kate?"

"As soon as you choose a color."

"What color would you like, Ben?" Josie asked. "Yellow or white?"

"What the hell does it matter!" he barked, his shoulders up, wary.

Josie backed away, fear in her eyes.

"Ben!" Kate touched his arm.

He shrugged her off and turned away. "It's just . . . sorry."

"What happened?" Kate asked.

He covered his eyes. "After the grenade went off . . . curtains blowing out like they were alive and . . ." He took a breath and whispered, "Not yellow. I don't want yellow."

Josie moved toward him and slipped an arm around his waist. "It's decided, then. White lace. Got that, Kate?"

Kate blinked away tears. "Got it. White lace." She was amazed at Josie's finesse.

"Let me show you the back room," Josie said.

In the bedroom, Ben touched the quilt and pillows Josie had brought in. He glanced into the mirror the two girls had hung. He sat and bounced on the bed, patted the spot beside him. "C'mere."

Josie squinted toward his stubby leg and turned away. "Let's go to the porch and sit in the sun."

Ben's cheeks flamed, but he picked up his crutches and followed her.

Josie perched on the wide bench swing. Ben sat beside her. Kate leaned against the wooden railing.

"You like what we've done?" Josie asked.

Ben put an arm around her shoulders and gave her a squeeze. "You bet."

They were silent for a while, watching the lake. A ship off on the horizon plied its way slowly north.

"Where d'ya think it's going?" Josie asked.

Ben stared into the distance, solemn. "Probably taking war supplies somewhere."

"Well, I'm glad *you're* not going anywhere." Josie hugged his arm.

He pulled away and put his hand into his pants pocket. He brought out a pack of cigarettes and shook one out. Josie didn't ask for one—maybe she didn't want him to know that she smoked—so Kate didn't ask either.

"We need some music," Josie said.

Ben sucked in deeply on the cigarette.

"If we had electricity, we could get a radio," she went on. "D'ya think we could get electricity down here?"

He blew out smoke. "Sure. I'll pull an extension from the house." He didn't sound excited about it.

"You can do anything, can't you?" She put her head on his shoulder, then sat up straight. "And when we have a radio and you get your leg, we can dance."

Ben's eyes clouded. "Yeah. Sure." He took a puff on the cigarette.

Kate was feeling uncomfortable, a voyeur. "I've got things to do at the house." She pushed off from the railing.

"See ya, Kate." Ben's tone perked up. He gave Josie a quick kiss on the cheek and whispered something in her ear.

"No, stay!" Josie rose and grabbed Kate's arm, pleading.

Kate didn't want to stay, but she sensed panic in Josie's voice. She returned to her position against the railing.

Ben frowned. Josie sat back on the swing, not quite as close to Ben as before.

"Say, why don't we go swimming?" Ben said.

Josie's eyes widened in alarm. She shrank away.

"Whatsa matter, afraid to see my leg?" He fingered the big safety pin. "I can show you right now."

Josie put out her hands against the sight. "No, that's not it. No, not at all." She floundered. "I just thought . . . maybe it would be hard for you to swim . . . until you get your new leg anyway . . ."

"I can do anything. You just said it yourself." He reached for his crutches.

"Not now," Josie said. "I'd have to go home to get my bathing suit, and my mother . . . she doesn't know I'm here."

"What'd you need a suit for?" Ben smirked and whispered loud enough for Kate to hear. "You didn't mind getting bare naked with me before."

Josie's face colored. "That was at night," she whispered.

"So what are you hiding? Night, day, what does it matter?" He sniggered. "If you're my girl, I can see you any damn time I want."

"Ben! Stop it!" Kate cried. "If I were Josie, I'd slap your face!"

Josie stood, lips trembling, and blinked back tears. Kate put an arm around her friend. *How frightening it must be for her, how embarrassing.* Was this what the war did to men? Kate thought of Clay—polite and tender. But Ben used to be like that too.

"C'mon. I'm sorry." He started to rise, then sat down again. "I'm used to kidding with my buddies. That's what comes natural now. I need to get over it. That's all. I'll get over it."

Josie sniffed. "How long will *that* take?"

"C'mon."

Josie sat on the edge of the swing.

Kate had to do something. "How about if we play Monopoly? I'll go get the game." Ben loved Monopoly.

"That would be fun," Josie said.

"Nah, I don't want to play."

"Cards, then. We could play Hearts or Gin Rummy . . ." Kate said.

Ben laughed. "One of the guys had a great deck of cards, pinup beauties. Not the kind you see in posters. Hah! Pokerface we called him. He was good at it." Ben was quiet for a bit. "Poor kid got hit bad. Wonder if he's still playing."

"I've never played poker," Kate said. "Why don't you show us how?"

"Nah, it's not for girls."

"Then what *do* you want to do?" Josie said.

He poked her side and leaned in. "You know what I want."

Josie pushed his hand away and wrapped her arms protectively around herself.

Kate's stomach lurched. What *would* he do if he were alone with Josie? Kate shared her friend's anxiety, yet she knew that Ben needed Josie to help him get back to his old self. "Let's talk about your wedding," Kate said, trying for a light tone.

"Yeah, let's get married." Ben squeezed Josie's thigh. "How about tonight?"

Josie slapped his hand away. "You have to be nice to me or I won't speak to you anymore, let alone marry you."

Ben's jaw tensed. "Well, then. Maybe you better go play Old Maid."

Josie jumped off the swing.

He grabbed for her, tried to tickle her. "C'mon, Josie. I was just teasing." His tone softened. "You know I'm a kidder." He stood and moved toward her. He touched her cheek, her shoulder.

"Oh, Ben!" Josie hugged him, crying. He kissed her hair.

Kate turned away and walked down the path toward the house, resisting the urge to look back.

CHAPTER THIRTY-NINE

KATE UNFOLDED THE LINEN NAPKIN on her lap to protect her white summer dress and bit into the messy barbecue beef sandwich. She closed her eyes and savored the dark smoky flavors, and when she opened them, Clay was watching her. She dabbed her lips with the napkin, embarrassed to be caught in such an unladylike moment of enjoyment.

They sat at an outdoor table overlooking Kangaroo Lake. The sky had cleared and the evening held that rich loamy after-rain scent of damp earth and roots and wild grasses. Loons bobbed on the lake's surface, diving down and coming up somewhere else.

When Clay had picked Kate up earlier, he'd asked about Ben.

"Lost a leg?" Clay repeated. He looked startled at the news.

"The Army's making him a new one." She rushed her words. "He says he'll be fine." She wiped away tears.

Clay put an arm around her.

"He doesn't want anyone to worry about him. But how could he possibly be fine?" Kate wanted to ask Clay's advice about how to help Ben. She looked at his tense jaw. No. It was too close, too close to his own coming war. Besides, this was their last night together before he left, and she didn't want to spoil it. Clay squeezed her hand. They were quiet on the drive to the roadhouse, and once there, they didn't speak of it again.

Dusk had shifted into a magical blue-gray twilight. Stars peeked out here and there. And then the moon rose full.

Clay's Navy whites shone bright. I must be glowing too, Kate thought. With Clay's admiring eyes on her, she felt beautiful. She sipped her beer and licked foam from her upper lip. "After the war, where do you want to fly?"

"Everywhere." He gazed off over the lake. "California, Mexico, Argentina—"

"That's South America!"

He laughed. "New Zealand, Australia . . ."

"Gee whiz! I wonder what it's like in Australia."

"That's what we'll find out." He took one of Kate's sticky hands and kissed her fingers.

We? Oh yes! "I could write about it." She had never thought of writing about faraway places. "I haven't read any novels about Australia, or Argentina. Maybe I'll be the first—"

"That's what I like about you, Kate. You just head right into life like an aviator into a storm." He grinned. "Bare feet and all."

"Could we go to Cornwall, where Daphne du Maurier lives? She's an author I like. Do you think we might visit her?"

"If you want to visit her, we'll do it." He touched the tip of her nose.

Was this really happening? Were they really talking about a future together? Kate was too excited to eat any more. She took a swallow of beer and closed her eyes to hold the moment.

"Look there," Clay said. "Is that an egret?"

She squinted at the tall blue bird stalking the shore. "Great blue heron."

"Smarty pants. That's what you are."

When a gentle breeze lifted the ends of her wispy hair, Clay smoothed a palm along her hair and cheek. "Smarty panties."

Panties. Kate was wearing the silk lacy ones Josie had given her for her birthday, which for months had lain wrapped in the original tissue paper, hidden in the back of her underwear drawer. She was used to heavy cotton ones; these were so light she felt naked under her dress. Yesterday in the cherry shack Clay had led her hands to his belt before she got scared and stopped him. She knew what he wanted, and she wanted it too. She hoped he had one of those rubber things the girls at school talked about because she certainly didn't want to get pregnant.

Kate didn't know what had happened between Ben and Josie after she left them in the cottage, but the next day, when she went to the bedroom, the sheets Josie had brought were still fresh, unused. The cottage smelled of wildflowers.

Wild. She smiled into Clay's eyes, sipping her beer.

His hands grasped hers across the table, his face serious. "You know I'll be leaving tomorrow."

The great blue bird rose up from the shore, spreading its wide wings, and drew its reedy legs together like a rudder and glided off across the still lake.

ON THEIR WAY HOME, Kate asked Clay to park the car near the cherry shack. She took off her sandals and led him barefoot along the edge of the woods to the cottage. "Do you mind waiting here? I have to run into the house for a few minutes."

Clay had never asked Kate why she didn't invite him in to meet her family, and she was glad of that. Her parents would have too many questions, reasons she shouldn't see him. He was older, an "out-of-towner," as Mrs. J had suggested, not to be trusted.

It was after nine. Mother, Father, and Ben were sitting in the parlor.

"How was the party?" Father asked. A party given by one of the girls at school. A lie. Kate hadn't asked the girl to cover for her. As long as she was home in time, she knew they wouldn't check. Their focus was on Ben now.

"It was nice."

"Glad you're home," Mother said. "We were just going up to bed." She put away her sewing and rose from the couch. Father emptied his pipe into an ashtray and followed.

"I'll be along." Ben sat on the couch under a reading lamp, a tray of carving tools on his lap, whittling away at a figurine.

Kate sat close. "What are you making?"

He rotated the figure, a carving of Josie's head.

"Wow, I can see her," Kate said. This would be a good time to talk with him about Josie and their plans. But Clay was waiting. She faked a yawn and stood. "See you in the morning."

"G'night, Kitty Kat."

She went up to her room and closed the door. After stuffing pillows under her covers, she climbed out the window and down through the branches of the oak tree.

Clay came forward along the path and took her arm. "Sweet little place you got here."

Crickets sang from the trees, mating calls.

Once they'd settled on the cottage swing, Clay pulled out a flask and handed it to her. The two beers Kate had drunk at supper had gone down easily. The whiskey was harsher. He offered her a cigarette and lit it with his own. She drew the smoke into her lungs, and Clay put an arm around her, sweet and gentle. She gave the swing a push with her foot. They were quiet for a while, his warm hand on her bare shoulder, his hip next to her hip, his thigh touching hers. The gentle lapping of the lake. The slow squeak of the swing. The first star. She closed her eyes and wished for Clay forever.

He sucked in the last of his cigarette and flung it onto the grass. "I'm going to miss you, Kate."

"Me too." It came out in a whisper.

He kissed her forehead, her cheeks, her mouth. When she kissed him back, he opened the top few buttons of her sundress and his palm brushed across the filmy fabric of her bra.

Kate's nipples came erect at his touch. Her insides rushed down in a flood of desire, and she couldn't help but move her hips toward him. He put a hand under her dress and moved it slowly up and up until his fingers played along the lacy edge of her panties and then teased around that spot, that embarrassing wet spot, and she sighed.

"Oh!" There, right there, the touch she didn't know she longed for.

He rose and put his arms beneath her knees and shoulders and carried her through the door, into the cottage, into the bedroom, and gently lowered her onto the bed.

Moonlight from the window softened the small room around them.

He unbuckled his belt and unbuttoned his white trousers and let them drop to the floor. His shirt and undershirt followed, exposing that strong deep chest she remembered, the dark curly hair diving down in a V.

Dressed only in his boxer shorts, he knelt over her and opened the remaining buttons on her dress. She arched up to help as he pulled it over her head. Exposed in her bra and panties, she slid between the sheets and he gently pulled the top sheet down and touched her skin, his face serious.

"I don't want to get pregnant," she breathed.

"Don't worry, my love."

My love!

When he took off her bra, he sucked in his breath and put his hands on her breasts and then his lips, his mouth. His hand moved down her tummy, under the waistband of her panties, his fingers in her pubic hair, finding that place. Swirling a finger in that wet place, pushing his finger up into her. Moonlight in his eyes.

When he lay beside her, he brought her hand to his shorts and she touched the warm thickness, full and alive. She watched his face, his eyes half-closed, dreamy, mouth open. And she grabbed it, pulled on it, wanting him, wanting him.

"Easy," he said, husky voice. He pulled off his shorts and showed her the way, touching it up and down, slowing her hand. Then he reached to his trousers on the floor and came back with the rubber thing and pulled it down over the length of him.

"Are you okay?" he whispered. Rapid breath. Excited eyes.

She could barely speak. "Yes." Her skin warm and tingling, her heart beating loud, her breath uneven.

"Oh!" When he moved into her she tensed.

"Sure you're okay?"

She nodded because she didn't want him to know that it hurt, tugging at her insides, burning. *What am I doing wrong?*

He must have known because he slowed and kissed her and touched her breasts and breathed into her ear. And she relaxed, and then it didn't burn so much and being so close—*Is this really happening?*—so close to Clay, wanting to please him. Her arms around him, his skin hot and slick. He moved faster now, burning her insides with his excitement, then he shuddered and cried out, straining.

He breathed hard, then slower, slipping out of her. He opened his eyes and kissed her face. He took off the rubber thing, and then his body returned to her, warm and solid, his arms around her. She pulled the sheet over them, together.

His face lay on the pillow next to hers. A hand in her hair, then on her cheek. "You are so beautiful."

She smiled.

"Good night, my sweet Kate." His eyes closed, and he was soon asleep, breathing softly beside her.

It had all led to this. All the beautiful suspense—the weeks and weeks of suspense—and these last few days—it had all led to this. She had expected to be marvelously content, like Amber in the book, but she only felt chafing pain and a rousing restlessness.

She lay awake in the moonlight, afraid to move, afraid to wake her lover, watching him as he slept. Dark curly lashes against his pale skin, tiny cinnamon freckles dotting his nose, a sleepy smile lingering on his lips. It must have been what he'd expected.

WHEN KATE OPENED HER EYES, there was Clay, propped on an elbow, waiting for her. He brushed stray hair from her face. "You were dreaming."

She blinked awake, mildly conscious of the illusory world she was leaving. "Where do we travel when we dream?"

He kissed her forehead. "This is my dream, right here with you."

The night was warm. She was sore down there and hot from their coupling, sweaty. "Let's go down to the lake."

He groaned.

"C'mon, lazybones."

Outside, they ran naked to the beach and paused on the shore, holding hands. The lake lay velvety still before them. Moonlight dusted rippling waves like diamonds.

Kate dove out across the surface and turned and floated on her back. Clay was soon floating beside her.

"It's cold!" he said.

She laughed and moved her arms in a slow backstroke. "Do you know the stars?"

"Tell me." He followed her pace.

She pointed out the Pleiades, Little Dipper, Big Dipper, Milky Way. "If you listen, you can hear them."

"What are they saying?"

"They're saying, 'Look at those beautiful lovers on the lake.' They're jealous. Wouldn't you be?"

A sudden flash of bright light pierced the sky. Then another.

Vivid green and blue streaks. Puffy clouds tinged pink. The lights got brighter, more intense.

"Wow!" Clay grabbed Kate's hand, floating together now. "I've never seen anything like that."

"They're showing off," she whispered. "Northern Lights. Aurora borealis."

The colors changed and grew and saturated the huge dome of sky with an electric green, vivid and close.

"It's you," he said. "A reflection of you."

"It's us." She laughed. "You and me together."

They swam to shore and walked to the cottage, to the bedroom perfumed with wildflowers, and pulled the sheet up around themselves beneath the breeze of the open window. Kate closed her eyes, content now, and breathed in the earthiness of the night.

SHE WOKE WITH THE SONGBIRDS. Sunrise already. She kissed Clay's cheek, and he opened his eyes. He ran his hand along her torso.

"I have to go," she whispered.

When his hand moved toward her breasts, her nipples tightened and she felt the wetness down where it was still sore, but not so much now. He kissed her lips, and she clung to him. Yes, not wanting to leave him, kissing him back, her mouth open.

He pulled away and reached for his trousers and brought out another rubber thing. And she opened to him, unafraid this time, no longer thinking, alive now to his fullness inside of her. This time he was slower, more gentle, and the soreness turned to a feeling like scratching an itch, and her insides came sighing down to that place and her hips went up to meet him, moving instinctively up and up. She held him tight, slick with sweat, her sweat, his sweat. Her legs moved up around his thighs, rocking with him. She shivered and shivered again and cried out, and he kissed her, breathing "Kate" in her ear, "Sweet Kate." And he pulsed into her, wet and fast, and then dropped, breathing hard.

And yes, this was what it had all led to, the anticipation, the suspense, it had all led to this. This amazing moment elastic with pleasure extended in time. She could live on this precious night forever.

CHAPTER FORTY

KATE CLIMBED THE TREE to her bedroom window and changed into her overalls. Down in the kitchen, she tried not to smile too broadly lest she give herself away. Mother greeted her as if nothing had changed.

Outside she walked barefoot on lush grass glistening with morning dew. A band of silver rimmed the lake's horizon where the Northern Lights had come out just for them.

As she approached the barn, Kate saw that the big door was already open. Ben sat on the high stool at the lathe, the radio playing.

"What's that you're making?" she asked.

"A new leg." He said it matter-of-factly.

Kate recoiled, afraid to look, until she realized he was talking about the chair. She went over to the bench and watched his large hands deftly craft the cylindrical piece of wood. "I like having you home. You like what Josie's done with the cottage?" She was eager to find out what had happened after she'd left.

"Sure." He switched on the noisy lathe, effectively cutting off the conversation.

Crossing the barn to Mia's pen, Kate paused at the place with the bloodstain. The hair on the back of her neck bristled whenever she neared it. She glanced toward Ben. He need never know.

While she pulled gently on Mia's teats, Kate's thoughts wandered. During past harvests, Ben, a fast picker, worked in the trees, but surely he couldn't climb a ladder now. She could ask him to help her in the cherry shack—it would give them an opportunity to talk about things, about his plans with Josie—and she wanted to tell him about Clay. She wanted Ben to meet Clay, to show them off to each other. They'd shake hands, swap stories—Ben coming home, Clay leaving. And when the war was over, they'd share experiences. Like brothers. Yes, brothers! But no, this was her last day with Clay. Introductions would have to wait.

Outside, the early sun shimmered across the lake, pooling on waves and ripples like liquid silver. Squawking seabirds hovered and wheeled away and back. Kate breathed it all in. Everything was good again. Ben was home and Clay loved her.

After breakfast Kate went to the cottage and pulled the sheets from the bed and brought them up to her closet to hide. She would wash them later.

She took time to bathe and wash her hair, then chose a lavender sundress, ribbony straps at her shoulders—Mrs. J said that lavender complimented her skin tone. She brushed her hair until it shone like gold and added her pink barrette.

The sun was bright, and sales at the cherry stand were brisk. Kate tried to focus on serving the customers, but her thoughts were on Clay. She closed her eyes and relived precious details of their night together. She was still sore down there, beautifully sore.

With every approaching car, she looked up, expectant.

Just before noon Kate heard the tractor, Father bringing fruit. And there was Ben, sitting on the flatbed amid lugs of cherries and a rack of pies. "Want some company?"

Kate's heart sank, but she couldn't very well say no. "That'd be swell."

After they unloaded, Father drove off and Ben stayed.

Sitting next to Kate behind the counter, Ben put a cherry into his mouth and spit the pit out onto the gravel lot. Watching him, Kate noticed that his face was thinner now, his rosy cheeks roughened. Squinty lines had formed on his forehead between his eyes.

"Did you miss the cherries last summer?" she asked.

"I missed everything." He plopped another cherry into his mouth, spit the pit. He laughed. "You wouldn't believe the fruit they grow around the Mediterranean. Figs, dates, persimmons, pomegranates . . ." He closed his eyes. "I liked the figs best. And so many different kinds of olives and nuts—"

A car pulled up to the stand. A family emerged—man, woman, three redheaded children. The woman marched forward. "Came for the pies."

"How many?" Kate asked.

The woman looked to her husband. "Two? Three?" After a pause, "Two then."

"Try some cherries." Kate pushed a plate of samples forward.

"I want some!" the pigtailed girl cried. The other children chimed in, stuffing their mouths.

The family left with three pies and four baskets of sweet cherries.

"You're pretty cagey, Kitty Kat." Ben gave her shoulder a light punch.

"If they try them, they'll buy them. That's what Mother always says." Kate sat back, bathed in the warm sun flowing in through open shutters.

Ben sat back as well and closed his eyes. "Feels good." His face relaxed into that smile she remembered.

"So how about you and Josie," Kate ventured.

Ben opened his eyes, serious. "In her letters she said she wanted to get married as soon as I came home." He regarded his damaged leg. "She seems okay with it—"

A passing truck backfired. Ben jumped—eyes wide, mouth

twisted—and pulled Kate with him to the ground. He was hurting her arm, holding her down, but she kept still. After what seemed like a long time, he let go.

He was shaking. "Sorry." He struggled to get up and into the chair. "Sorry, I just—"

"It's all right, Ben." She put a hand on his arm.

"It's not all right," he said, barely audible. He sat forward and wiped his nose on his sleeve.

Kate touched his shoulder. He breathed in deeply and gave a big sigh.

After some time he said, "Everybody back home . . . You just go on as if . . ." His shoulders fell and his voice softened. "But you couldn't possibly know what it's like."

Kate faced him. Maybe he didn't want to tell her. Maybe she didn't want to hear. Maybe she shouldn't ask, but she did. "Tell me, then. What's it like?"

Ben ate a cherry, spit the pit. Then another. "Charging machine guns. That was my specialty." His voice grew stronger, proud. "I learned to hear the difference between the amateurs and the professionals."

"The difference?"

"It's like this," Ben said. "*Bup bup bup.* Pause. *Bup bup bup.* Pause. That's a professional. But an amateur will hold the trigger too long—*bup bup bup bup bup*—and the barrel floats up, giving me room to rush in underneath. Take him out."

Take him out?

"That last time. Approaching Rome." His voice came in a monotone, as if he were reciting a story he had told many times. "Summer flowers covered the hillsides. When we passed an apple orchard, I thought of the cherry trees back home. The sun had just set. Dusk." He stared off into space. "Salami—"

"Salami?"

"That's what we called him. Nino Salvatore Salamme. He had this crazy New York accent. We were together from the beginning—

across North Africa, over the Mediterranean to Sicily, through the mountains—and then we were headed to Rome. Two years together. The last survivors of the original platoon. My buddy." Ben paused for a bit, grinned. "He had this big Italian family. Lots of sisters. Showed me pictures. I told him I already had a girl. He had relatives in Rome he'd never met. Wanted me to meet them too."

"And did you?"

"We made it to the outskirts of Rome, but . . ." He bit around a cherry pit.

"We were in a field of high grass, scouting out the enemy, covering for each other. The action had slowed. I was reaching for my canteen when I heard a gunner. We fell to the ground, waiting, listening." Ben paused. "He was tapping out too many shots. When I heard him do it the third time, I gave the sign for Salami to throw a grenade. He pulled the pin and stood . . . *why the hell did he have to stand up?*"

Ben was silent for a bit. A car passed by, tires humming.

When he spoke again, his words came out in a whisper. "That's when the machine gun cut him." Ben looked straight ahead. "Grenade rolled from Salami's hand. Live grenade, ready to blow. I dove down and grabbed it, flung it toward the sound of the machine gun, but the gunner got me before the grenade got him. I was smelling burning meat and something metallic. And my leg was on fire. Then the grenade blew the earth sky high in the distance, and that's the last thing I remember."

"Oh, Ben!"

Ben jostled and shifted in his chair. "You look out for your buddy." He slumped back, an arm across his eyes. "I shoulda died instead of him."

"Don't say that!" Kate grabbed him. "You're home and—"

He shook his head.

After some silence, Kate whispered, "Did you ever have to shoot anyone? Close up where you could see his eyes?"

He turned to Kate, then away. "You gotta think of them like rabid dogs." He stared into space. "It's hard to look at their faces and pull the trigger, but you know they'll kill you if you don't."

Kate shivered. "Like Old Tramp?" she said, referring to the puppy she'd found when she was six. He stayed beside her every day, every night, best friends. He followed her to school and waited outside and followed her home. When Tramp was nine, he disappeared. Kate was frantic, searching the shore, the woods. When he finally returned, he was snarling, foaming. Father corralled him and said he had to be shot. Ben got his gun. Then Old Tramp was dead. That night Kate was crying, and she heard Ben crying too.

"Yeah, like that." He nodded. "You can do it if you think of them as rabid dogs." He pulled a pack of cigarettes and a lighter from his pocket.

"May I have one?"

"You?" He grinned. "You're growing up too fast, little sister." He tipped the pack her way.

A car pulled up, and a couple approached the stand. Kate hurried them along, giving them what they wanted, taking their money.

When the customers left, Ben said, "Look, Kate. Maybe I shouldn't 'a told you all that—"

"I asked—"

"It's not your fault. None of this." His arm came warm and strong around her shoulders.

"It's not your fault either." She worked to hold back tears. "You did what you had to do. And we have to keep going here at home too. Take care of things."

"Yeah. But now . . . it's just hard for me to sit here knowing they're still over there, and . . ." He looked up and let out a long whistle. "Would you get a loada that automobile!"

Clay! Kate's heart jumped.

The red convertible pulled onto the gravel, and Clay stepped out.

"Hey, he's in uniform. Musta been wounded, like me."

"No, he's . . . come and meet him."

Ben followed on his crutches.

Clay came quickly forward. "Hi ya, Kate!" He put an arm around her waist and kissed her on the cheek.

Kate felt it all again, the electricity of his touch. She wanted to melt into him, but Ben was right behind her.

"Well, whaddya know." Ben smiled. "Little sister's got a guy."

"You must be Ben." Clay put out his hand, and the two men shook. "Kate told me you were coming home. I've been looking forward to meeting you."

"Ben, this is Clay."

"Good to meet you," Ben said. "Navy, eh?"

"Yup. Going to be a pilot." His eyes went to Ben's leg, and his face colored. "I'm sorry about your leg."

"Ah, I'm okay." Ben said, lifting his chin as if proud of his injury. "Pilot, eh?" He slapped Clay on the back. "Tell you what. Whenever we saw those planes swoop in to help us out . . . well, it's a beautiful sight."

This was going well. As much as Kate wanted to be alone with Clay, she was glad the two were meeting. "How about we sit at the picnic table," she said. "You two go ahead. I'll be along."

The men moved toward the table in the shade of the maples, and Kate stayed behind, ostensibly to fill baskets, letting them get to know each other.

Watching them together—Clay moving easily, Ben hobbling alongside—Kate's breath caught. *What if Clay comes back a cripple?* She gripped a straw basket so tightly it crumpled in her hand. She feared that almost as much as Clay not coming home at all. She shook her head with guilt. She thought of what Josie had said about duty. No, that wasn't it. She loved Clay. She would never give him up, no matter what.

"General Mark Clark's Fifth," Ben was saying in answer to a question Clay must have asked.

"We saw you guys in the newsreels, cheered you on."

Ben offered Clay a cigarette. Clay accepted the light. After some low conversation Kate couldn't quite make out, Ben said, "How much longer before you ship out?"

"Gotta finish OCS, then flight training—"

"Huh. What are you, eighteen? I thought you looked older."

"I'm twenty."

"Twenty?" Ben's voice had an edge. "What have you been doing?" He crushed out his cigarette on the table.

"College . . . ROTC—"

"In school?" Ben stood up on his crutches. "And looks like your plan is to stay in school . . . OCS, pilot training, then some other special this or that, waiting it out—"

Clay was standing now as well. "Hey, I'm in."

"Sure took your sweet time about it."

"Ben?" Kate hurried to the table.

Clay glanced at Kate. "Better get going. It's a long drive."

"But you just got here!" Kate panicked.

"Let him go!" Ben shouted. "Back to his . . . his country club."

Clay turned away and headed for his car.

"Clay!" Kate rushed after him. "You need to understand. Ben . . . he's not . . . it's just that . . ."

Clay got into the car and looked up at her. "He doesn't want me here right now." He started the engine.

"But *I* do! I don't want to lose you—"

He took her hand, kissed her fingers. "You'll never lose me. You and me in the cottage last night. That's what I'll be thinking about." He let go of her hand. His tires crunched forward on the gravel. Kate watched his taillights trail off down County Trunk Q, smaller and smaller, until they disappeared.

"Oh!" Kate whirled toward Ben. "Look what you've done! Clay is a good person."

"Is this what you call taking care of things?" Ben was breathing hard. "We're over there fighting and this . . . this pretty boy's driving around in his fancy car . . . impressing all the girls . . ." Ben banged on his left thigh. "I can't believe I lost this for the likes of him!"

"You don't understand—"

He grabbed her wrist. "You think a rich guy like that is serious about a simple farm girl like you?"

"You're hurting me . . ."

"Damn fucking officer! He'll never see action." Ben's grip tightened on her wrist. "Guys like him are why enlisted men get 'Dear John' letters. Know what that means?"

Kate twisted from his grip. He grabbed for her again, but she ducked away. "What's the matter with you!" she shouted. "What did you do with my brother?"

"Damn OCS brat. He's a sonofabitch! You stay away from the likes of him." Ben swung his arm, nearly lost his balance, righted himself. "From all of 'em, ya hear?"

He's possessed. That's what it is. Possessed by war ghosts.

"You hear me, farm girl?"

Kate slapped his face hard and watched him wobble with the shock of the blow. Never had she hit anyone, let alone her brother, but no one had ever been so cruel. He caught himself and put a hand to his cheek, his eyes wide.

A car rolled onto the gravel. Kate turned toward the stand, her palm burning.

The couple wanted to know the prices of everything and sample every kind of cherry. Kate's hands shook as she picked up their coins from the counter. Surely they saw she was crying. When they finally left, Kate went outside. Ben was far down the lane, hobbling toward the house.

"Good. Hobble away," she said under her breath. Maybe I am a simple farm girl, but Clay wants to be with me. He could be with any old prissy debutante, but he wants me. She rubbed her wrist. He

wants to read my stories. Like Father, and Miss Fleming. He appreci-
ates me. "Barefoot and all," she said aloud.

Kate brought the OPEN sign into the shack and pulled the shutters closed. She got on her bicycle and pedaled north along County
Trunk Q.

At Island Road, she veered down toward the lighthouse and rode
to the end, set her bicycle against the tree, and waded across the channel.

Josie was at the edge of the woods picking wildflowers.

"I have to talk with you," Kate said.

They sat on the grass in a patch of sunlight, and Kate told Josie
what had happened. "Would you please speak with Ben about Clay?
Ben always listens to you."

Josie frowned. "He's different now."

Kate froze. "Of course he is. Think what he's been through. He
did his duty, now we—"

"I know, I know. I feel terrible! A coward, a traitor . . ." Tears
streamed down Josie's face. "He was romantic and considerate and
fun and happy and . . . Mama asked me how he could possibly run
the farm now."

"He'll get a new leg, and—"

"It's not that . . . well, not only that . . ." Josie wiped her cheeks.
"I loved him the way he was. I loved him *so much!*"

"I know." Kate took Josie's hand.

"But now . . . he's so bitter. Mean. I don't know what to say, how
to act. I can't even be myself around him."

"Josie, we have to give him time. That's what Father says. He'll
be fine."

"When?" She pulled away. "When will he be fine? How long
does it take?"

She lay down on the lawn and curled into herself. Ringlets of
dark hair fell against her pale skin. Her tears rolled sideways down
her cheeks. Her full breasts heaved against her white cotton blouse.
She was so pretty, any boy would choose her.

"C'mon, Josie." Kate bent forward and stroked her friend's hair. "You should have seen the way Ben perked up when Craig visited. That's what he needs. To talk with the other boys who've come back."

Josie moaned. "I love being with him, in his arms. He's the only one I ever . . . we were meant to be together." Josie sat up and pulled out a hankie and wiped her face. Her white blouse was grass-stained, but she didn't seem to mind.

"I'm leaving end of August," Kate said. "If you want me to help you with your wedding dress, we better get started. A summer wedding." Kate recalled Josie's excitement whenever she spoke of the wedding. Dancing with Ben. Well, there'd be no dancing now. "Let's go up to your room and look at that *Bride's Magazine* with the dress you like."

Josie turned away. "Maybe later . . ."

"And those kitchen curtains. White lace, right?"

"I haven't decided."

"Decided?" Kate repeated. "Look, we'll go to Mrs. J's together and pick out the fabric. We could go now."

"Stop!" Josie put her hands to her ears.

"What's wrong?" Kate's words felt hollow as soon as they left her lips. Hadn't she just slapped her own brother? Everything was wrong.

"It's not his fault, I know. It's not fair. Not fair for either of us." She was sobbing now, shaking with sobs. "I feel so . . . so guilty! I told him I'd marry him. I love him, I really do. But I loved the *other* Ben!"

Everyone loved the other Ben, Kate thought miserably.

"He did his duty, and I should do mine. If I only knew whether he'd ever be the same again. If I knew that . . ." Josie blew her nose. "I've been waiting for him, and I'm older now, and all the boys are gone . . . and I don't want to lose you either!"

Kate put an arm around her friend's shoulders.

"I'm afraid of him," Josie whispered.

Kate rubbed her wrist where Ben had grabbed her. "Oh, Josie!" Ben needed Josie. If she were to leave him . . . "Let's give him a chance."

Josie sniffled. "What if Clay comes back angry like Ben? What will you do then?"

Kate stiffened. Oh, why had she goaded Clay into joining up?

Josie's mother called from the house.

Josie let out a ragged breath and wiped her nose. "C'mon." They walked arm-in-arm to where Josie's mother waited.

Kate greeted her. "Hello, Mrs. Lapointe."

"Josie has things to do," Mrs. Lapointe said sternly. "Come along, Josie."

"We'll talk more later," Josie said over her shoulder.

CHAPTER FORTY-ONE

CHARLOTTE HAD CARRIED her heirloom seeds forward year to year, and now, standing amid the bounty of her garden, she examined the ripe tomatoes in the morning sun. She picked a plump one from the vine and bit into it, dribbling sweet juices onto her chin and apron. She closed her eyes and savored the rich flavor, a guilty pleasure, then filled a bushel basket with the ripest ones to blanch for canning.

Walking to the kitchen, Charlotte looked off toward the orchard. The men were working near the house. She hadn't seen Karl since the night of the telegram. She had been so focused on Ben. Yet thoughts of the root cellar would flit across her mind like afternoon shadows, and tactile memories would glide across her skin. Now, in the warm summer breeze, there he was, his good strong body.

No! It was over with Karl. It had to be over.

STEAM ROSE FROM THE POT. Charlotte was about to dump tomatoes into the boiling water when she heard the thumping of Ben's crutches on the wooden porch steps. The door opened. He seemed agitated. She pulled the pot from the burner.

"What is it, Ben?"

"Damn Nazis all over the place! Can't stand to hear that fucking German talk!" He put his hands to his ears. He hadn't said anything about the prisoners since his return, perhaps because he hadn't come in contact with them. But now they were in the trees just beyond the back porch.

Charlotte ignored his swearing. "They'll be gone soon."

"Now is not soon enough." His eyes bored into hers. "Where's the one you let into the house? Which one is he?"

"It's over, Ben. Kate's tutoring is done." Charlotte touched his arm. "I have hot water here. Would you like me to pour it into the tub for you? A good warm bath before dinner. Some mint tea—"

He pushed away. "A bath? Mint tea? What the . . . Didn't you hear what I said?" His eyes flashed at her as he grasped his crutches and swung away down the hall. Soon she heard him thudding up the stairs, one step at a time.

Charlotte went out and scanned the orchard. There he was, up on that sorry tractor, picking up lugs. She walked to the end of the row where he was riding and stood, waiting for him to see her. When he reached her, he pulled on the brake and climbed down off the metal seat, leaving the engine rattling.

She had to shout for him to hear. "Thomas, we need to send the prisoners away as soon as they're done with the cherries."

"I've committed to housing them through the apple harvest."

"Well, uncommit!" she yelled.

Thomas reached up and switched off the tractor. "What is it, Charlotte?" He took her shoulders, concern in his eyes.

"It's Ben," she said. "He can't bear to see the prisoners . . ."

"They'll be away from the house tomorrow—"

"Thomas, he's agitated, angry. He wants to know which one came into the house."

"Oh, Charlotte. You didn't tell him—"

"Of course not." She took his arm. "Thomas, things have changed since you made that commitment. Your son is home. Isn't he more important than the apple farmers?"

"Yes. Yes, of course." Thomas glanced toward the PWs. "When we're done here today, I'll go down to Gus's farm and let him know. We'll find them another place."

"Thank you, Thomas." Charlotte touched his cheek.

He pulled off a glove and put a warm hand on hers.

"Thank you," she said again.

ON HER WAY BACK TO THE HOUSE, Charlotte sensed someone following her. "Karl! Get away!"

When he stopped, she looked into his wide eyes and mouthed out, *Root cellar.*

Karl's dimples deepened. He headed in the direction of the barn. Charlotte stood on the porch and watched as Thomas disappeared down the row on his noisy tractor. The PWs had moved further on as well. Charlotte crept around to the root cellar, down the stairs, and lit the kerosene lamp. Soon Karl appeared.

"Charlotte, I am sorry for your son." He took her shoulders. "That we . . . a German soldier did that."

"It wasn't you, Karl."

"No, not me . . ." He hugged her. "I want to meet your Ben."

"No, no. That cannot happen." Charlotte backed away. "Karl, you'll be leaving sooner than you thought. As soon as the cherry harvest is done."

"But I will stay here, close to you—"

"What?"

"My beautiful Charlotte!" He pulled her in and kissed her mouth. Suddenly his hands were on her breasts. She hummed with desire as he unbuttoned her dress and cupped her breasts and kissed the nipples. "Charlotte, we can save each other." He surrounded her with warmth.

"Save each other?" she breathed.

"We go together. We take your boat." He kissed her neck. "I will hide here until you are ready, with enough gasoline." He grabbed a blanket from the barrel.

"No, no, no." She had never thought of leaving, not really. This was her home. Her family needed her. She would never leave.

He kissed her again, and she sighed and lost all thought, and soon he was inside her. Leaving, leaving. Her hips pumped up with the knowledge of his leaving. And when he collapsed and rolled next to her on the blanket, he breathed into her ear, "Come with me."

"No, Karl."

As she lay there, facing him, he slid his hand along the side of her body. Gentle.

"Karl . . ."

He pulled her to him, hard and forceful. She shook her head and pushed away, rising and straightening her clothes. *What was I thinking?*

"I can't."

CHAPTER FORTY-TWO

AS KATE TOOK THE SHEETS DOWN from the clothesline in the side yard, she tried to picture a happy future for Ben and Josie—together in the cottage, laughing children around them, lacy white curtains fluttering, a fresh lake breeze wafting into the kitchen where they would enjoy hearty suppers. Mother might want them to move up to the house, but Ben—he'd have his new leg—would build an addition on the cottage instead.

A quick movement caught Kate's peripheral vision: Karl emerging from the root cellar! She watched as he straightened his tan shirt and trousers, smoothed his hair. He glanced about. When he saw her, he stopped short. She stared at him. *What was he doing down there?* He smiled and waved, as if nothing was amiss, and marched off across the orchard.

Her thoughts were distracted by the sound of a motorboat. Yes! There was Josie, coming to talk with her after all. Kate ran toward the front yard, but hesitated when she saw Ben swinging out of the barn on his crutches. Josie tied up the boat and walked slowly, head down. Ben waited at the foot of the dock. They spoke for a few moments and then went to the cottage.

Kate returned to the clothesline, keeping an eye on the path along the shore, waiting to see what would happen next. She unclipped a sheet from the line and dropped it into the clothes basket along with the wooden clothespins.

Time. People said that time healed everything, but how did that work? Would Ben ever be his same old self again? Or would he be different . . . forever?

How could she expect Josie to take that chance, to spend the rest of her life with someone who might never heal? But if Josie didn't marry Ben, what would become of him? And the orchard . . . his future . . . he couldn't run it alone.

Before Josie, plenty of girls had wanted to be with him. But that was the old Ben, the fun Ben. Not this angry, aggressive Ben. And if Josie left him, he'd be angrier still. Crazier maybe. Who would want to live with that? Who would help run the farm when Mother and Father could no longer do it?

Kate froze with the answer. *It would have to be me!* She brought her hands down from the line, dizzy with the thought. She hugged herself. She wanted her own life, an exciting life she could write about. She didn't want to give up school and come home to take care of things, as Father had. And Clay . . . he certainly wouldn't want to live on a Wisconsin farm, not with the whole world to explore.

Oh, Josie, please say yes!

Kate heard raised voices. She looked up.

"Let me go!" Josie was rushing from the cottage, running along the path toward the dock, sobbing openly, her dark curls flying askew, her pretty blouse hanging off one shoulder—was it unbuttoned, or torn?

Ben swung quickly after her, his shirttail flapping outside his trousers. "Josie!" His voice sounded rough, pleading. Was he crying?

At the end of the dock, Josie got into the boat and pulled on the cord and the motor growled.

"For better or for worse," Ben wailed.

"I can't! I just can't!" she called back before speeding away.

Kate left the sheets and ran to the dock. "Ben!" She reached out for him.

"Leave me alone," he shouted, pushing her aside.

Helpless, Kate backed away and watched him hobble off into the barn.

CHAPTER FORTY-THREE

CHARLOTTE WAS STERILIZING CANNING JARS when she heard the thud of Ben's crutches on the back porch. She stopped herself from opening the door. Let him do it.

He came into the kitchen, unsteady, his face full of hurt.

Charlotte wiped her hands on her apron. "Ben, I've spoken with your father, and the prisoners will be gone by the end of the week. We won't need to see them ever again."

He looked away.

"What is it?"

He stared out the window and shook his head.

"Come, sit." She pulled out a chair. "Have a ripe tomato. So sweet. I saved some fresh ones for dinner tonight."

"Ripe tomato," he sneered. "That's what she is. That's all she is."

"What are you talking about?"

He leaned against the kitchen wall, closed his eyes, whispered, "It's over."

Charlotte stopped, her heart pounding. *Please, God, tell me this isn't about Josie.*

He stared down where his leg should be. "She doesn't want me."

"Oh, Ben, that can't be!" Charlotte shook her head. "It's just a little lovers' quarrel. You've been apart so long, you need time to get to know each other again."

"She doesn't want me anymore."

"Of course she does. She's confused. I'll go over there. I'll talk some sense into her."

"No, you won't!" he yelled, his face close to hers.

"Ben!" She stepped back in alarm and caught her breath. "Josie doesn't realize . . ." She spoke rapidly now. "You're strong and capable. Your children will have a good future—"

"It's over," he said firmly.

"It doesn't have to be over . . ." She paused at the squeak of a door, the wood box opening from the outside.

"What was that?" Ben jerked forward.

"Let's go into the parlor."

Ben moved toward the open window and peered out. "One of those Nazis!" He hissed, pushing in front of Charlotte. He yanked open a drawer and started rummaging through it. "Stay down. I'll take care of him."

"No, Ben. It's not . . . What are you looking for?"

"Shh!" He quietly closed the drawer and opened another.

"It's all right, Ben. While you were away, he helped me with chores—"

Ben stopped, eyes wide, mouth agape.

Charlotte glanced out the open window and shook her head at Karl. "Not now."

"Charlotte—"

"What did you call my mother?" Ben barked through the screen.

"You must be Ben—"

"He knows my name?" Ben's face was tight, veins bulging on his neck. "*Fick dich!*" he yelled out.

"Karl, please go," Charlotte said.

"Karl?" Ben snapped. He opened another drawer. Flatware. Closed it, opened the next.

Karl looked at Charlotte, then headed off toward the barn.

"What's happened here? What the hell's going on?" Ben yelled.

Charlotte turned her back to Ben, moved toward the rear cupboard, gently opened a drawer, and slipped the revolver into her apron pocket.

Ben slammed a drawer and held to the counter, breathing heavily.

When Charlotte reached out for him, he evaded her and went into the parlor, crutches thumping angrily on the wood floor.

Through the window, Charlotte saw Karl entering the barn. She moved cautiously, quietly, from the kitchen to the dining room to the front hall, and slipped out the front door. She hurried across the yard. Chickens clucked and scurried. Mia bleated. Kate's rabbits jumped to the far side of the pen.

Late-afternoon sun filtered dimly through the barn windows, creating a patchwork of light on the floor. It took a moment for Charlotte's eyes to adjust. With the animals outside and the stalls empty, the barn was quiet. The dusty scent of hay drifted down from the loft. Ben's whittling knives and carving tools were scattered across his workbench along with an open pack of cigarettes.

"Karl!" He was hanging the ax on the wall alongside the pick and saws and butchering tools. "Karl, you have to stay away from the house!" She ran to him and grabbed his arms, frantic.

Ginger Cat scampered from out of the shadows and dashed away. Kate's Mama Bunny scratched nervously at her bed in the hutch.

Charlotte looked into Karl's eyes, pleading. "You need to go. Keep close to the other PWs. Stay by the guards."

"Let me talk to Ben—"

"Go now!" she cried.

From outside, she heard the goat bleating.

"I don't know what he might try to do . . . I don't want anything to happen to my son." She touched Karl's hard cheek. "I don't want anything to happen to you."

He took her hand, his face close to hers. "Charlotte—"

"Get away from my mother!" Ben stood at the open door, his face in shadow.

Charlotte rushed toward Ben to block his way. He swung forward, dodging her. She took a step and tripped on his crutch and fell to her knees. The revolver slipped out of her apron pocket and clattered onto the wooden floor. Charlotte reached for it, but Ben dove onto his stomach and grabbed it. He whirled away from her and sat up, his two hands on the gun, pointed at Karl.

Karl put up his hands. "Ben, I am not your enemy."

"Tell that to my dead buddies, you Nazi bastard!" Ben's eyes were steady on Karl.

Karl moved slowly forward, arms open in front of him. "The war is over for us."

"That's what you think!"

Karl eyed the butchering tools.

No!" Charlotte cried.

"I've killed plenty like you!" Spittle flew from Ben's twisted mouth.

"You and me—" Karl said.

"Shut up!" Ben's words were controlled, the revolver focused.

"Your family, they've been kind to me . . ."

"Yeah, I see that." He glanced toward Charlotte, then back to Karl. "Well, that's over." He cocked the revolver.

"Ben—" Charlotte cried, rushing forward.

Karl lurched toward Ben, grabbing for the gun. The two men struggled, rolling on the floor, wrestling.

"Stop!" Charlotte cried.

A shot exploded in her ears.

And then something else. The cry of a wild animal. A wounded animal.

He was lying on the wooden floor, clutching his chest.

"Ben!" Charlotte bent over him, searching for the wound.

He was gasping for air.

"Shh. It will be all right, Ben." *Oh my God oh my God . . .* She unbuttoned his soaked shirt. Blood pulsed from a hole in his chest. *Oh my God . . .* Tears clouded her vision. She slipped her apron over her head and held it against the wound. "You're going to be fine."

Pulse . . . pulse . . . pulse . . . and then a sucking sound. *What's that?* His breath rattled, irregular.

The sucking stopped. "See, it's better already." *Please, God. Please!*

His gasping stopped.

"Ben?"

Nothing.

"Ben?" Charlotte looked into his eyes. His wide blue eyes. His beautiful blue eyes. They stared back at her. Darker now. Empty. "Ben!" she cried. "Ben!" She shook him. Blood bubbled from his lips.

Then the screaming came. Loud and close. Her own voice screaming.

"Charlotte—" Karl touched her shoulder.

She glared up toward him. "You killed him! My baby! You killed my baby!"

"Charlotte, *nein!*" His eyes on the revolver.

She grabbed the gun. Pointed it at his heart.

Screaming from the barn door. Steps rushing toward her from behind. "Mother, nooooo!"

CHAPTER FORTY-FOUR

GEESE FLY IN FORMATION. All afternoon, maybe yesterday too, their plaintive calls haunting the sky. How do they know when to leave? How does anyone know?

The air is chilly, the shadows long. Charlotte steps through brittle garden vines. She remembers planting fall vegetables—beets, radishes, squash—but she doesn't recall harvesting them. Her mind searches for the memory but finds only static, like a radio tuned to a bad station. Like in the cold white room where they tied her to a gurney and put wires on her head and a strap of leather in her mouth—"bite down"— and her head exploded in a fiery rage. Smoldering white.

She spies the end of a squash protruding from under a thicket of gray crumbling leaves. She stoops to pick it up. Decaying juices ooze onto her fingers. She drops it, wipes her hands on her dress, looks off toward the barn.

The yard is strewn with red and gold leaves, maple and oak. Her steps are slow, unbalanced. Where are the chickens? The goat? She peers into Kate's rabbit pen—empty.

She pushes aside the wooden barn door. Heavier than she remembers. She scans the dim expanse. A dead place.

The workbench is cluttered with carving tools and gnarled hunks of wood. She picks up an oval piece, a head without a face. He hasn't finished this one yet. She touches an open pack of cigarettes. He must have left in a hurry. And a matchbox. She takes out a match and strikes it against the flint and watches the flame flare and travel down the wood and watches her fingertips blacken and holds on until the flame goes out and there's nothing left.

Her eyes follow a ribbon of light that points to a dark patch of floor. She rushes forward and falls to her knees and scratches at the dried blood. Sobbing. Wooden slivers shooting under her fingernails. All that remains of her beautiful boy.

THE RIBBON OF LIGHT IS GONE NOW. The window, the color of sunset.

Her face lies against the hard wooden floor, damp where someone's been crying.

"Charlotte!" Thomas's voice, coming from outside.

She crawls across the floor and scoots under the workbench.

"Charlotte." The voice is in the barn.

She stays quiet until it leaves. She waits until she hears it again, far down the path.

"I'm coming," she whispers. "I'm coming, Ben . . ."

She gets out from under the workbench and walks stiffly across the dim expanse, out the big door, down to the boathouse. Slow and deliberate.

The sunset ripples on the lake like blood.

She takes the can of gasoline back to the barn. *I'm coming . . .*

SHE LIES ON BEN'S BED.

Whispers come out of the walls.

Faces flit in and out. Kate. Thomas.

Doctors.

The sheriff.

When they ask, she doesn't answer.

"CHAR?"

She sits on the couch in the parlor, turns her head slowly.

"Char, let's go for a walk." Thomas stands before her.

Would you walk with me? Painted horses go round and round. Calliope music piping. *Tom, Tom, the piper's son, stole a pie and away did run.* Or was it a pig? No matter. She should have recited that one. Not Tommy Tucker looking for a wife. Too late. Too long ago. *And then what happened?*

She looks about the room. Dust on every surface. Cobwebs in the corners. *Why would he want to walk with me now?*

"C'mon, Char." He helps her up and puts her hand in the crook of his arm.

He walks her through the living room and out the front door and down the porch steps. Morning light throws sparkling diamonds on the lake. "I remember this," she says.

He pats her hand.

They walk slowly along the path.

She stops at the cottage. "I want to go in."

"All right." He leads her up the steps and through the door.

Someone has cleaned it, painted it. It just needs a little dusting. *Who's moving in?* She tries to remember.

There's a picture over the couch—a watercolor of a house with a white picket fence. Kate must have put it there. She was fixing it up, something about kitchen curtains. She gropes for the memory. *Curtains...*

"Is Kate moving in here?"

"No, Charlotte. Kate's away at school."

The kitchen window is bare. "I need to make curtains."

Thomas smiles. "That would be lovely, Charlotte. A sewing project."

She picks up a wooden figurine. This one has a face . . . it looks like . . . Josie . . .

"Ben?" She glances about. "Ben! Where's Ben?"

"Charlotte, let's go—"

"Ben!" The voice is screaming now.

Thomas is carrying her back to the house.

SHE STANDS BEFORE THE PARLOR WINDOW. She reaches out and touches it, the War Mother's Flag, blue with the white star. Ben's flag.

And then it comes again, heat rising in her veins, the trembling, blood swelling up, pulsing fast. *His eyes staring from the casket deep in the ground that will soon be frozen. Staring at her.* She falls to the couch, rocking and rocking, moaning.

When she looks up again, the window is empty. Something is missing.

"Thomas?"

IT'S QUIET NOW. The house quiet. Even the birds have left.

When she reaches for Bingo, he jumps away.

On the other side of the window a breeze rustles the maples. Leaves flutter in a rain of red and gold. Kate likes to rake colored leaves. Pretty little girl in pigtails dragging the rake around. Following her father. He tosses her into the air and she squeals with glee. He reads her nursery rhymes. She learns so quick. "She can make a cherry pie / Quick as cat can wink its eye . . ." But she never cared for making pies. Kate and Thomas making rhymes together. *He stole her away from me.*

Charlotte hears the back door open, close. Thomas. Heavy rhythm of his step. Water pumping in the kitchen sink. Wood thumping into the stove. Smoky aroma, cherry wood.

Cherries. Cherry pies. Cherry jam.

The cherry trees are bare now. She stares out at the orchard. Thomas's orchard.

"Char." Thomas stands in the doorway. Not as tall as he used to be. What's happened to him? "Come in to supper, Char." Then he's gone.

She smells fish, rice with butter, tomatoes. Hears his chair scrape against the kitchen floor. Utensils clicking on his plate. *Not waiting for me.*

She heard him talking with someone about that place, Clarington Home. Not a home at all. No, a gray cluster of low buildings out by the railroad tracks, high stone wall, crazy faces behind barred windows.

Kate, it was Kate he was talking to. Kate and Thomas. Conspiring against her.

She's afraid of them now.

Pretend. *Pretend I'm just fine.* She takes a ragged breath and rises and holds to furniture and walls.

The kitchen smells warm. A plate of food at her place, a glass of water.

"Rainbow trout," he says. "Fried the way you like it."

She slouches onto the seat of her chair. Thomas puts down his fork, stands, takes his plate to the sink. Then he's back, sitting across from her. He empties his pipe into the ashtray and refills it, scratches a match against the box. Cherry-scented puffs float into the air.

"Why don't you kill me," she whispers.

"Eat, Charlotte."

She picks up her fork, takes a bite. It tastes of fresh fish and butter and salt. She should like it. But it doesn't matter now. She chews slowly.

"I sold the farm," he says.

What farm?

"Artie, he's got a cherry orchard up near Sister Bay, remember?

He'd like to have this place." Thomas sucks on his pipe. *Puff . . . puff . . . puff.* "Got two sons. Doesn't want to break up his land. One will stay with him, the other will live here."

Not in Ben's room. That's my room now.

"Good that Artie's willing to take it on this time of year, seeing we're going into winter." *Puff . . . puff . . . puff.* " 'Course I'll leave him everything in the root cellar. Kate did all that canning after—"

"Kate? Where's Kate?"

"You know where she is, Char. Down at the university." He sucks on his pipe. "She'll be back, Thanksgiving break, help me pack things up, take whatever she wants."

Pack things up?

Blood rushes, heat in her veins, dizzy. She clenches her fists to stop it. Thomas doesn't like to hear the moaning. Fingernails cutting into her palms.

Thomas tamps down the ashes in his pipe, relights it. Puffs for a while. Puts it down. "I found a place for you."

"For *me* . . . ?" She stares at him.

"Charlotte." His hand reaches across the table and closes on hers. "Please understand . . ."

She moans.

Thomas takes a red handkerchief from his pocket and blows his nose, wipes his eyes. "They have the help you need."

She lets it come, the blood racing and the dizziness and the moaning, she lets it happen. And rocks and rocks. Because it doesn't matter anymore.

After a while it's quiet again. Her hands in her lap.

Thomas empties his pipe. Puts it on the table and stares down at the ashes. "I never did want this farm."

EPILOGUE

THE TRAIN SWAYS GENTLY SOUTHWARD through snow-covered fields and forests, frozen lakes and rivers, backyards with tire swings and bedsheets stiff on clotheslines.

Kate stares out at the passing scene.

She could have stayed, could have run the farm with Father, taken care of Mother, but Father said no. Her staying would make no difference. "Your mother lives in a dark place. Nothing more we can do."

Kate touches the cold window, wipes away a patch of fog. Snow devils gather and stir across the darkening landscape. A coming storm.

She reaches into her satchel and pulls out the notebook Father gave her. Like everything else in his little campus bookstore, it smells of cherry tobacco. She enjoys working with Father between classes, and joining Father and Miss Fleming for Sunday dinners.

When she can, she spends time with her new friends—sharing meals in the student union, sledding on Bascom Hill, walking in the Arboretum. She often stays up late with the girls in her dormitory, sitting in their pajamas, smoking cigarettes, talking about literature and philosophy and politics and the meaning of everything. So many opinions about so many ideas she'd never even thought of before. They share hopes and dreams and letters from boyfriends off at war. Everyone has a story.

Kate has shared some of her letters from Clay, certain parts anyway. And she's shared stories about growing up on the farm, but not the bad parts, not the parts about Mother and Vehlmer and Karl and Ben and Josie. Not yet. Maybe never. Telling them about the cherry orchard was bad enough. One of the girls piped right up: "I remember reading about a Nazi murder at a cherry orchard . . . a boy shot, the mother went crazy . . . wasn't that Door County?" "The details were exaggerated," Kate told them. "Journalists angling for a lurid headline. Badgering the poor family, can you imagine?"

The train rushes through a tunnel, darkening the compartment. Kate glances toward the window. Staring back, her mother's face.

"Takes after her mother," they all said.

She shivers into her sweater, opens the notebook, and picks up her pencil. "The last time I saw her, a face in the window . . ."

When did Mother's darkness begin? That mad Nazi attacking her in the barn? *Dear Mother!* No, it was before that. Before the prisoners ever came. That first year without the harvest, when Mother had to sell two of her goats. No, that wasn't it. It was about Ben. When Ben left, that's when it started.

And when he came home . . .

Kate closes her eyes and drifts along with the sway of the train, the rhythmic sound of the wheels.

Birds cry and flutter. A pistol shot? Not a rifle for deer or pheasant, but a pistol. Running to the barn . . . faster . . . Ben! Mother . . . no! Karl's eyes wide. The second shot. A scream—

She jerks forward. The whistle screams again. Outside, bare-branched oaks cast long shadows across snowy fields.

Everyone agreed about what happened, what must have happened. The Nazi killed Ben, and Mother shot the Nazi in a fit of grief. Crime of passion. *Poor Charlotte. For a mother to witness such a thing!* That was what they said aloud, but Kate heard the whispers too, noted the looks. *That woman brought it on herself, inviting those Nazis onto her land, into her home even!*

The sheriff came with questions, but Mother only cried and moaned and rocked and whispered gibberish about the barn, the stain, the root cellar, the boat. Kate heard the clues, but the sheriff didn't seem to pick up on them. Or maybe he didn't want to.

Whether Father made any sense of it, Kate couldn't tell. When the sheriff finally turned to Kate, she didn't confess what she thought she knew. It didn't matter anymore.

The Army took Karl's body away, took all the prisoners away. The harvest was nearly finished. Kate and Father picked the last of the cherries.

Ben lay in the parlor for viewing. Mother sat close, rocking, muttering, fingering his collar, smoothing his hair. When reporters came with intrusive questions and flashing bulbs, Father smashed one of the cameras and shouted at them to go away.

Fire and ice. If only she could burn away the images. Kate turns from the dark thoughts and looks out at the icy world rolling by. No, they're frozen in her mind.

Karl coming from the root cellar—the more she thought about it, the more she was sure that Mother must have been down there with him. If only she had confronted Mother then, if she had told Father, Karl would have been sent away, Ben would be alive, and Mother . . . If only . . .

The train slows and settles into the next station. A man in the compartment a few seats ahead stands, gathers his things, and disembarks. Another boards. They move about as if nothing's happened. The way Kate once moved about.

A blond woman with two children hurries into the car and sits across the aisle, excitement in her face. The brother and sister scramble to the window, giggling over some secret. We used to do that, Ben and I.

The whole town came to his funeral—Mrs. J, Old Man Berger, Olga the butcher's widow, plenty of girls who once pined for Ben, Craig with his caved-in face, and a few other war-wounded boys.

Josie cried inconsolably. "It's not your fault," Kate tried to convince her.

The doctor sedated Mother so she could go.

Afterward, people brought food and flowers to the house, tiptoed into the parlor where Mother sat staring at the War Mother's Flag. They whispered among themselves, the townspeople, how terrible it all was. Then there was nothing more to say. After an awkward time they got up and left and the house was quiet.

A few days later Kate found Mother in the root cellar tearing apart a good woolen blanket with the edge of a broken jar, tomatoes and blood dripping from her hands.

It was Father who saved her from the burning barn, carrying her into the house, with Mother screaming, "Leave me to hell!"

Kate sold all her rabbits, save for Mama Bunny, which she gave to Josie. When it was time to leave, she packed up her clothes and books and bicycle. That was all she needed. She went upstairs for a last look and chose one of Ben's carved figurines—the rearing horse he had started before he left.

The locomotive gives a last toot and a young couple pushes through the door. The boy, not much older than Kate, wears a tan Army uniform. They sit close, holding hands. The girl's been crying. She drops her shoes to the floor and tucks her legs up under her plaid wool skirt on the leather seat. The boy puts an arm around her shoulders. Must be shipping out. He strokes her hair. Will he come back as sweet, as loving as he is now?

When the couple kiss, Kate turns away. She pulls the worn photograph from her sweater pocket—Clay, so handsome in his officer's uniform, standing next to his plane somewhere in the Pacific. Far away. So far away.

"We'll go flying," he told her that day in the cherry shack. "Wherever you want to go." She closes her eyes, her skin tingling with the memory of his touch, rain all around, lights flashing beyond the storm. Electric.

She sends him stories, and he comments thoughtfully on each one. "The mermaid—that was you, wasn't it, finding your way to my party. How awkward you must have felt, swimming through the land without legs among the leggy ones. I had no idea."

He writes to her nearly every day, mailing packets of notes whenever he's able. "The dewy soft valley of your back . . ." "How your eyes smile at me over your shoulder . . ." "The way you plunge right in . . ."

She opens his latest letter and reads it yet again. "I do not have the words to describe the lush islands I see from the air—rugged jungles, deep purple waters, tall grassy meadows flowing like rivers. I want to bring you here, after the war. You will find the words. That's what I love about you, Kate."

It used to be, "That's what I like about you." Now it's "love."

That one word doesn't matter. No, not nearly as much as the way he shares his world with her, imagines a world for them together. He will be flying, she will be writing.

Her story is just beginning.

ACKNOWLEDGMENTS

FOR THEIR STEADFAST EDITORIAL support and inspiration, I'm indebted to Brent Barker, Kevin Arnold, and most importantly, Antoinette May, who never stopped believing.

To my agent, Harvey Klinger, who made it happen, I am truly grateful. *Onward!*

To my editor, Rachel Kahan, for pushing me to go deeper. I thought that the great literary editors of old had left the building—what a fabulous surprise.

I thank Ann Jinkins and Maggie Weir, curators of the Door County Historical Museum, for their review and advice on the historical accuracy of the manuscript. I thank Cliff Ehlers for sharing his experience in working a cherry orchard in Door County during World War II. Also, Laura Kayacan, at the Door County Library, for providing a wealth of information about the place and time.

I'm also thankful to writing buddies Rob Swigart, Sandy Towle, Sally Henry, Jim Spencer, Robert Yeager, Pam Mundale, Monika Rose, Genevieve Beltran, Kathy Fellure, Amy Smith, Sally Kaplan, Lou Gonzalez, and Jennifer Tristano.

For their input on the final manuscript, I thank John Sanna, Pam Sanna, and Ann Iverson.

For deepening my writing experience, I am grateful to Vermont Studio Center for a month-long residency, to Middlebury College for Bread Loaf in Sicily, and to Squaw Valley Community of Writers.

To Larry Greene, longtime friend, advisor, and writing pal, for steering me in the right direction time and again.

To Mom and Dad, who have always been there for me.

And hugs to my daughter, Katie, my greatest fan.